·To:

Evan Phillips &

With best wishes from,

Frederick. A. Read

This Special Edition of
We Come Unseen
is limited to 500 copies and in
support of:

Registered Charity No. 210760

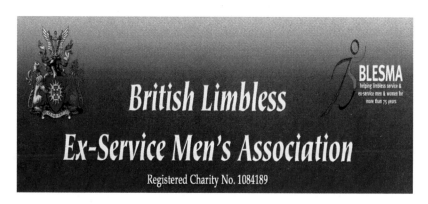

British Limbless
Ex-Service Men's Association
Registered Charity No. 1084189

We Come Unseen

Frederick A. Read

a Guaranteed *book*

First Published in 2010 by
The Guaranteed Partnership
Po Box 12, Maesteg, South Wales, CF34 0XG
www.theguaranteedpartnership.com

Typesetting by Christopher Teague

ISBN (Limited Edition): 978 1 906864 16 3
ISBN (Trade Edition): 978 1 906864 14 9

Printed in Wales by Print Evolution

I have often looked for an opportunity of paying tribute to our Submarines. There is no branch of His Majesty's Forces which in this war has suffered the same proportion of total loss as our Submarine service.

It is the most dangerous of all Services that is perhaps the reason why the First Lord tells me that the entry into it is keenly sought by Officers and men.

I feel sure the House would wish to testify its gratitude and admiration to our Submarine crews for their skill and devotion which has proved of inestimable value to the life of our country.

(Extract from a speech by the Rt. Hon. Winston Churchill, Prime Minister)

Author's Statement

We from the world of Submarines have no active role or involvement with the current conflicts and troubles in the Middle East.

As an ex Submariner and the author of this novel, I wish to take this opportunity, dare I say on all our behalves, to give a salute and offer a tribute to those that are, and for it to be accepted in the kindred spirit it is given.

Dedication

To all our brave Warriors who marched over the hills to far-away foreign lands, only to return limbless, or paid the ultimate sacrifice and come back feet first.

For these noble warriors who risk their very lives each hour of every day while carrying out their duties, yet find themselves fleeced, and under-equipped by the very politicians who sent them there in the first place.

It is my wish to make a donation towards two special Forces Charities which provide the needs and support to the families of the warriors who have carved their names in glory.

'WE WILL REMEMBER THEM'

Also…

To all the illustrious Royal Navy SUBMARINERS both past and present, with a special mention to the 'A' Boats that formed the SM7 Squadron based at Singapore.

In particular: H.M.S. Andrew, Anchorite, Auriga, Ambush and Amphion.

Acknowledgment

Many thanks to Rev Janice Gourdie for her help in providing my Biblical references that were used to great effect during WW2 as part of the Submarine Signal code system.

To all my fellow Shipmates from the Royal Naval Association who continue to subscribe to my Naval 'Adventure' series, who have given their names to be used within and as described, to help me create this special novel.

To my dear wife Anne, who endures many a lonely hour whilst I'm reminiscing of my 'Days of Yore' in the writing of this and all the others in my 'Adventure' series of novels.

Author's Note

For the benefit of the reader who is a non-Submariner and are not familiar with the issuing of orders or command within their service: each order given must be repeated back in case of being misheard. Then once done, that person must report back to having carried those orders out, and receive an answer from the person who gave that order or command.

Thus to cut down the lengthy and cluttered narrative, the phrase "Aye aye sir!" will be used throughout to suffice this protocol, and for the story to unfold without this undue impediment.

The custom of quoting Biblical quotations within the command of the Submarine Service, was not only used to send succinct signals to and fro, but also for the recipient to be able to interpret the signal or command according to the situation it refers to in conducting required actions or operations currently underway.

This yarn as narrated by the Character called 'The Signalman' who will be referred to as 'T.S.'

BE AWARE!
I am non Politically Correct (P.C.) therefore this book is not suitable for those that are.

Foreword

A soldier who fights on land, has trees, ditches, outcrops of rock, buildings or other objects for him to hide behind to protect himself and perhaps keep hidden from his foe. Sometimes he would have to dig himself a little hollow in the ground to provide his shelter.

For those magnificent men in their flying machines, they have the clouds to hide in, and the sheer speed to be able to get out of trouble.

Whereas a ship slap-bang in the middle of the sea can be seen for several miles by the naked eye, and be detected much further by electronic devices.

Those sailors on board have nowhere to hide, and can be preyed upon by any larger more powerful ship, by an aircraft, and even a missile. But their biggest threat comes from the most deadliest of predators, which lurks below the waves; a Submarine.

Size for size, a Submarine packs more punch and is able to create more devastation to any surface vessel than even the most powerful battleship, which is the reason why it is classed as a major warship.

Surface vessel Captains may know there are submarines around, but would not know where they may strike or even when, because these denizens of the deep rule the undersea world and can pop up anywhere they may choose, and live up to their motto:

'WE COME UNSEEN'

Part One

1

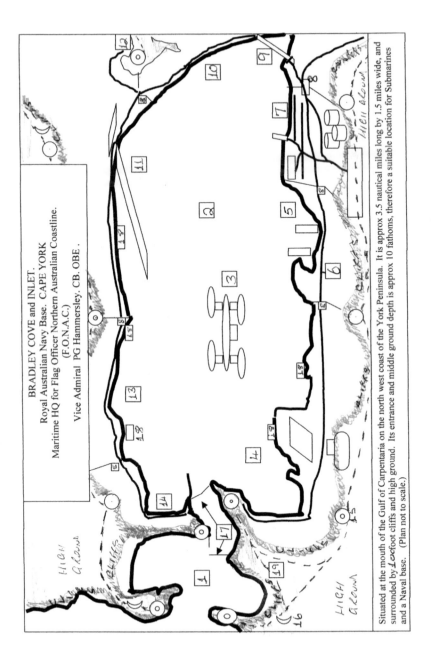

BRADLEY COVE and INLET.
Royal Australian Navy Base. CAPE YORK
Maritime HQ for Flag Officer Northern Australian Coastline.
(F.O.N.A.C.)
Vice Admiral PG Hammersley. CB. OBE .

Situated at the mouth of the Gulf of Carpentaria on the north west coast of the York Peninsula. It is approx 3.5 nautical miles long by 1.5 miles wide, and surrounded by 1ecfoot cliffs and high ground. Its entrance and middle ground depth is approx 10 fathoms, therefore a suitable location for Submarines and a Naval base. (Plan not to scale.)

Plan Legend
(Not to Scale)

1. Cove with sandy beaches.
2. Inlet with a sandy beach along the village and airfield area.
3. Submarine Depot ship and her Squadron.
4. Admiral's H.Q. and Naval camp area, with a stores wharf and warehouses, and an underground Communications Centre.
5. Submarine repair yard area with 2 floating docks, warehousing etc.
6. The main road and railway around the base, with the rail / road link south to Townsville.
7. Underground munitions dump, fuel storage tanks area, motor transport and railway sheds.
8. Main gate access to each area.
9. Bailey bridge over river and outflow from waterfall.
10. Married Quarters and village area.
11. General Naval Air Transport Seaplanes (GNATS) Squadron and landing area with a slipway, hangar, and earmarked for a future Airbase.
12. Power station and Incinerator area.
13. Marine and Artillery Barracks area.
14. A Fast Patrol Boat / Minelayers Base and camp area.
15. Base Defence Gunnery positions.
16. Mobile Radar stations.
17. Boom Defences and Diving School.
18. Landing jetties.
19. Gun/Radar access tracks.

In the Beginning

The year is around 1941 when the might of the Japanese Imperial Forces were creating havoc and destruction with their invasion on the mainland of China, Korea and other Oriental countries in their quest for expanding their Empire. They had realised that if they were to destroy the mighty and powerful fleet of the American Navy based on the Sandwich Islands, (the Hawaii's) gaining space for them to grab as much land and territory, and certainly all the islands in the Western Pacific, before things got too much for them, they could sue for a Peace Treaty whilst holding onto their ill-gotten gains.

Siam had capitulated within 3 days of the Japanese invasion, enabling them to make their way south through the Malay Peninsula to grab the sea gateway to the Pacific at Singapore.

Despite the war with Germany, which took up most of the British resources, the British War Cabinet decided to despatch 2 Royal Navy Battleships to help stave off these Japanese advances, and to help bolster Fortress Singapore.

It was also the decision of the War Cabinet to re-inforce those ships with several of the brand-new type of Submarine, that was by far superior to any which had been built before.

They were to arrive at the Naval Base in Sembawang, Singapore and from there, conduct a naval warfare scenario such as was experienced by the infamous German Wolf Packs that nearly won the recent 'Battle of the Atlantic' for Germany.

By the time it took these Submarines to arrive off the coast of Ceylon, they were faced with the news that not only both those battleships had been sunk, but the 58,000 troops of the British garrison at Singapore, under the command of General Percival, had surrendered to the Japanese, making a total of over 250,000 allied troops that had been captured by the invasion forces of the Japanese 21st & 25th Army.

* * *

Therefore it was decided that they would form a new squadron to bolster the Submarine Squadrons already in Australian waters, mainly from their base at Sydney.

These boats made the long voyage 'in company' down the entire length of the Atlantic Ocean, then across the Indian Ocean and up to the northern coast of Australia, stopping only for fuel and supplies along the way.

Of the 8 that went out in company with their own depot ship; two of them and their depot ship had made their destination in the bay at Exmouth on the Western Coast to make up the squadron there.

Two more had to stay awhile at Darwin, leaving the remaining four to continue on towards their own final destination.

These four made their way along the northern coast of Australia, before entering the Gulf of Carpentaria, towards the tip of the York Peninsula to make their rendezevous time and the arranged meeting with their pilot who would escort them into their hastily prepared base.

These new submarines were to be known as the 'A' Class boats, and specifically designed to operate with the Pacific theatre of war in mind, and would match the US Navy's long range 'Gato' and 'Guppy' Class patrol submarines. Thus taking their place alongside all the other 'Class' of RN Submarines who were continuing to carve their names in glory time and time again against the might of the German Wermacht and her Axis allies in the Mediterranean Sea.

Chapter I

New Home

The boats sailed in line astern with S64 in the lead, as her captain had a vast seniority over the other boat's captains, thus maintaining the R.N's tradition of keeping a pecking order within the Officer's ranks.

When the cross on the sea chart was reached for them to arrive for the r/v, they found that they were almost in front of a small cove.

"Captain – Navigator. We have arrived at Lat 12 Degrees South, Long 142 Degrees East and appear to be ahead of our r/v schedule. Bradley Cove is now just off our port bow, sir!"

As T.S. was recognised as the top lookout on board, it was part of his duty to keep a sharp eye out for any approaching vessels or aircraft.

It wasn't long before these 4 brand new 'A' class boats were met by an Australian Navy Fast Patrol Boat (FPB) skimming over the waves towards them at very high speed.

"Sir! There's an FPB approaching on Red 15. She's flashing us to give our recognition code." T.S. reported swiftly.

"Very well Signalman! Make the appropriate reply. Captain - Officer of the Watch (OOW)! FPB approaching us on Red 15! We're exchanging recognition signals. Suggest a welcoming committee."

"Am coming up!" came the terse reply.

"Sir! He says that he's our Harbour Pilot, and to follow him." T.S. reported.

The Captain arrived on the bridge to see the neat turn of the FPB, sending sprays of water through the air as the vessel changed her course abruptly.

"Make to him. Hello Sailor! Have a daisy chain behind me. Will follow you like sheep. Baa, Baa!"

T.S. flashed the signal and read back the reply for the Captain to laugh at a speedy yet cheeky response.

"W/T - Captain! Contact the others and tell them to we've met up with our pilot and for them to follow my wake, and exact courses."

"Aye aye sir!" came the metallic reply from the intercom.

The snake-like convoy of boats were led into the small cove before entering a narrow, fjord-like entrance on the top end of the York Peninsula, facing the Carpentaria Gulf, which meant that it was virtually concealed from view seaward, and afforded a deep-water area suitable for a squadron of submarines and their depot ship in the surrounding high ground that led them into a narrow inlet, which itself was topped by a wide 'Y' shaped valley.

This was a Naval base that was still in the making, and manned with Navy personnel from each of its four elements. It also had an Army presence and a special workforce of civilians to run the base[•].

In the middle of the inlet was a moored depot ship, with two pontoon platforms lashed to each side of her to make one landing stage for each boat that arrived.

She was a one-time Australian cruise liner of 670feet long by 85 feet wide, weighing around 20,000 tons, with two tall funnels, but her cargo derricks removed and instead of her civilian livery colours of paint, she was painted in a uniform 'ships side' grey to tell everybody that she was now converted into a Submarine Depot ship. Her cargo holds were converted into workshops and storerooms, and although previously able to carry 1,400 passengers, she now only had enough accommodation space for up to 6 boat crews, plus her own totalling around the 950 mark

She bristled with A.A. guns, and ladders over the sides to each of the pontoons that were secured to her. She had 4 large cranes positioned by each pontoon for loading or unloading stores or equipment.

[•] See the diagram and legend.

This was to be their new home for the duration of the hostilities against the so far 'all conquering' Japanese armed forces. Once the FPB saw the last boat had cleared the gorge and entered the inlet safely, she turned round and left them to return to her own 'home'

There were buildings being constructed on both sides of the inlet that looked like a giant construction site.

"This looks like a nice cosy berth No1. All brand-new by the way things are being built, even as we speak, and a lovely big liner as our home!"

"Aye sir! Far from the maddening crowd too!" Welling replied affably.

"Captain – W/T! Signal from Cdr S/M. Says we've to secure alongside Trot 2, which is Starboard side for'ard. Says to pass their Starboard side down towards the bottom of the lake and turn to make your approach. You will turn when you reach 5 cables astern of me. You will use a red marker buoy where you make your turn. Each one of you will be instructed to use this marker buoy as your 'Carousel' or 'Merry go round' if you prefer, but take it in turns and approach us from astern to your own designated Trot number. You have a good 2 fathoms under your keel to do so."

"Roger that W/T.

The depot ship dwarfed each boat as they passed down her starboard side in procession, and with a slow and careful turn, approached their allocated 'Trot'.

"Signalman! Standby to pipe."

"Aye aye sir!"

The protocol of saluting from one vessel to another requires the junior of the two captains piping the side, or 'Still' by using a Bosun's Call, then waiting for the response from the senior officer. Once done, then the salute is completed by a response call, known as the 'Carry on', which is the cue for the crew on deck to resume their duties.

S64 glided slowly towards her pontoon landing stage, and for the final string of orders to be given.

"Stop main engines! Group up! Starboard 10! Half astern Starboard, Slow ahead Port." Hosie ordered, as the boat swung round to line herself up with the pontoon.

"Stop together! Port 10! Slow astern together! Stand by fenders, and get a heaving line across both ends and get the breasts secured. Midships! Stop together. Start the for'ard capstan and winch us in slowly. Provide fenders for our friend approaching our stern, don't want any collisions as part of our grand entrance No1."

The boat was now being berthed neatly alongside her 'trot' and gave a small nudge against the woodwork of the pontoon to let everybody know they had 'arrived' at last. This was being done in succession by each boat as they too arrived alongside.

A slender 15 foot gangway had been slung across the small gap between the boat and the pontoon, and secured just aft of the 4inch gun sponson.

"Finished with main engines. Secure from Harbour Stations No 1 and get the boat opened up!" Hosie concluded, as he leaned over the side and spoke to an officer who was waiting to greet him.

"Aye aye sir!" Welling, the No1 responded[•].

"Afternoon sir! My name is Lt Trevor Bell RANVR, your relief Navigating officer. As you can see, each boat has its own pontoon and access ladder up onto the depot ship. When you're ready, Cdr S/M Harry Harley will meet you along with the other captains and their officers on the Quarterdeck." Bell informed in a broad Australian accent.

Hosie looked down at the large berthing parties that had gathered on each pontoon, then towards his waiting reception team, and Bell who greeted him.

"Thank you Bell! It's nice to see you Reservist mob getting

[•] He also gets called the 1st Lt, because he is next in line of command from the captain.

9

your noses into the world of boats. This place looks a nice holiday resort we've come all this way for. It seems that we've just left one side of the globe at war only to find there's going to be one here too." Hosie responded amiably.

"We can't have everything sir. I'll be your navigator until you have given a weathered eye over the new set of sea charts for this part of the world. In the meantime sir, we've got a few weeks to get ourselves ship-shape. For now you are requested to send your Cox'n inboard for his instructions on the crew's accommodation etc, then await the visit of our Linseed Wipers, Poultice Wallopers and other nefarious Scab Lifters to come and give you all the once over. Officers are excused this, so if you'd care to bring your officers ashore with you, a Snottie will meet you at the top of the ladder to show you the way."•

"Thank you again. Good as done!" Hosie concluded and announced that he was going below. This was the cue for the rest of the bridge crew to relax and clear the bridge of any equipment etc before they too went below.

The boat had her for'ard torpedo loading hatch opened up, along with the seldom opened engine room hatch, and their ladders secured for her crew to climb up onto the main casing to gaze around at their new surroundings.

"Don't tell me we've sailed half way round the bloody world to end up in some God forsaken arsehole of a place. It's like a bleedin' building site! Just look at all the sand they've dumped next to the 'oggin. I'm buggerin' off before the ruddy cement arrives." A stoker opined as he walked swiftly from aft to gather around the gangway.

T.S. was on the bridge scanning around the place through his powerful binoculars, when he heard that remark below him, and recognized the voice.

"We've just passed through that gorge in front of us, and

• 'Snottie' is a nickname given to a midshipman or officer cadet.

there's a nice village at the other end of the inlet. Maybe there's a gaggle of gorgeous Aussie girls, Sheilas' I think they're called, ashore just waiting to get to know you Brian!" he remarked, emphasising the word 'gorgeous' pointing to the village astern of them.

"Yes, Stoker Sandom! You've been bragging about being the 'mess-dick gigilo' since we left Simonstown." another person said, which was hotly denied by Sandom, but it started a round of banter which seemed to release the tension of the past few weeks at sea, and lift it all from their shoulders.

Their spontaneous banter was broken by a tannoy announcement made from the control room.

"Do you hear there! Nobody is to leave the boat until certain procedures have been sorted out. There will be a Doctor and a team of Sick Berth Attendants to come aboard and give you all a once over, so have your pay-books ready for scrutiny for them to see your medical notes. Red Watch, temporary harbour routine." the voice of Cox'n James ordered, before he switched his mike off and went inboard as previously ordered.

T.S. had remained on the bridge, satisfying his curious mind as to his surroundings, and observed the shore cables being taken on board and connected up to the boats circuitry, thus shutting down the batteries. The gangway was fitted with a telephone and a microphone system for the Trot Sentry (otherwise known on surface vessels as the Gangway Quartermaster) to use as and when. He watched as James came down the main ladders and onto the gangway with reams of papers under his arms, and go below into the control room.

"Do you hear there! Leading hands of each mess muster in the control room!" he announced, but didn't wait long until they had arrived.

"Right then! Here is the depot ship's layout detailing where your mess-decks are, the galley or other important places you'd need to find. Take these to display them in your messes then have everybody stand by for the Squadron M.O. and his team.

Once done so, and finding all you reprobates too fit for words, according to my victuals and the chef's cooking, the boat will be cleared for the proper duty watch roster to start up." James stated, handing out the various bits of paperwork of instructions whilst receiving ribald comments from the men about the pending medical inspection.

Once the men had dispersed, leaving only the T.S. and James in the now deserted control room, they heard footsteps coming along the accommodation passageway.

Hoare, the Sonar officer was first to appear into the control room, leading the way for a Female Medical officer who raised several whistles from the crew as she passed their mess-decks. Immediately following behind her was a team of medics.

"Cox'n. This is Major Sandra Hodgson who is the local Army M.O. and is representing the Australian Health Board, accompanied by her Naval team from inboard, namely POSBA Watson, and LSBA Caughey who will take down your 'er' particulars so to speak. You will use the wardroom for your inspection Major, but as the crew are a bit woman hungry at the moment you might find a few 'hairy moments' if you like." Hoare announced with a grin, showing her where it was, before leaving them.

"G'day Cox'n. We've got another boat's crew to screen, so if you'd kindly have your men lined up for us to conduct our inspection, the sooner we can all go home. POSBA Rob Watson here will see that no impropriety occurs, and LSBA Tom Caughey over there will check their inoculation details etc, so have your men get their pay-books ready." Hodgson stated as she introduced her medical team and started to unpack a load of medical bags that they brought with them.

"I'm Cox'n Roy James, the boat's so called 'Doc', but it's nice to have the professionals to fall back on as I'm only a 'First Aider' so to speak."

"Not to worry, we're here only to check your men are fit and in compliance with immunisation protocols. You can leave us now if you wish and let us get on with things, as I'm sure your men are champing on the bit to get ashore."

"That's fine by me, but given there's a pretty female Doc on board, what does your inspection entail? No offence Doc, but decorum and all that."

"Just stripped to the waist that's all. Er, from the waist up that is, but I feel that the Doc can speak for herself." Caughey said with a smile.

"I'm a qualified unarmed combat expert, should their, um, need arise." She said candidly.

"Well just make certain you are gentle with my men, as our Captain might find himself short of crew when he sails next time. Must go now Doc, have several other caps to wear now, and get the men organised." James said with a nod and left the wardroom to start the inspection.

"C'mon lads! There's a pretty nurse waiting to feel your body and check out your other particulars, you lucky bastards! Hurry hurry! The sooner you've been cleared the sooner we can get inboard." James chuckled as he poked his head through the curtains of both the stokers and sailors mess that separated them from the main passageway, producing an immediate stampede with arguments as to who would be first.

He met T.S standing in the queue and beckoned him to follow him into the fore-ends.

"What's up Doc?" T.S. asked breezily.

"There's a shipload of mail being sorted out in the mail office inboard. But it can keep until tomorrow, when everybody musters back on board."

"Thanks Cox'n! From what I've seen from the ship's layout, it's a right camel trek to and from the mess let alone to and from the galley and the bathrooms. It's going to take us a good couple of days to get used to it all. Em! What time are we mustering in the morning?"

"I'm just about to announce that. Just listen up!" James said and left to go back through the queue of bodies to reach the main microphone in the control room.

"Do you hear there! Once you have had your medical, clear the boat and get yourselves introduced to your inboard accommodation. 2nd Port watch will start the Harbour watch pattern using TROPICAL ROUTINE, and uniforms. That is to say, muster at 0700 and finish at 1300 for those not on duty. Duty watch will wear No 10A's, but 10's if going ashore at any time. You will be victual led inboard but your rum ration will be issued on board as normal. You will be expected to observe any inboard procedures such as fire drills etc, and you will be under the scrutiny of the depot ship's Master at Arms and his Regulating Branch team. So keep your noses clean and out of trouble. That is all!" James concluded to make his way for'ard again.

T.S. stood there half-naked with Hodgson poking and prodding him and wielding a cold stethoscope across his chest, whilst Watson was taking his pulse and temp, and Caughey wrote furiously into a large logbook. He had to poke his tongue out, say 'ahh!' bend down and touch his toes. Finally, he had to sit on the wardroom table to have his knees 'tapped' with a rubber hammer Watson was wielding, with Caughey questioning him about his jabs.

His eyes had somehow been attracted to the exquisite female curves that were tantalizing him and making his mouth water when he saw her upturned breasts playing peek-a-boo, being semi displayed under her white open necked blouse.

She followed his gaze and discovered that she had one button too many undone for her normal prim attire.

"You poor boys! No wonder you're all standing to attention, so to speak! Cooped up in this ruddy steel coffin for weeks on end must play havoc with your love life. Never mind, if I know you sailors, once you've been ashore for a few days all will return to normal. So stop dribbling down my tunic and stop trying to looking down my bosom." She said with a sigh and a disdainful look at him, but to took time to re-do the offending button.

14

"Sorry Doc! Haven't seen such a glorious vista like that since leaving Blighty some 8 weeks ago." He responded with a cheeky grin.

"Next!" Watson shouted, as Caughey gave him his pay-book back, saying.

"You need a second Malaria injection. Report to the inboard sickbay by the end of the week."

T.S went to the senior rates mess to speak to his PO Tel when he bumped into the Cox'n coming out of it.

"Ah Cox'n! I was going to ask the PO Tel but maybe you can help. What about our pay routine etc?"

"On board as usual, but using Aussie dollars."

"What's wrong with the good old Sterling then? I'd rather trust the old Pounds Shillings and Pence than Mickey Mouse money."

"No! It just saves you from exchanging money at rip off prices."

"From the way your bumpf has it, we can only spend it in the NAAFI canteen. Where are we going to spend it all? By the looks of it, the nearest civilisation is down the inlet. Liberty boats and all that." T.S. moaned.

"All sorted, so trust your old Cox'n. Mind you tell the lads."

"Good on yer Cox-Swine, and here's us thinking you were a hard hearted so and so." T.S. said, emphasising his word 'swine'
James laughed at the candid remark, but with a smile and a wink, whispered

"Don't tell anybody else then. Loose lips sink ships and all that!" then went.

T.S. gathered his belongings and joined the queue to tramp up the steep ladder onto the main upper deck of the depot ship then down several hatches and ladders to reach his allocated mess deck.

15

Chapter II

Dhoby Time

T.S reached the bottom of a steep ladder and looked around a large spacious area that was to be the boats crews mess-deck whilst on board this newly acquired depot ship.

"What no micks?" Brown, asked in amazement.

"You forget Ken, this is a converted liner. No such things as hammocks in this type of vessel, but I was expecting single cabins and a cabin Steward service at least." T.S responded with a laugh.

"It looks as if we've been sorted out into 'Boat's crews and Branch messes instead of all mates together. Wonder why?" Underwood asked in puzzlement as he located the small closed off area marked S64 COMMS.

T.S spotted that they had the for'ard outside mess Starboard side of the large accommodation compartment, with three racks of two 6 foot long by 3 foot wide wooden bunks that were built to the ships side bulkhead, and featuring a curtain covered porthole for each of the top ones.

"This one is mine!" T.S stated defiantly claiming one of the top ones, at the same time as Leading Telegraphist Boyall and Hemmings the Leading Radar Plotter claimed the other two, much to the chagrin of the other 3.

Their mess was a standard 20-foot by 10 foot and had a small bulkhead separating them from the next area down. There were two columns of 3ft wide by 3 foot high and 2 foot deep steel lockers on each side of the gap to make a secluded area, and help form 3-foot gangway to separate the mess opposite. To complete the mess-deck they had a 7foot long by 2foot wide table flanked by two wooden benches in the middle of the open space. Thus each Boat's crews were put into 8 small messes of 6 men and in 6 columns down the length of the ship. There was a gangway ladder that was shared between 2 columns and placed front and rear of the entire compartment.

"So we're Starboard side for'ard on deck 2, in the after mess deck compartment, with our individual mess number of 2S22. Hmm! Sounds about right to pinpoint our mess on the Damage Control Layout at least. We appear to be well situated as we're nearer to the heads and the galley, with that ladder coming down between us." Hemmings said, as he examined the location map they were given.

They quickly stowed their gear into their chosen lockers and started to strip off their clothes which smelled of diesel and other fumes that clung to their clothing from the close confines of a submarine.

One by one they walked, some wearing what passed for a clean towel, others just a smile, along the main passageway and making their way down into the next deck that had their allocated heads (bathroom) area, carrying their dirty clothing, and toiletries.

To have a shit, shave, shower and shampoo after several weeks without access to fresh water, or worry about the shortage of it, was sheer bliss for them all. Soon the scrubbing brushes and the standard issue of green soap was out, for 'Jack' dhoby his kit then himself clean again.

An abundance of hot water from the showers and the different posh soaps rubbed all over their bodies, rinsed off with more warm water, helped them start feeling more like human beings again instead of smelly diesel-driven animals who had just emerged from the deep. This was also the time for those who didn't request to grow a 'Set' had to shave his beard off, T.S. included.

When he had finished shaving, he discovered there was a good-looking, blue-eyed bloke looking at himself in the mirror.

"There you are Signalman! Thought you jumped ship in Colombo! Let's get the dhobying down into the drying room and then for some scran." He said to himself but got a ribbing from the others.

"Stop talking to yourself or the big man wearing the badge of the King's hat on his arm will come and take you away." Telegraphist Underwood remarked

17

"You're only jealous of my good looks Ron!"

"Fer Chris'sake! I'm surprised you haven't broken the ruddy mirror." Brown, the other Telegraphist quipped and flicked his towel at the bare bum of T.S.

"As you appear to be the only one to know where the drying room is, how about you taking my dhobying too?" Boyall requested, who was swiftly joined by several of the others.

"Yeah right! And for my next trick which is also impossible for you lazy lot." T.S. replied, and after wrapping himself up in his damp towel he sauntered off out of the compartment, along a passageway, down a gangway ladder and into a dimly-lit yet hot compartment that was full of drying clothing. He spotted a light at the end of the compartment coming from another one leading off from it.

He investigated what it was and to his surprise, found a large compartment full of washing machines, with several Chinese looking men dashing away with their smoothing irons.

A scantily dressed man with a small Billy goat beard came over to him enquiring what he wanted.

"Didn't know there's a Dhoby Wallah on board! I've just arrived here on board S64, with 3 other boats that have come to form the squadron here." T.S. replied evenly.

"Ah so! We have a daily dhoby collection, return them following morning fully ironed, Monday to Saturday morning. We charge one-shilling English money for each bundle collected, even if it's just the one item. We'll give you your own dhoby mark and you pay me every payday. No pay no dhobying." The garlicky, curry-laced breath of the man wafted up,as he spoke in Pidgin English, yet with an Australian accent.

"Sounds right by me. Anything else I should know, like a tailor, a barber or cobbler for instance?"

"Yes! 'So So' can make you a nice suit or whatever you want, and 'Shoe Shoe' can make you new sandals or whatever."

"That's brilliant! Wait until I spread the news about all this. By the way, are you people 'Ship's company' or do you work from ashore?"

"We Local Entry people down from Hong Kong and been with this ship for several years."

"Well Mr, er Mr?" T.S asked, searching for his name.

"Me So Hi, my brother over there is So Lo 'cause I'm bigger than him and No 1 Son."

"Well pleased to meet you Mr Hi, I'm T.S. off S64 as I've told you."

"No! My name is Hi! In China my last name is So." He grinned and shook hands with T.S.

"Okay then Hi So, pleased to meet you. Maybe you can pay us a visit in the morning in 2 deck, and here's my mess-deck number and my name. You will find that that is the accommodation for 6 boats crews, but you'll have to find out about the Senior Rates and the Officers quarters yourself. Must go now." T.S. stated and commenced putting his dhobying onto the drying racks, only to be met by more of these messmates that had arrived.

"Guess what lads! We've got a Chinese Laundry in that compartment behind me. He'll be collecting our clobber each day and have it washed, ironed and mended the following day. Says it's only 1 shilling a bundle. He also says that there's a cobbler and a tailor on board too. So it looks as if we'll have a cushy life on this tub." T.S. announced, and got a loud cheer from them.

"And here's me ruining my finger nails on that washboard too. I feel like a real scrubber now!" Hemmings quipped, putting on a lisping voice, with one hand placed on his hip and waving his other hand limply, making the others laugh at the pretence, only for him to duck and try to dodge the shower of items that were thrown his way in fun.

They were nicely surprised to find that instead of the usual surface vessel method of 'Broadside messing' where all the food is taken from the galley and dished up in the mess decks, they had a dining room to use, with a cafeteria type of service to serve the food.

From the furnishings, they guessed that it was a throwback to when the ship was a liner catering for rich fare paying passengers.

"Blimey! We've even got Yankee type of dishes to yaffle from, white Pyrex I think they call it. And real silver lined knives and forks too." Graham Parry, one of the Leading Stokers declared!

"Would you just look at the polished lino on the deck? Look at those lovely curtains. Are you sure we're in the right place. It looks all 'Officers Mess only to me" Dave Brawn, the Leading Sonar Operator quipped.

Brian Mackenzie, the boat's Leading Chef appeared from behind the serving counter assuring them all that this really was their dining hall.

"Just a gentle warning to you all. For the time we spend inboard, Scratcher (the boat's 2nd Cox'n) will detail 2 mess-deck dodgers assigned to clean the mess-deck, heads and bathrooms including this dining room. This will also apply to the other boats and you'll all be working together in one big gang. In the meantime each one of you are responsible for clearing away your own mess and placing your used crockery etc in the receptacles provided along that bulkhead over there. Any spillages must be mopped up immediately and not left for others to tread in and probably slip on their arse into the bargain." he announced, with an approving nod from the General Service P.O. Chef who was standing in the background.

Soon the crew were tucking into some real Aussie tucker, of 'T' bone steak, egg, chips and mushrooms, followed by a large slice of melon for those who wanted it, but most importantly all swilled down by a couple of tins of ice cold beer.

"That was one feast worth coming all this way for. Our compliments to the Chef!" T.S. said with a loud burp towards the PO chef, who simply grinned as his response.

"Did you notice one thing peculiar about this place Ron?" Boyall asked, but gave T.S. a sly wink as he flashed up a 'duty free' cigarette.

"Not really, what is it?" Underwood queried.

Brown sat there with a smirk on his face and announced that he knew the answer.

"Okay Ken, clever clogs! What is it?" T.S. asked with a groan.

"When we came in to sit down what did you spot was missing from all this. I mean table wise?" Brown teased.

"I did notice that all furniture, the lights and pictures on the bulkheads weren't swinging around for a change, if that's what you mean." Boyall stated, looking around innocently at what he was supposed to see.

"Partly! In fact it's the first meal we've had without a rubber mat to stop our food from sliding around all over the place. We'd have to go down at least 200 feet for that, yet here we are on the surface and not the slightest movement." Brown declared. Boyall, who was sitting a few places away from Brown sighed then shoved the group of condiments and sauce bottles roughly, one by one towards him.

"Try that for size, clever bugger!" he said with a laugh, as they all slid off the table to land in Brown's lap spilling some of their contents onto him.

"Oops! Somebody must have moved the ship when you weren't looking Ken!" T.S. quipped.

Underwood looked at the mess on Brown's shorts and tutt-tutted, saying that obviously they couldn't take him anywhere.

It was getting dark now with everybody settling into their bunks for their first full night's sleep in over 2 weeks, without any instant disruptions to waken them up.

There were batteries of electric fans revolving over their heads to keep the place cool, but T.S. opened his porthole, then with his newly found 'wind-scoop', shoved it out to catch the cool breezes coming over the water that lapped gently some 15 feet below his porthole. He managed to spot a further row of portholes below him that were much nearer to the water to guess they were in the deck where the store-rooms and perhaps the dhoby wallahs accommodation spaced.

He was still thinking of the day's events whilst looking up at the deck-head at the fans, enjoying one last cigarette before getting some kip, but managed to hear the faint but shrill tones of the Bosun's call made by the duty Quartermaster, telling everybody to 'pipe down' and get to sleep.

"Chris!" he asked Boyall who was head to head with him in the next column of bunks.

"Yeah! Wassa-matta! Can't sleep?" he asked sleepily.

"I've got a plane load of mail to bring on board in the morning, let alone sending off ours. Any chance of a helper?"

"Better wait and see what the Cox'n' and Dave Lewis has got in store for us. Don't forget we're all mustering to de-store the boat including all those ruddy spares we brought with us, getting ready for certain internal modifications to it. All hands on deck so to speak. Let alone Brian Westwood having Bill Crank to strip down the 632 which will make the office a slight squeeze to get in and out of."

"But the REA will be too busy sorting out the new sonar arrays we've brought with us. Bill will have enough on his plate let alone the main transmitter. Oh well, it would be best if I'm out of it altogether, and just do my own tasks then" T'S concluded, flicking his dog-end out of the porthole fell into a deep sleep.

Chapter III

Alongside

T.S. was excused by the direct sanction of the No1 from the de-storing, given that he had a 'personnel morale' duty to perform, in the shape of taking off the outgoing mail then collecting a large pile of incoming mail.

He climbed slowly up the steep ladder with a backward look at the hive of activity below him, and likened it to an ants nest, with men scurrying backwards and forwards to satisfy the ever hungry demands of the cranes that were taking away whatever was placed into its nets. He crossed the main weather deck of the depot ship to glance at the port side where the other two boats were, to see that their crews were also involved with the same activity of de-storing.

With his blue nylon bag slung across his back like a kit-bag, he located the duty gangway quartermaster and asked for the whereabouts of the Mail office. Having followed his instructions, and finding his way to the office he passed the very place he needed to pay a visit to, which was shut for the present, according to the 'opening hours', by the order of the Canteen Manager, Barrie Morris.

"Hmm! I'm not duty watch today, so I'll maybe visit him around the 1st dog watch hours, and before supper." he said, making a mental note of the 'opening hours' and reminded himself that he needed Aussie dollars to spend there.

He reached the compartment, knocking on the wooden door that declared its function and who was in charge, then stepped inside.

He saw an exasperated Leading Patrolman angrily throwing items of mail, seemingly willy-nilly at a large collection of brown bags that were filling with each throw.

"Leading Regulator Magnes?"

Magnes looked over to see T.S standing there.

"Bloody Submariners" he growled, then with a change of mood.

"What's up Sparks? What can I do you for?" he asked when he saw the Branch badge T.S. was wearing.

"I'm T.S. and Postie off S64, with some outgoing mail to hand in also collect any incoming mail for us."

"Glad you've arrived, in fact you're the first of your lot to do so. Yes, I've got several bags of mail to be collected, but not until I've sorted it all out. What's in your outgoing mail? Any registered or specials?"

"No, just normal stuff. Mind you, I'm not sure of the correct stamps per weight of items, or whether it can all go by sea or not."

Magnes stopped his mail sorting and came over to a large table, ordering him to empty his bag out onto it.

Magnes sifted through the large pile picking out the items he thought would be a problem.

"Hmm! You've done well Sparks. Let's hope the other posties are just as good. I'll sort them out for you but in return you'll help me finish the sorting of this lot." Magnes stated with an Australian drawl, waving his arm across several unopened brown mailbags.

T.S looked at it all, took off his hat and asked to be shown what was what.

Soon he was throwing mail items into the brown mailbags, almost like a professional Dart player, just like he had seen Magnes do when he arrived.

It took a good half hour to complete the task, but in the meanwhile the two men were now on first names terms.

"All sorted this end Des! Didn't know we had all this mail, and only from Colombo too." T.S said as he counted at least 9 brown mailbags ready to be taken away, with even more for the other boats that came with his.

"Actually, some of it is sea-mail that must have been diverted from Simonstown. Most of it Red Cross parcels."

"Lovely! Home comforts can't be bad! Any chance if it being put onto a 'sky hook' and lowered onto our pontoon for me? Otherwise it's going to take me up to the ruddy dog watches to shift it all. In fact Des, maybe you could arrange for it all to be dropped onto the boat's pontoon. I mean, if it's going to take me several return trips all the way up here, then magnify it three times for the others, you'll never finish this side of the 1st watch."

Magnes looked at the large collection, realising that what T.S. had said was true, so agreed for it to be lifted over by the duty crane driver, providing the crane driver was still 'turned to'.

"The crane drivers are busy de-storing the boats at the moment, so I suppose you could ask your boss, er Chief or whomever to get things organised on completion of it. It's nearly stand easy on board now, so if I take a bag now, maybe you can get my lift down by say, Tot time' which is around 1230 ish."

"Now that is a very good idea. I'll cost you at least a 'wet' if I do."

"And here's me thinking that a man wearing the insignia of the King's hat on his arm is above blackmail, or is it Sea-mail. If you want a gulper of my tot Des, then who am I to argue, but bring some of the famous Aussie Golden Nectar I've been told about, I'll show you round the boat."

"I'm going R.A. as of tomorrow, but thanks for the offer. Maybe next time, and I'll hold you to it."

"Fair enough Des! My boat is on the Starboard for'ard trot No 2. See you probably tomorrow. Oh and by the way, I'm short of stamps, have you got any?"

"Actually I'm out of most of them right now. If it's only for yourself then I suggest you try seeing Barrie Morris the Canteen Damager, he might have a few left. Other than that, there's the new civvy post office being made into the Base Mail Sorting Office, down at the married quarters village they're making, as that's where I'm getting mine from."

"First day inboard Des, so give us a chance. Perhaps the other posties will be in the same proverbial boat too. Maybe you can arrange this too?"

"As my original statement when I first saw you, Bloody Submariners!" Magnes sighed, but agreed to try and get it sorted for him.

"Cheers Des! Incidentally, as we're victual led inboard, where is the post box for us to use instead of on board the boat?"

"There's one outside the canteen flat, and one here just outside my caboose. No stamps, no postage. Over weight mail will incur extra charges, but you know the score on that."

"Right then Des, I'm off. Thanks for the info, see you anon!" T.S concluded, then swung the heavy mailbag over his shoulder, left the compartment to act just like Santa Claus, with his big bag of goodies and other presents.

Chapter IV

Growing Up

Over the next couple of days, thanks to the exchange of knowledge, the boats crew got to know their new surroundings, on board the depot ship at least. For all element of the services occupying the inlet had their own things to deal with and grow up with new and daily additions to their own little domain. But for the boat's crews, in order of precedence, it was the mess deck, heads and bathroom, galley, NAAFI, then the workshops and who to see there, then back onboard again for 'tot time', especially for when the golden eagle shits into your hat (payday).

It was also a time for the boat's crew get to know one another, with a series of musters, lectures, and other interactive events, soon this very new Submarine Squadron was formed.

Every boat was thoroughly cleaned and given a new coat of jet black paint on the outside and 'poxy' white on the inside, with their Pennant number painted on both sides of their fins to denote who was whom.

Even the depot ship was seen to in the same manner, just to complete the turn-out.

This took a full week and was a fractious time because some of the 'wet paynte' ended up not on the metal but on the person, especially when everybody was trying to look neat and tidy in white tropicals.

After that week of frenetic activity, came the big 'DIVISIONS' where everybody had to dress up in funny white suits with the inane title of 'ice cream suits'. All were looking like snowmen, and some were smart as a guardsman but not quite as tall.

This parade was to be held ashore on a prepared area earmarked for the Admiral's Command HQ for the entire base, be they Coastal Forces, Marines, Fleet Air Arm, Submariners, or the local Artillery Battery.

Whilst the boats crews were RN, the depot ship and the rest were by the grace of the R.A.N. So instead of listening to the stirring music of 'HEARTS OF OAKS' or other such naval marches as performed by a band of the Royal Marines, they heard the strains of 'Waltzing Matilda' and other strange unlikely antipodean sounds. All of which was kindly provided by the brass band of the Artillery camp from the opposite shore of the inlet, cheered on and witnessed by the host of civilian workers with their families who had gathered from the newly constructed village at the bottom end of the inlet.

The Squadron Commissioning Ceremony had passed, giving everybody a feel good factor and for a gay 'bonhomie' attitude between the 4 services occupying the shores of this inlet. All of a sudden almost everybody inherited a nickname, some which were obvious and some really as daft as the person who inherited it, but nobody minded one jot.*

It was also a time for a bit of recreation, where each 'Unit' entered their names into the locally organised day time sporting activities, but in the evenings, it was darts, dominoes, skittles, watching the latest movie, dances, the much loved evening 'barbies' that were held on the lovely sandy beaches of the cove.

Maybe the cynics would portray it all as a propaganda or P.R. stunt, but in reality, it was just human nature taking over to bolster all those going off to fight the reportedly most ruthless of foe, the all conquering Imperial Japanese Forces.

This was especially true for all concerned, as there were still several very important tasks or other preparations to be made to be able to conduct such a deadly game of war, and as each day passed they were getting more ready for the task.

One afternoon T.S. was taking his turn as the duty 'Trot Sentry' standing by the now vacant gangway, as everybody had

---

* Gay. As in the traditional Centuries old expression of being happy and carefree and not the politically-correct term for being homosexual.

gone inboard, leaving only the 'duty watch' on board.

This would consist of an Officer, a Seaman P.O. plus any 3 sailors, a Telegraphist, an Electrician, an E.R.A. or either a Chief or P.O. Stoker depending who's on board plus 3 Stokers, all deemed to be able to move the vessel away in an emergency or a crises that threatened her safety.

He heard a loud resonant sound coming from a ships horn, and saw a massive tanker with a small launch in front of it, coming slowly towards him. He informed the duty P.O. who came rushing up onto the casing to see for himself.

P.O. Woods, the Sonar Operator's head of department (P.O. U.C) looked at this spectacle for a moment ordering that the hatches be shut to prevent any waves from the wake entering the boat.

"How the hell did she get through the narrow gorge? More to the point, where do you suppose she'll anchor Slinger? I mean, the oil jetty and fuel bunkers are not quite ready to take her yet?"

"Probably anchor down towards the floating docks and the refit area, where the water is still pretty deep, I guess."

"Hmmm! According to the Harbour State signal, there's a freighter due in tonight as well, and another one tomorrow. It's going to get very crowded around here." T.S. informed.

"The Aussie navy must be lining up something special if they're sending large supply vessels our way. Perhaps, they may just be parking here to get out of the way in the Gulf!

"Well, let's hope that when we get back off our first patrol, we've still got a parking space."

"We'll soon see when the other 2 boats arrive. 4 pontoons between 6 and all that."

"Nothing new there Slinger. We're used to hot bunking, so why not a case of the 'hot trots'. Maybe get to tie up alongside outboard, once in a while."

Woods had observed enough to give his decision.

"Let it pass, then wait until the wash has gone before you have the hatches opened up again." he concluded and went below via the fin door and down the conning tower hatch into the control room.

T.S. stood awhile watching with fascination the heavy laden tanker drop anchor then to transform herself into a source of light bulbs shining everywhere, with sea boats being launched with crewmen eager to get ashore, although he couldn't figure out where considering there was only a small NAAFI canteen bar in the village.

During these 2 weeks 'pastoral' time alongside, the inlet was transformed from a peaceful creek and valley into a bustling area of activity. Nissen huts by the score, AA gun batteries positioned above them on the cliff tops, landing jetties, marker buoys along part of the waterway, even an air base complete with large hangars, barracks, or other warehouses along the entrance both sides of the inlet; all seemed to appear almost overnight, like mushrooms in a cow field.

To get from one side of the inlet to the other there was a small ferry service for passengers, with a road and light railway track going down around the shoreline for train and vehicular traffic. The R.A.N, Fleet Air arm, Submarine Squadron, Marines, the Artillery regiment and a civilian village had shoe-horned themselves into this small inlet with radar and radio aerials placed in suitable locations along the cliff tops as were most of the defensive ring of AA guns.

The arrival of a squadron of MGBs, MTBs and FMLs caused a stir as they first raced down the length of the inlet, followed closely by the slower Minesweepers, before spinning round to make their way to their new base on the right hand side of the inlet. Next to arrive, with much to the delight of all on deck at the time to see it, were six Seaplanes who emerged through the fjord and landed on the water, only to taxi their way ashore to their new hangar on the shoreline. They were followed by two lots of six Fairey Aircraft that landed on the newly constructed airfield, to be stowed away in their own hangars lined up next to the airfield control tower.

T.S. was on the bridge looking at each Fast Patrol Boat passing, managing to note their pennant numbers and whether they were gunboats torpedo boats or minelayers just in case he was needed to identify any of them in the future. He also did this with the aircraft recognition markings, discovering that 6 were Swordfish torpedo bombers, and 6 were Fairey Fighter bombers.

What seemed to make the picture complete, was the arrival of three tugs of various sizes, then what looked like a few Torpedo Loading Vessels followed by a couple of small coastal tankers. Then one afternoon whilst on duty again, he saw a large plume of smoke coming from the right hand side of the airfield, and on using his binoculars, he discovered that it came from a tall chimney, which he put down to being the new communal incinerator and power station. Not long after that, the inlet had its own lighting from it instead of relying on the individual camp's generators to do so.

Very early one morning around 5 am when he was sitting quietly, he heard the huffing and puffing of a steam engine, which stirred him up from his stool on the gun sponson. With the aid of his trusty binoculars he saw a large steam engine was hauling several flat wagons loaded with boxes or round objects that looked like large footballs. He watched it enter the area where the underground ammo dump was made from a disused copper drift mine, guessing those round objects must be mines, with the long boxes to be full of torpedoes for both the boat and MTB squadrons.

Along came the day when finally, the 'pièce de résistance' was put into place, when the tall flagpole out in front of the HQ building sported a large white flag quartered in a red stripe and 1 red ball in two corners of it. This then would be the badge of office for a Vice Admiral, and anybody of a lesser rank would render unto him. King of the castle or top of the pile of brass hats and red tape if you prefer it.

This was another excuse for a full Base Parade, whereby everybody not on duty had to be on parade to welcome the new Flag officer, Vice Admiral Peter Hammersley to take command as F.O.N.A.C.

This was also another time when several 'outstanding favours' were called in and tots were collected from those who were able to wangle themselves out of it, or managed to find a decent excuse not to attend. Thus instead of the intended 2,500 out of a possible 2,900 personnel from the base on parade, there was less than half of that number, S64 and her crew, somehow 'inherited' a host of 'observers' who managed find their way on board to scrape out of it due to operational training with the Marines. The local hospital, especially the sickbays from each camp were inundated with requests to be 'excused boots' creating an epidemic which worked for some but not others. Ingenuity and inventiveness was at its height from all levels during that time, yet rapidly disappeared immediately after the event. As long as the Admiral was chuffed with his reception was all that mattered, and as it transpired he was more than pleased, therefore nothing else was done or said about it afterwards.

Chapter V

Incidentals

Everybody at the base were conducting their allotted tasks in life, with a quiet fortitude knowing full well that it was the proverbial calm before the storm, waiting for when the 'shit hits the fan', with everybody armed to the teeth, ready to 'Kick Ass' as the new phrase goes when 'Hank the Yank' turned up on Australia's doorstep having been kicked up the ass and taken over by the Japs in the Philippines. When they arrived it was the first time in centuries and the last time for Australia ever to be invaded albeit with a friendly one, as the Americans built several air bases along the northern coast-line.

Each task, be it big or small, meant that it was one step nearer to be ready for sea, and a hectic time for some.

For instance; T.S. was in the control room with James, bagging up the censored mail ready for posting, when Lewis the PO Tel came along.

"Ah Signalman! I need you to go inboard and see the 'Jack Dusty' (storeman) to get some signal pads, writing sticks and other items. Here's the list of everything needed."

"Glad you asked Dave, I need to have my 5inch Aldis lamp fixed or replaced as the trigger on it is broken. Any chance of a stores chit to add to yours?"

"That's a point! This is my last one, so better add it to the list. But I'll give you an authorisation note. If not then you'll have to see the LREM."

"I'm on my mail run just now, will do it when I get back."

"Well, if you do see Bill Crank, tell him I need him to come down to the office."

"Roger that!" T.S. confirmed, then completed his immediate task to go for'ard, passing the wardroom.

"Are you the duty Sparker today Signalman?" Bell, the new Navigating Officer asked, poking his head out through the curtain that marked the 'door' of the wardroom.

"No sir, Brown is, but he's required on board and not allowed to go inboard unless it's for his scran."

"Then I'm afraid you'll have to do. I need you to come with me to carry the confidential waste ashore. I've got transport to take us down to the incinerator."

"What time sir? Only I've got an errand for the PO Tel to do after my mail run." T.S. sighed quietly.

"The duty pinnace will take us ashore to the Flagstaff jetty at 1500, for pick up by the duty transport truck. Shouldn't take long, as I've got to be back for 1600." Bell explained.

"Fine by me sir! Where shall I find you?"

"Meet me here in the control room at 1430."

"Aye aye sir!" T.S. acknowledged then threw his blue mailbag over his shoulder, made his way to the mail office inboard.

"Just my flippin' luck! I'm supposed to meet up for some quality time ashore with the Army Signaller twins, Jackie and Sylvia, er Bramall I think their surname is. Yesterday's barbie was definitely the best so far, maybe I'll get to show them my badges if they show me theirs!" He sighed wistfully.

Whilst he waited for the mail to be ready for collection he had time to nip down into the Stores office where he encountered the Jack Dusty, issuing items to the sailor in front of him.

"Cheers Doug. Maybe this new set of 10's will fit me better that the other ones " the sailor commented and left.

"Hello Doug, got a few stores req's for you." T.S. said cheerfully.

"Leading Stores Assistant Pointon to you, pal." Came the annoyed and harassed reply.

"Sorry and all that! Only trying to be friendly, as I did hear your name being mentioned." T.S. said defensively.

"Well, whatever! What can I do for you Sparks?" Poynton said less aggressively, taking the chit he was given.

"Sorry pal, you've come to the wrong stores. You'll need to go either to the MSO, the Comcen or the Base Supply Office

(BSO) ashore for what you want, as I don't do Boats stores let alone Comms stuff. Only loan clothing, bedding, slops and the like."

"Bloody handy stores office this is, considering this is supposed to be a Submarine Depot Ship after all." T.S. groaned as his thoughts were of a long trek ashore just for a few measly pads of paper, pencils and other office requirements.

"Look pal! If you've got any drips or complaints about it then go and slap a Drip Chit into the Master At Arms Office. Can't you see I'm busy, now bugger off! Next!" Pointon shouted, pointing to the person behind T.S.

T.S. shrugged his shoulders then left the compartment for the next lap of his journey.

On his way back, loaded up with mail for the ships company, he met up with Crank.

"Bill! I've got a message from Dave Lewis, who he says you're to go and see him in the office. I've asked him to give me a chit to get a new Aldis, but says that you might be able to fix it for me."

"What does he want me for this time? As far as your aldis is concerned, you might as well ditch it overboard as it's totally knackered with all the signalling you've been doing since we left Blighty."

"Just doing my job Bill, that's all. Dave was muttering about a new ballast lamp for the main transmitter if that's any good."

"Bloody hell! I clean forgot all about that. Thanks for the reminder. Better go and see him first though as the REA has me lined up to fit a new LF/ MF transceiver in the W/T office, let alone getting a spare filter fitted on the radar display unit." Crank moaned.

"It's all go at the top then!" T.S. commiserated, and leaving Crank he staggered his way back down onto the boat under the weight of the boats mailbags..

"Here we are Signalman. Get the sacks of waste ashore whilst I go and phone for the transport." Bell ordered, leaving T.S.

struggling with several bags of out-of-date codebooks and other items needing to be destroyed by incineration.

Within minutes, a 3 ton truck arrived, much to T.S's surprise, the driver was a WAAF, and very pretty too from her shapely profile he noticed, but then no red- blooded 'Jack' couldn't help noticing such fine details.

"Afternoon sir! I've already got a load in the back for the incinerator, so just have yours piled onto it. There is room in the drivers cab for you both, so climb aboard when you're ready." She informed them, then waited for the loading before fitting the tailgate up again and all three crowded into the cab for her to drive away.

They passed through each area's main gate, which were manned by the new base's Police Security teams.

As T.S. was sitting close to her he was able to sneak the odd look down her ample cleavage, which only whetted his appetite for the twins he hoped to meet up with later.

"What's an Air force girl doing over at the F.A.A. base, er, driver?" T.S. asked.

"Call me Edna, Edna Clarke that is. I'm a signaller, part of the advance party from our Squadron of Hurricanes due here at the end of the week." She said with a melodic voice.

"How did they get all the way here to Australia, Clarke?" Bell asked politely.

"They were originally sent out in sections by ship to help reinforce Singapore. But were redirected to Darwin, reassembled ready to be flown here for final location. Seeing as you've got a ready-made base here for your aircraft our Group Captain decided to come here and help out 'Hank the Yank' defend his bomber squadrons dotted along the northern coast, from Cairns to Darwin." She told them. On noticing T.S. sneaking a quick look down her cleavage, she rewarded him with a slap on his bare knee just below his white shorts.

"Down boy!" she said with a smile, but carried on driving her lorry out through the main naval base gate (South), over the

Bailey bridge passing through the new village to be met at the main gate (North).

"Hello Patrolman Lewis! Here's my chit to get to the incinerator." Clarke stated in a business- like manner showing her pass.

"Hello Edna, didn't know you were part of the Transport section? When's the next dance you girls are putting on? Only I've got my wife and kids arriving tomorrow as we're moving into married quarters in the village and she likes her dancing." Lewis replied when he recognised her.

"No Vince, I'm just filling in for a pal for the day. Yes you certainly can do a stand- in for Fred Astaire. As a matter of fact, we've got one organised for tonight, with luck another one next weekend. Tonight's' at 1900 at the village NAAFI complex, not sure about the next one though, as we've got a half squadron of Yank planes visiting us then. So get your dancing shoes on and maybe I'll let you tango me awhile for old times sake, if you like." She said with a smile, as he opened the gates letting her drive through to continue her short journey along the perimeter fence of the airfield to the incinerator.

"Sounds all nice and cosy Clarke! Is it an invitation dance for all comers or what?" Bell asked.

"You've got one being laid on at the main Officers Mess tomorrow at 1930 I think sir. We girls are in short supply, roughly 1to 10 of you boys at the moment, so we must share our social lives with all the boys on the base not just the few lucky ones. That way we girls can have fun from all the camps, at least that's what the Admiral's Secretary Evonne Broad has told us. She by the way is also the base's Entertainments Officer, who hopes to bring some of the ENSA mob up here soon."

"Rats! And here's me thinking I've pulled a pair of them for myself. Maybe you know them Edna? They're twins called Jackie and Sylvia Bramall, from the Army Signals Unit." T.S. grumbled.

"Why yes! They're the twins that I've shared a few shifts with in the new underground communications centre behind the

Admiral's office. Good swimmers they are, and just as pretty as the rest of us." She said with a grin.

"Never mind, you can always stand in line with all the other hopefuls. By your badge you're a Naval Telegraphist, so that makes us all Comms ratings in one big pot. And stop looking down my top." she added, trying to change the subject, slapping him on his knee when she saw him trying to sneak another look down her blouse.

"It seems this place is blessed with hills that are of outstanding natural beauty." T.S. grinned, flicking his eyebrows and winking at Edna, who blushed guessing at what he was referring to, before giving him another slap for his cheek.

"That's not fair! It's all slap but no tickle." T.S. said, rubbing the red hand mark she made on his knee.

"We girls must keep you boys from getting too fresh!" she replied, returning his wink with a smile

"Show some restraint and behave yourself Signalman, or you'll get out and walk back!" Bell ordered, as the vehicle stopped by the large open mouth of the furnace, which was right in front of the vehicle.

Bell looked at his watch, then ordered T.S. to help Clarke to offload the truck by throwing all the sacks into the unquenchable flames that occupied the abyss below them.

Soon they were back on board the depot ship for T.S. to take his leave from Bell, to get himself ready to meet his double date.

T.S. was standing in the queue outside the NAAFI shop when he spotted an object lying near a gash bucket, investigating what it was, he discovered it was somebody's pay-book.

"Better give it to Barrie in case Stoker Bell or whatever his name is from the water stained ink, decides to retrace his steps looking for it." he muttered.

This, he decided was the safest option because if he took it to the Master at Arms office, Bell would be in for it.

He spotted Stoker Ted Lewis in the queue, showed him the

pay-book and asked him if he knew Bell, who maybe off one of the boats.

"Ted! You seem to know every stoker in the squadron, do you know this one?" T.S. asked and showed the pay book to him.

"Hmm! I know of an ugly bugger called 'Quasimodo' Bellringer off of S63, but in this case, this name doesn't ring a bell with me. Sorry and all that. Why not try Barrie Morris the canteen manager, he gets to know everybody on board let alone the Master at Arms." Lewis offered, and was thanked for his trouble.

"Sorry Sparks, this is not a lost property office! Best place for that is up in the M.A.A's office." Morris stated with a shake of his head, which dashed any hopes of saving the stoker from grief.
Once T.S. made his purchases left the canteen flat, he had to with reluctance, report this to the M.A.A. but secretly hoping not to bump into him in case he got picked up for a 'hair cut', or some other cock-a mamie excuse.

T.S. knocked on the M.A.A's office door then on entering the office, he found a Regulating Petty Officer, commonly known by the rest as 'Deputy Dawg' to the big white Chief of Police.

"Excuse me RPO, I wish to hand in an article to the Sheriff, but as you're here you might as well have it." he said and saw a neat little sign on a desk stating that this RPO was Ray Isted.

"Sheriff! Who are you calling the M.A.A. the sheriff?" Isted shouted indignantly.

"Sorry RPO but all our Cox'ns on boats gets called that, as that is what he does on board when enforcing a 241. He even gets called the Grocer, because he is the one who makes out the shopping list for our chefs to get our scran on board. Then again he gets called the 'Doc' as he's the one that runs our 'Rose Cottage' handing out plasters etc. So I mean no disrespect to the man whose job it is to act as the local Police Chief." T.S. replied defensively, which made Isted give a little smile before he wound his neck back in again.

"What is it you have to hand in then?" he asked in a more civilised tone.

"It's a pay-book that I found in the NAAFI canteen flat. I was hoping to return it to him without getting him into trouble." T.S. said, handing over the item.

Isted looked at whom it belonged to, then told him it didn't belong to any of the Depot ship's crew, but judging by the manky state of it, it probably belonged to a Submariner.

"Oh well then RPO, I'll take it back and find out which boat he's on, to save you the bother. Maybe I'll get a 'gulper' for my troubles too."

"Here you are then and best of luck, if not then the stoker has less than 24 hours to report it." Isted agreed, handing the book back again.

"You'll do no such thing RPO! A pay-book is a very important document that contains a man's service identity and records and is part of his kit issue." roared a voice from behind a screen at the back of the office.

"Who are you? What do you want? If you've found a pay-book it's your duty to surrender it to this office and for the offender to report its loss before we issue a 241 on him. In case you don't know what a 241 is then it's a…"

"It's an offenders charge sheet MAA. I know as I've typed quite a few of them in the past."

"Well get yourself out of this office before you have to type one out for yourself, and next time have more respect for my office. I could charge you with insolence towards a Senior Rate, now get out before I change my mind. And get your ruddy 'air cut!" the big burly M.A.A. bellowed, pointing to the door.

"Nice to have met you RPO. I'm on my way Sheriff. One 'air cut coming up. " T.S. sighed and managed to duck some missile that the MAA threw at him as he disappeared out of sight.

"Remind myself not to go near that place again. Next time I'll see the Cox'n." he muttered and made his way down to his mess deck.

"Glad you're back Signalman, only we've got to go ashore to the Comcen to fetch those stores you didn't get for us." Boyall stated, donning his cap.

"Come off it Chris! I've been on the go all bloody day, and only just escaped from the Sheriff's office without being put on a 241. It's the last bloody time I'll act as the duty Samaritan that's for certain." T.S. said, stowing his NAAFI purchases into his locker.

"The thing is, we've all got to go and meet up with Dave Lewis there, including Ron who's on duty, as we're being given a spiel from Cdr S/M's Chief Tel, er Bob Goodman, of the '*Neptune*' fame I think. Anyway, according to Dave Lewis, he's pie hot. Has to be to be the Squadron's Chief Tel, I suppose." Boyall explained.

"Yeah! We've got the chance to cop an eyefull of all those delectable female signallers, instead of looking at our own home grown ugly one." Brown commented and gave T.S. a meaningful look, then followed Boyall up the ladder and out of the mess deck.

"Well as a mater of fact Chris, I've got to get into the BSO to collect a couple of bridge ensigns whilst ashore anyway, so I might be parting company with you on completion of this exercise."

"You'd better clear that with Dave Lewis. I think he's going to give us a back up spiel of his own when we return on board."

"You seem to forget Chris! As I'm T.S. I only do Seamen's watches not W/T office watches."

"Hmmm! Good point, but you'll still need to be around for certain relevant facts being dished out, being part of the Sparkers branch on board."

"Okay then! Were the rest of you around when I was taking a Ship Recognition exam and Inter Allied visual signalling protocols before we left Ceylon, and even last week?"

"That's your domain as T.S. not ours."

"Exactly Chris! My case rests!"

"Fine by me, but it's Dave Lewis to decide." Boyall concluded as they all climbed into the next pinnace to take them from the depot ship to go over to the Flagstaff landing pontoon.

Part Two

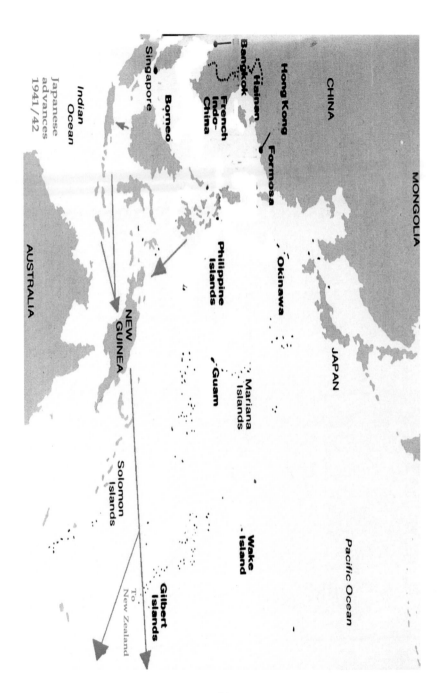

CHINA

MONGOLIA

Hong Kong

Hainan

Bangkok

French Indo-China

Formosa

Singapore

Borneo

Indian Ocean

AUSTRALIA

Japanese advances 1941/42

Okinawa

JAPAN

NEW GUINEA

Philippine Islands

Mariana Islands

Guam

Solomon Islands

Wake Island

Gilbert Islands

To New Zealand

Pacific Ocean

The Royal Navy's A-class submarine (S64)

Bad Neighbours

The year is around 1942 when the Japanese Imperial Forces were conducting a 3-pronged attack in the process of Island hopping to encompass, Java, Indonesia, the Moluccas, the Celebes Islands even the neutral lands of Portuguese Timor and part of New Guinea. Let alone the Gilbert and Solomon Islands, the Marshal Islands, the Caroline Islands, New England and the New Hebrides on their way south to threaten New Zealand.

During that time the combined A.B.D.A. (Australian, British, Dutch, American) fleet consisting of 9 cruisers and 24 destroyers tried to prevent the Japanese Invasion of Portuguese Timor and New Guinea. They were under the command of the Dutch Admiral Karel Doorman from his 12 inch heavy cruiser the *De Ruyter*, but were thrashed not only by superior numbers but also by the battleships and other much heavier ships and aircraft carriers of the Japanese, causing them to lose this crucial 'Battles of the Java Sea'.

Admiral Karel Doorman went down with his ship, thus ending any effective naval presence there by the Allied forces.

Of the 9 cruisers from the allied force, only 3crusiers plus 8 destroyers managed to escape being sunk, but not before they were given a heavy mauling in the process. They all ended up taking shelter in the relatively safer waters in the Gulf of Carpentaria. Those were the RN 6 inch light cruiser *Encounter*, the RAN 6inch light cruiser *Perth* and the RNN 9 inch medium cruiser *Den Helder*.

Chapter I

Slipped Out

The monsoon rains bucketing down during the very early hours of one morning deluged the black shadowy silhouette of S64, as her captain Lt Cdr Hosie slipped his boat from the mother ship's apron strings to sail silently away into the inky waters of the oceans that lay before her.

During those dark hours S64 made her way from her base, before stopping to get herself ready for a special covert operation that required all the skill and cunning needed to bring a successful conclusion to it.

"Captain! We've arrived at our designated area and adjacent to our own patrol area." the O.O.W reported.

"Very good! What's our battery strength?" Hosie asked.

"We've completed the second reduction. Both batteries at 100%, all gas cleared from the boat."

"Okay. Stop engines and go to diving stations. I'll be down in a minute."

"Aye aye sir!"

"Stop together! Clear the bridge! Diving stations! Stand by to dive! Uncotter 1, 3 & 5 main vents. Report when ready!" Welling commanded whilst Hosie made his way down from his little pressurised cabin just above the control room.

"Diving officer on watch! Fore-planes turned out and both planes manned!" Welling reported as Hosie climbed down the little chrome ladders into the control room.

"Very good No1! Press the klaxon twice and take us down. Come to periscope depth!"

The raucous tones of the klaxon alarm reverberated throughout the boat to let everybody know that the boat was about to submerge under the waves.

"Open 1, 3 & 5 main vents!"

Scarlett, the Outside E.R.A who was the one responsible for

operating the diving panel controls, pulled a few levers, and the noise of air escaping from the ballast tanks, told him and everybody else that the boat was now on its way down below and into the depths of the sea.

"1 Main vent open! 3 Main vent opened! No 5 main vent opened!" came the reports from the various parts of the boat.

"Upper lid shut with both clips. Tower cleared! Lower lid shut!" T.S reported, as the officer coming down from the conning tower arrived safely into the boat and allow the boat to dive.

"Very good Signalman."

"Captain! We have about one hour before sunrise but the horizon seems clear!" S/Lt Mike Sample the Torpedo Officer and Gunnery Officer as the off coming officer reported.

"Thank you T.O! Has the wireless office completed their signal broadcast yet? If not then raise the whip aerial!"
Hosie went over to the navigation table, busied himself with it whilst the wireless office made their report.

"Captain – W/T! Signal schedule completed, 4 incoming signals." Lewis the PO Tel reported some moments later.

"Very good W/T. Okay No 1. Let's see the trim. Group up! Half ahead together!"

"Starboard 10 steer 215. Keep a periscope depth of 50feet!"

The boat slid down into the murky depths of the ocean to be concealed from any eyes, be it human or electronic that might be looking their way.

"Periscope depth! Bubble slightly aft. Flood 70 gallons aft!" Welling ordered, then waited until the boat settled herself almost onto the magic reading of a 'zero' bubble.

"In trim!" he reported.

"Very good! Sonar! Keep a special listening watch astern of us!" Hosie ordered, continuing to scan the world above him until he was satisfied nothing was in sight.

"Down periscope. Let's take a 'Bathy' reading. Navigator, what depth have we got? Run the echo sounder for 5 seconds."

The clicking of the echo sounder recorded the depth beneath them onto a small ribbon of paper, indicating that the depth was 400 feet, and just as the N.O. reported the same figure.

"Take us down to 300 feet No1!"

"Aye aye sir!" Welling responded and started to read out the depth every 10 feet until the required depth was reached, then reported the fact to the captain.

"Let's hope we've got a good selection of thermals this time. Return to 100feet."

The boat rose slowly back to the required depth for Welling to report it.

"Very good No 1. Fall out diving team. Group down half ahead together. Maintain present course until 1300. I'll be in my cabin until then. Have the steward to bring me up my breakfast." Hosie ordered.

"Aye aye sir! Rig the control room ladder and open the lower lid!" Welling ordered, which prompted the messenger sitting next to the helmsman to carry out the orders.

"Captain – O.O.W. Time is now 1300 sir!" the duty officer informed via a special voice pipe from the control room up into the captains little cabin in the tower of the pressurised hull.

"Very good! Bring us up to periscope depth. No more than 50 feet." was the return command.

Hosie climbed down the little chrome ladder, ordering it to be removed once the lower lid leading into the tower was shut and clipped.

"Anything on sonar ?" he asked

"Nothing astern sir! A few faint traces coming from our port side, sir!" S/Lt Rod Hoare the Sonar Officer (S.O.) reported.

"Let's see what we've got then. Up after periscope!"

The big after periscope slid silently up from out of its well, as Hosie waited to engage his electric chair to it, thus enabling him to propel himself round and round whilst looking at the world above the waves.

He stopped a couple of times on his first round, before he was satisfied that there was nothing to bother himself with, ordering the periscope be lowered again.

"Captain – W/T! We have 1 special signal designated 'Officer's eyes only' signal for you, and 2 Operations Immediate' signals also for your attention sir."

Hosie acknowledged this information, then strode purposefully towards a specially sealed area some 8 feet by 6 feet which was situated behind the control room, containing the realm of the communications world within.

"What's up Lewis?" he asked as he appeared into the very cramped little office space.

"I have one special signal designated 'officers only' for you sir!" Lewis answered, holding out the pad with the coded messages on it.

"You do the honours to decipher it, whilst I read the tape as it comes out. Better clear the office though." he ordered.

"Clear the office and let the Captain sit next to me. I'll call you back when we've finished." Lewis ordered, which meant that the on watch Sparker had to stand outside in the passageway until he was ordered to return.

Lewis typed swiftly and accurately keeping his hands on the keyboard with his eyes on the signal pad that needed decoding, whilst the captain took the expanding ribbon from the decoding machine and read what was said.

"Hmm! Looks as if we're in for a short unexpected excursion, as our spot of hunting has been put in abeyance." He said as he finished reading the ticker tape.

"Okay, I'm satisfied. Do the honours and stick it down, then have it typed out and brought into the wardroom for me. What about the second one?"

"This looks like a follow on from your first one sir." Lewis replied, commencing to decipher it too.

When he had finished, he processed that one also as the captain thanked him and left the office.

"What was that all about POTS?" Brown, the current 'on watch' sparker asked.

"Can't tell you Ken! Sufficient to say that the skipper will be acting upon certain information that will involve us going to action stations before long. Best wait until the skipper announces his intentions first, before you start blabbing. Official Secrets protocol and all that, so bear that in mind."

"I thought that signal was something special, and I'm glad I recognised it to call you."

"Yes! You did well, but it's part of your ongoing training if you wish to reach the dizzy heights of being the Leading Tel of the boat just like Chris Boyall. Once I've typed it out in proper format and folded it so that you can't look at it, you'll take it to the skipper in the wardroom."

"But I've got two more 'O's and 1'P's to sort out Dave, er sorry, POTS!" Brown informed him swiftly.

"Fair enough! Belay my last! Get yourself for'ard and get Chris to come down and help you, whilst I finish off."

Lewis wrote down all the morse code messages coming from the high-speed tape recorder, deciphering and typing them out, then took them to the captain.

Hosie took the signals and read them slowly and carefully before he got to his feet and went swiftly into the control room to the chart table, with Lewis in hot pursuit.

Taking hold of his well-used Bible, Hosie scanned through the dog-eared pages until he found his reference: Matthew 19:14, "Let the children come unto me…"

"We've to maintain radio silence. But it means that we've got to go and collect a few passengers once we've dropped our own off." Hosie said almost to himself, before he turned to Lewis.

"Thanks Lewis! Keep them handy for me in case I need to refer to them later. Maintain radio silence."

"Aye aye sir." Lewis replied, returning to the sound proofed steel box that was the wireless office.

"Starboard 10! Come round to 020. OOW! Come to periscope

depth then raise the snorkel mast. Run main engines and put on a running charge, as we'll be probably go deep for a while."

"Aye aye sir." replied the officer on watch.

"Anything on sonar?" the captain asked through his intercom microphone to the sonar room that was below the deck of the control room.

"Several faint cavitations for'ard of us." came the reply.

"Very good! Get the after periscope raised when we've reached 50feet. I want to take an all round look before we start snorkelling. In fact get the Shuff Duff mast raised then man the D/F. We might be able to pick up something from there even if the sonar cannot be more precise." He ordered.

Hosie sat in his electrically propelled seat, taking a long look around world above him until he was satisfied, before he ordered the periscope to be lowered again.

He went over to the chart table, joining the N.O, who was plotting various courses and notations onto the large sea chart that was stuck onto a table the size of a 'house' door.

"Captain. As you can see by our dead reckoning, our targets for landing are 3 and 5 hours away. If the location for us to pick up our extra passengers lie approximately on this other course it will take us about 2hours or so to r/v. Suggest we pick them up first, as given our present position we're nearer to them than the landing sites."

Hosie confronted with this dilemma, took several minutes to study the chart before he came to his decision.

"Apparently these extra passengers have vital information that we need as of last week sort of thing, which means that we should pick them up first. Then again, we have to get our onboard passengers off before we get spotted and perhaps clobbered by Tojo and his pals. We don't have the room to accommodate these extras, so we'll have to make our drops sooner than planned. Lay on a course for me." He concluded.

"Signalman, ask Captain Waterhouse to come to the control room." he ordered, sending T.S. on that errand.

"You asked for me sir?" Waterhouse asked civilly.

Hosie explained his dilemma to Waterhouse, then, between them came up with a suitable plan to alleviate the problem that was unforeseen.

"Actually sir, we do need an extra hour ashore due to the monsoon conditions. I'll go now to get my men ready."

"Very good! Speed is of the essence Captain, so we'll try to bring you closer to shore than planned."

"Thank you sir!" Waterhouse concluded, leaving to get his men together.

The transit time it took to reach their drop off point seemed to evaporate and Hosie returned to the control room.

"Stop snorkelling No 1! " Hosie ordered, which precipitated the shutting down of the main engines, and the boat reverting to battery power.

T.S was in the fore-ends at the time, looking around to see that instead of 2 racks each side of the gangway loaded up with sleek 12foot long torpedoes, each packed with 600lbs of high explosives, he found them loaded with 2 man canoes, and other vital equipment needed by the 12 Marine Commandoes who were to use them.

He gathered them around him to give them some signalling instructions needed between them and the boat.

"We will be listening out to know when to return and pick you up again. These radios have been set to our special frequency so all you've got to do is switch on, but don't forget to connect them to your battery first! When we arrive, and you're ready to come out to meet us, use a red filter over your torch to signal me. You will use the letter 'M' to signal me, with my reply being the letter 'S'. Bring your radios back, but you can destroy, bury or dump the batteries overboard. If there's a problem in getting off the beach, then we'll just have to come and get you. Sufficient to tell you, I know how to handle a machine gun. That instruction, however, is part of the final briefing with your Captain." T.S. concluded.

"No1. Go to Action Stations. Have the fore-ends strong backs unshipped, and prepare the canoes for discharge via the for'ard torpedo-loading hatch. Prepare the wardroom ready for the marines to muster and have their weapons ready. Up after periscope!" Hosie ordered smoothly, and started to examine the world above the surface of the water that was now being pockmarked by large drops of rain pelting down upon it.

"Navigator! I have a promontory with a prominent rock face bearing 350. A small stream coming down onto a shingle beach bearing 005, and what looks like a small islet just off the mainland bearing 015. By the looks of it, the beach is deserted, but I can see some sort of hut just in behind the front screen of trees bordering onto the beach. Ask Captain Waterhouse to come and see it." He advised.

Waterhouse appeared and looking through the powerful periscope took his time to scan the rest of the immediate area where he was to land.

"Just to the left of the beach, about a mile away, there's another small piece of shingle beach which offers plenty of overhanging vegetation for me to use." Waterhouse stated, standing back for Hosie to look..

"Yes, that's perfect! What depth of water have we got?"

"According to the chart, we have a 20 fathom line before we reach a 10 fathom line, rising steeply to give the beach a short shelf of about 1cable." Bell replied after a brief moment.

"Which means Captain, that we can take you almost alongside. But you'll need to be quick about it, say 5 minutes before we pull the plug and get away." Hosie informed.

"5 minutes? What's keeping you sir!" Waterhouse joked and called his Marine sergeant over to him.

"Sergeant, you have less than five minutes to effect your clearance from the boat, so use all our men for this launch as we're still in daylight. My team will have the dusk to help give us a few extra minutes for our launch. Good luck to you and your men, Ken. I'll see you back on board here in 4 days time.

54

Happy hunting!" he ordered quietly.

"Aye aye sir! Give those Japs what for! See you anon then Terry, er, I mean sir!" Hillman replied softly. He was rewarded with a faint smile before giving Waterhouse the traditional salute and left.

"Stand by to surface! Report main vents! Stand by in the gun tower to unclip the upper hatch. Stand by the for'ard torpedo-loading hatch. Once the gun tower is clear, open the hatch to get the men out, then wait until the gun sponson is clear for them to wait there. I'll let you know when the loading hatch is clear, so have the canoes out for the marines to take them from you. Once the ballast tanks are clear of the water, get the canoes loaded and onto them, ready for when we pull the plug." Hosie ordered over the tannoy system.

"Surface ! Blow 1, 3 and 5 main ballast!" Hosie ordered as he kept looking down onto the for'ard casing of the boat.

There was a large hissing noise as the compressed air was blown into the ballast tanks to clear the water out of them and for the boat to rise swiftly out of the water.

"Gun tower clear. Open the gun tower hatch!" Hosie ordered, then seconds later he gave the sequential order to effect the discharge of marines and their canoes.

"We're on the surface. Torpedo hatch clear. Open the for'ard torpedo loading hatch."

"For'ard torpedo loading hatch opened and canoes on their way out." came the report from the fore ends.

Hose watched through his periscope and saw the marines manhandling their 3 big 2 man canoes and 3 inflatable dinghies onto the saddle tanks, then load up their extra equipment before they climbed into them waiting until the boat sank beneath them and for them to paddle away.

"Gun tower cleared and upper lid shut, both clips secured." Came a voice from the little space in front of the control room that was the wardroom.

"For'ard torpedo loading hatch shut all clips secured, strong backs being rigged." Came a report from the fore ends via the tannoy system

"Take us down slowly No1 we don't want to drown our men. Open 3 and 5 main vents." Hosie ordered, then watched as the boat slowly disappeared under the water, the canoes floated gently off the ballast tanks.

"They did well No1. They were clear away and us dived within the 5 minutes we had practiced on achieving, and we thought the 5 minutes was a record. Open 1 main vent. Slow astern together!" he ordered, for the boat to sink down quicker and back away from the island.

Giving an all round look to make sure nobody was sneaking up behind him, he saw that a boat full of armed men had emerged from the beach the marines would have landed on, and grinned when he saw that the marines had already landed and were hiding their canoes from sight.

"Just in time boys! " He breathed, then watched the motorboat full of Japanese soldiers sail past him and away, unaware of what had taken place a few precious minutes earlier.

"Starboard 10 steer 055. Group up full ahead together. We've got our second landing party to deliver before we collect our guests." Hosie said cheerfully.

Once again, the slow creep towards a deserted shoreline for a quick periscope reconnaissance before they surfaced to launch the second team of Marine Commandoes who were part of the elite Special Forces, who eventually, would become known as the famous S.B.S.

They were going ashore to create mayhem on the unsuspecting Japanese, who had taken the pains to gather together oil storage tanks, and ammo dumps forming part of their military and weaponry force

"Let's go and get our passengers now No1. Starboard 10 steer 090." Hosie commanded, before he had the after periscope lowered again.

"It's dark up top, with no lights showing No1. Anything on sonar?"

"Nothing reported sir."

"Very good! Have the galley flashed up and supper over with by 1930. Then prepare for our guests. "

"Ditching gash from the for'ard gash ejector sir?"

"No! We'll keep it until we're in deeper waters, in case the tide carries it ashore."

"Aye aye sir!"

Chapter II

Matthew 19:14

"We've reached point Echo sir!"

"Very good! Let's go to periscope depth and take a peek!" Hosie said quietly, following the N.O. into the control room.

"Go to red lighting! Up for'ard periscope." He ordered, which was promptly obeyed.

Hosie danced swiftly around the orifice of the periscope well, holding onto the periscope as he moved around it.

"I have a red flashing light to port of me. Get T.S."

T.S. arrived and was asked to see if the flashing red light was a visual communication from shoreward.

"They're flashing the code letter sir. And by the look of it their boat's sinking under them." T.S. stated.

"Use your torch on red filter and make to them. ' See you to port 1 cable away, so stand clear' "

T.S. flashed the reply and reported that they understood, and stood back for Hosie to take over the periscope again.

"Take us up No1. Have P.O. Anderson (the 2nd Cox'n) and a casing party muster in the control room. They will bring the passengers down via the fin door and conning tower hatch. We must be away just as quick as we launched our marines."

"Aye aye sir!"

Hosie watched the boat rise out of the water almost alongside what looked like a large seagoing fishing boat that was seemingly over full of people.

Soon the first passengers arrived down into the control room to be met by James and the Steward, then by the sound of their voices, very scared children who were manhandled down the vertical ladder.

T.S. saw the wide-eyed, terror-stricken faces of the children, which didn't go unnoticed by Cox'n James

"Signalman, get the Baby Chef down to assist the Steward.

Then fetch the Chief Stoker." James ordered.

T.S. came back with both men and returned to his Action Station.

"Ah Bill! We'll be using the Stokers mess to keep our passengers together and out of harms way. Get your Stokers into the fore ends until we get back. Baby Chef! Assist the Steward in providing them with food and whatever else they might be needing." he said softly, so as not to alarm the children any further.

An officer wearing the remnants of a naval uniform arrived, went over to the captain to report.

"Bloody glad you came along sir. We wouldn't have lasted much longer in these conditions, as our engine ran out of fuel, and the children are in a bad way." The officer said to Hosie.

Hosie greeted each arrival before turning to him

"I'm Lt Cdr Hosie, captain of S64. You are safe now and will be landing on Australian soil within 24hours. In the meantime kindly introduce yourself."

"I'm Lt. Brian Buckle, a pilot from 635 Squadron that was based at the Naval Air Station at Simbang, Singapore." He said, then introduced the escapees.

"This is the ship's engineer from the ship we escaped Singapore in, Engineering officer Keith Ellis with his wife and child."

"I could do with an Engineer Officer Keith. Maybe we can fit you in the squadron somewhere."

"It'll make a change handling diesels instead of steam reciprocating engines." Ellis grinned, as he and his wife shook Hosie's hand.

"This is Nursing Sister Liz Dovey formerly from BMH Singapore, with 5 orphaned children they've managed to rescue. She has some very disturbing stories to tell the authorities. Stories that will involve the War Atrocities tribunals."

"Welcome aboard Sister Dovey. Tell your children they are now safe."

She thanked him then took the children away from the gathered crowd.

"This is army Captain Arthur Griffiths with his wife and 2 children. He was the C.O. of a Gunnery Battery C.O. in Jahore Bahru when the Japs turned up and literally butchered his men. He managed to escape to get his family away."

"Glad you came along, maybe you'll teach my gunners a few things or three." Hosie said with a smile and shaking hands with him and his wife.

"Here is Detective Inspector Helena Richmond, her husband Police Sergeant Ted with their 2 children. They were part of the Singapore Police Force who were involved with training Indonesian Police units in Djakarta and Surabaya. Thank goodness Helena has the gift of being a multi-language interpreter because it was her talent that got us through several sticky problems." he declared.

"Pleased you made it." Hosie remarked, shaking hands with them.

"I have some very valuable documents to hand over Captain." Helena Richmond announced, and promptly handed over a small yet bulging canvas valise.

"No doubt our backroom boys will make some use of this." Hosie said appreciatively.

T.S. had seen the wide-eyed terror stricken faces of the children which didn't go unnoticed by Cox'n James.

The last two passengers to arrive down were introduced by Buckle as an Aircrew flight engineer Fred Cayton and Co Pilot Cliff Williams, both from the civil aviation company Air New Zealand, and duly welcomed by Hosie.

"Welcome aboard gentlemen. We may be a little bit cramped, which I suppose is no change in your profession. But I hope you'll enjoy the cruise."

"It's about time we found something that actually works around here." Cayton remarked as he gazed at the workings of a submarine all around him.

60

"We don't issue parachutes on board our aircraft captain, but do you issue lifebelts?" Williams asked nervously, following the gaze of Cayton and seeing his new surroundings.

"Goggles and flippers on board these type of vessels I'm afraid, so if you really need a parachute, no doubt our Cox'n could fit you up with one that works underwater. But there's no need to worry as we've got a deal with King Neptune and his pals." Hosie quipped, then added.

"You must have been a very lucky party of people. How come you got down this far and for us to come along to pick you up?"

"Myself, Arthur, er Captain Griffiths and family, Inspector Richmond and family, Engineer Ellis and family, the nurse and the children are all that's left of a ship load of some 300 escapees from Singapore. We got as far as Surabaya before the Japs bombed us, so we had to abandon the ship. No matter where we decided to put ashore, the Japs were always there before us. When we did manage to get ashore, some local policemen who were enjoying a picnic on the beach met us. As luck had it they had been trained by and who managed to recognise Sergeant Richmond. They escorted us to some local airfield that was out of the way of the Japs. It was there we met up with Fred Cayton and Cliff Williams. Their cargo plane was in a hangar being repaired, so between us, we managed to get it going and take off before the Japs arrived on the scene. The plane was still very dodgy to fly and we were short on fuel. Rather than risking us ditching out in open waters between the island and Australia, we decided to keep to the shoreline, island hop so to speak, follow them across to New Guinea, and with luck reach Port Moreseby where Fred had one of his airline passenger stops there. Besides, due to the Jap Air force we were forced to try and keep ahead of them. We only got as far as Bali when we were shot down by one of their Zero's. The Japs had somehow beaten us to get there before us, as we seemed to be just that one step ahead of them until that point. Maybe it was a different Jap force as a pincer movement coming down from Borneo or wherever. It was thanks to Griffiths, we managed to slip away from the murdering Japanese troops and stole a fishing boat when the owner was in the process of being rounded up by the Jap soldiers. With Helena's languages as stated earlier, we managed to bluff our way past several Jap motorboat patrols, as we pretended to be local fisher folk out catching fish. The stories that need telling is everything we saw the Japs do not only to us but the local people as well. The same goes for Helena Richmond with her story of what happened at Surabaya and Bali. They are nothing but a murderous bunch of sadistic rapists and butchers that no other army in the world would want to belong to let alone come near to." Buckle explained at length.

"Welcome aboard Lt, and thank you for your courtesy of letting me know who my passengers are. Get your party for'ard and we'll soon have you all fed and watered with the children tucked up in bed before long. I would appreciate a small hand-written report on your escape, but more importantly, if you could write down what naval strength you might have seen in or around the Bali area. Only we're a bit scarce on that type of info as most of our 'Coast watchers' have been captured, and if what you say, killed."

"From what I have seen, especially during our flight, there's a massive fleet of battleships, carriers, and cruisers having a go at another smaller group of what looked like cruisers which were being sunk left right and centre. Behind them was what looked like a large armada of ships and landing craft making their way to the shores of Java and some on their way towards Bali." Buckle said with a far-away look in his eyes.[*]

"Apparently Helena Richmond was handling some irregularities at the Japanese Embassy in Singapore when they invaded the place, and managed to grab hold of several military directorates as issued by the Emperor himself. As mentioned,

---

[*] What they had seen was the 'Battle of the Java Sea' and the Japanese Invasion of Java.

they appear to be of vital importance to our Intelligence boffins, but I fear they may be out of date by now. That's all I can add just now sir!" he concluded.

"Well done. You and your people just follow the steward who will show you to your quarters and provide some food for you all. We'll talk more when you're feeling up to it." Hosie advised, before he ordered the boat to turn around and head back to base. "OOW. Charge the batteries up, and go to patrol routine. Tell the engine room to make as much revs as possible to get us the hell out of this area. Keep the bridge cleared in case of a crash dive. No lights of any kind to be shown topside."

"Aye aye sir."

To remain on the surface then to dive at a moments notice, is what is called 'riding on the vents', which are basically large flaps on top of the ballast tanks that are shut to keep air in so they can float, or opened to allow the air to escape thus for the submarine to sink under the water, referred to as 'diving'.

"Red watch patrol routine."

The escapees were being nursed and well looked after by all the off watch crew from for'ard. The children's tattered clothing got replaced by items of uniform from the crewmembers and adapted or tailored to fit them just perfect. They were given pieces from the slabs of chocolate that went to make their 'kai' and even lots of jelly with tinned milk for them to eat. The adults were also given items of clothing to wear, even the women had theirs adapted to suit their natural body shape. All of which was done mostly by the married crewmembers, with the single men trying to play with the children, but they seemed to be in some state of shock and withdrawn into themselves.

The crew's only reward was to hear from first hand, the horrendous and blood curdling events that these poor people had witnessed as related by the two women:

Of how all the patients in BMH Singapore were bayoneted or butchered as they lay in their beds, pregnant women included.

Of the way all the nurses were rounded up, gang-raped and forced to jump off the three-storey building to their deaths. Of how all 58,000 British troops that surrendered, were forced to line the entire route of the Japs victory parade, and should any Jap soldier take a dislike to any of our boys, they were shot in the head or bayoneted, and even hacked to death by a large sword, just where they stood. It was reported that over 1,000 of them were murdered in that way. Of when the Japs entered Palembang and onwards to Surabaya, they butchered every man and boy, raping every woman or girl they came across. Of witnessing the capture of several local military men who were trussed up and suspended from tree branches, only to be used for bayonet practice by the laughing Jap soldiers. They were pillaging and looting as they went along. The tale of such conduct by the Japs seemed never ending, and each member of the crew vowed to avenge those victims given the chance..

"How come they're able to do all that our passengers have told us sir?" T.S. asked Bell the duty OOW on the bridge, whilst he was the lookout.

"We from the Western world have a code of conduct which is dictated by what is called 'The Geneva Convention'. This means that any land or captured troops are to be looked after in a reasonable manner until the outcome of the wars have been reached. Anybody transgressing this code would be brought before a War Crimes' court and be taken to task for those crimes. Although the Japanese signed the 'Hague Treaty', they ignored it, because their code for war has a different outlook, and religious beliefs. To put it as best as I can, the Japanese warrior does not ask for nor give 'Quarter' and will fight to their last man to uphold that indoctrination of theirs. Therefore, to them there's no surrender and anybody who gives way to them, would treated literally as trash, to be disposed of as any Japanese warrior sees fit."

"But what about after the war is over sir? I mean, if we're conducting a war in Europe with those bastards the Nazis, with this one against the Japs as well, and we win; Does that mean that we have to treat the Nazis with kid gloves because of this 'Convention', but butcher all the Japs we come across?"

"Hardly! Although if what we've been told holds up in the courts. then that would only be fair. No! Those Japs will face the same 'War Crimes' courts and be handed out their punishment according to those deeds they were guilty of. Mostly by hanging or shot by a firing squad. This will be done in full view of the rest of the world who will be looking on, to see that 'fair play' and even-handedness be meted out."

"Fair play sir? Just wait until I've got my Lewis gun lined up on them, or even my Vickers, I don't care, but I'll bloody well show them fair play!"

"Now now! Keep a cool head or you'll be had up to be put on a 241 for doing just the same thing as the real butchers."

"Well, it certainly stinks of unfairness so it does, sir!"

"Yes it does, but then who are we to argue. Best do the jobs we've been trained for." Bell concluded bringing another period of silence between them.

The overnight surface transit back to base proved that the boat had managed to cover most of the distance of her return leg, but had to become invisible when sunrise came upon them. This was a precautionary step so as not to be followed back to their base.

"Helmsman I need to speak to the OOW!" Hall the P.O. Gunner and the duty watch P.O. in the control room, ordered.

The helmsman moved aside so that Hall could do so.

Just up in the left hand corner of the control room and right by the helmsman's left ear, is a voice tube that goes up through the pressure hull ending up on the bridge. This is the means of contact between the bridge and the control room. This double-flap valve gets shut each time the boat dives, then re- opened when somebody arrives back onto the bridge again once surfaced.

"OOW – P.O. of the Watch here. We need to ditch gash sir,

65

as it's positively 'chucking up' in the fore ends. Permission to ditch gash?" Hall asked.

"We may have to stop for this! Better check with the captain."

"Aye aye sir."

"About time too! Maybe we'll get it done after an early brekkers, 'cause I'm ruddy starvin'. Maybe clean the boat then dive for a pleasant dive time." Brawn, the Leading Sonar Operator opined.

Hall came back with a brief instruction from the captain and reported the fact to the OOW on the bridge.

"Very good! Make the appropriate order! Came the reply.

"Hands to early breakfast. All gash will be ditched in 30 minutes via the fin doorway. Blue watch will muster in the control room at 0630."

This order seemed to wake the boat up and the smells of food being cooked in the small galley wafted around the boat via the ventilation system.

There were some very bleary eyes on men who had only recently come off watch who tried to get some kip before the rigours of the day set upon them. But what exacerbated the situation for them were the cries and wails from the children who had been disturbed from their sleep, and the women escorting them down to the officers' bathroom to have their toilet and a wash before the water was switched off again.

The hive of activity was phenomenal inside this boat, as there were loads of other 'ship's husbandry' to undertake before the boat dived again.

Guyan, the Chief Stoker came to the control room speaking up the voice tube to the OOW.

"OOW – Chief Stoker! Our sanitary tanks are full and need pumping out. Permission to shoot shit sir?"

"Might as well Chief! Don't forget to vent outboard!"

"Aye aye sir!" Guyan responded, then went into the engine room to operate his pump manifold.

T.S. had just come into the control room to relieve Brawn who was the current helmsman, so that he could have his breakfast.

"What's for brekkees? " Brawn asked.

"Either shit on a raft (braised kidney on fried bread), or powdered scrambled egg. Either way, take it or leave it"

"Hmm, Hobsons choice again. What happened to the fresh victuals we took on board? I mean, we could have some fresh bacon 'n' eggs and maybe some arigonies (tinned tomatoes) on fresh toast."

"C'mon Dave, we've had passengers on board to scoff that lot. We've got a war on you know!" T.S. replied with a chuckle, then surprised to hear the hiss of air.

"What's that Dave?" he asked with a startled voice.

"Bill Guyan is shooting shit. He's to vent outboard."

"Bloody hell, hope no bastard's in the traps!" T.S. remarked, thinking of the consequences if they were.

"Now I know where the Chef is getting his brekkies from then! Anyway, we're on course and speed. See you later." Brawn quipped, then stood up for T.S. to take over the helm.

Before T.S. could sit down there was a loud bang, followed by a large scream and several expletives being uttered from the heads area opposite the W/T office.

Within seconds a stoker came running into the control room covered in shit and bog paper, swearing and cursing as loud as he could.

"You fuckin' bastards! I told you there was a dodgy flap valve in trap 2. Now the fuckin' lot's been blown right up my arse, covering the entire bulkheads as well!" he yelled and continued to swear loudly.

This spectacle was too much for even the hardest to withstand and were gagging for fresh air because of the smell. Yet within moments and because of the comical sight, everybody started to laugh at this man's mishap. This was laughing at another's misfortune at its best!

"You cupid stunt! You should have known to make sure you held the flap valve in it's shut position when you heard the tank being blown. You'd better get it all cleaned up before we dive, erm, whoever you are." Hall said angrily, yet tried to control himself from laughing but failed miserably, for him to join in with the rest of them.

Bell came rushing into the control room to sort out the problem, but even he couldn't stop laughing at the poor man's dilemma.

"Have the off watch stokers clean the area down, we'll be diving in 10 minutes so better get a move on." Bell ordered after a moment to collect his decorum again.

Guyan came sauntering into the control room unaware of the drama, and reported up to the bridge that 'Shit was shot' and the tank vented outboard.

It was only then he noticed a body covered in excrement standing in the corner of the control room by the diving panel, cleaning himself off with several wads of rags he was ripping out from a bale of them.

"Ah, it's you Holdsworthy. Wondered when you'd get round to fixing that flap valve. You finally got your own back then I see! Get yourself cleaned up and help the rest to clean up your mess, then report to me afterwards." Guyan said with a deadpan face. He just managed to clear the control room to go for'ard to the senior rates mess, when he too joined the rest of them and laughed at the poor shit-laden Stoker.

Hosie appeared into the control room from his cabin remarking on the stench the boat had somehow collected, and ordered all off watch crew to muster in the control room to clear it, then report on how such an 'accident ' had occurred He was angry to have his boat remain on the surface instead of dived, with sunrise breaking upon them.

The boat was stopped, the gash ditched overboard and the boat cleaned up with fresh clean air circulating around the boat before Hosie finally dived.

Again he watched his vessel submerge into the dark waters, as the sun started its rapid climb into the skies above them.

"Stand by to Snort. Running charge and 'float the load' Make revs for 10 knots and maintain this course for 3 hours. I'll be in the wardroom if you need me No1." Hosie ordered before leaving the control room.

"Captain – W/T. Received a signal from Coast watcher 27. Says a few Jap fishing boats have been snooping around his part of the shoreline all night and are now heading back home again. Keep a look out for them in case they are in your area."

Hosie went over to the chart table looking where this Coast watcher was situated, reckoning the possible track of these fishing vessels.

"Hmm! It seems as if Tojo is getting more adventurous in their snooping around. I wonder what they're up to. Better stop snorting and go deep in case they've got their nets out for a spot of real fishing." Hosie muttered to nobody in particular.

"Stop snorting. Group up half ahead together. Port ten, steer 210." he ordered whilst keeping his all round scan from his main periscope.

"Run the echo sounder for 5 seconds. Anything on sonar?" he ordered, waited for the result of the depth to show up.

"400 feet, that's good. Navigator, put that depth onto the chart we may need it again. Take me down to 200 feet No1." and slapped the handles of the periscope as the signal for Scarlett the 'Outside Wrecker' at the diving panel to lower the mast back into its deep well below them.

"Aye aye sir!"

"Several faint cavitations coming from starboard. Suggesting they're fishing boats."

"Confirmed. 3 small ones and one big one. Any chasers astern of them?"

"No. But a faint cavitation port side some way off." Came the reply.

"Keep a special track of the fishing boats! They might have a net streamed astern of them." Hosie concluded before he left the control room to go into the wardroom.

T.S. was at the controls of the fore planes when the voice of the sonar operator cut into his concentration.

"Control room – Sonar! Faint swishing noises ahead at Green 10. Suggest fishing nets being dragged."

Hosie happened to be in the control room looking at his sea chart at the time and took immediate charge from the duty 'dived' OOW.

"Periscope depth!" he ordered and had the after periscope raised so that he could have a brief glimpse of the reported hazard.

"It's a second lot of fishermen. Flood 'Q'. Port 20! Full ahead together! Go to 400 feet but no lower. Steer 270." He ordered swiftly, feeling the boat lurch downwards, going further into the depths of the sea.

Once the boat had levelled off at the required depth and steering the course ordered, Hosie had the sonar room listen to see if they could judge what the fishing nets were doing, to find whether or not they had escaped the nets, or to be scooped up into them like a giant whale.

The silence and concentration in the control room was broken by the voice of a little girl who was passing for'ard through the control room.

"Please Mister, don't let those vicious men get us! Please! Huh?" she asked pleadingly as she started to tug at Hosie's arm.

Hosie spun round looking down at the little girl and her mother with surprise, becoming angry at being distracted at a very perilous moment.

"What are these passengers doing in the control room? Steward! See that no passenger comes through here again without my permission. Issue gash buckets for them if necessary." he ordered angrily, but still bemused about the words the little girl used.

T.S. started to chuckle only to receive a withering glance from Hosie, but told him that the child probably meant ' Fishermen'. This seemed to let the steam out of him for him to take control of the situation again.

The little girl started to cry but was hushed by her mother as she took her child from the control room, saying that the captain would not let them.

The engine and propeller noises from the fishing boats were getting much louder and seemed to come from their starboard side. A scraping sound was heard from the starboard side of the hull, which told them that the fishing nets had nearly snagged them as they eventually passed astern and into oblivion again.

"Bloody hell! That was a close one. If they had've snagged us, we would have been forced to drag them under, or even surface and sink them with a gun action. At least now we can remain undetected a little while longer. I have that feeling the Japs are up to something and I'd like to know what. The sooner we get alongside and in front of the boffins then we'll know what it is." Hosie breathed.

"Maybe they're just fishing sir. Perhaps if we go upstairs and take a look?" Hoare suggested.

"Yes lets! Port 20 and steer 170. Half ahead together. Come to periscope depth."

The tense moment was swept aside by the control room crew who felt better that they were going back up to periscope depth again.

"Periscope depth!" Hoare prompted, but did not need to as Hosie had already observed the upward movement of the boat for him to order the after periscope to be raised.

He spun around to look aft noticing that the fishing boats were small objects in the water now, for the boat to be out of danger. That was until he spun around looking ahead of himself.

He saw 4 fast patrol boats almost in line astern coming fast towards him to call for T.S. to be temporarily relieved from the fore planes to get his ships recognition book out to identify them

T.S. looked through the eyepiece of the periscope for a moment before giving his opinion.

"Its okay sir, they're a squadron of M.G.B's from the base. I have their pennant numbers written down." he reported, then produced his notebook with the details.

"Hmm! I didn't expect to see them. They're a bit out of their area to do so." Hosie remarked, taking re-possession of the periscope again.

The fast almost humming noises from the MGBs propellers finally faded away for Hosie to judge that it was safe to start snorkelling again.

He looked at the control room clock then at his watch, before issuing the orders to snort to get his boat back on track, heading on the final lap towards the base.

The control room crew had been relieved with a fresh crew and the boat settled down for a spell of relative ease, as Hosie completed his consultation with Bell at the chart table.

"If we have no further interruptions and at this speed, we should be rounding point Kilo in about 3 hours. When reached, stop snorting. I'll be in my cabin if you need me."

"Aye aye sir." Bell responded, taking over the officer on 'watched dived', then scolded the fore-planes man for not keeping a proper depth control.

"C'mon! We've got a decent trim, so settle down and stop porpoising. It's playing havoc with our eardrums. The vacuums you're causing unnecessarily will alarm our passengers who are not used to such discomfort."

Underwood the on-watch Sparker came into the control room asking permission to raise the whip aerial so that he could get a better radio reception.

"Permission granted, but as soon as you've completed your schedule, lower it as we'll be making another 'wake' on the surface that could be seen for miles should an aircraft happen along.

"Aye aye sir!" Underwood responded to go swiftly back into his little sound-proofed box that was the W/T office.

Mike Sample the Torpedo Officer (T.O.) had relieved Trevor Bell and was keeping an eye on things occurring in the control room whiles he kept spinning around in the electric chair turning the periscope to wherever he wanted to look at above the waves.

"Stop snorting! Lower the W/T mast! Group up full ahead together and dive to 100 feet." He ordered.

"Captain – OOW! Aircraft approaching starboard side. Have stopped snorting and dived to 100 feet." he reported swiftly.
Hosie came into the control room and making a swift appraisal as to what had taken place, he just grunted and thanked Sample for his quick reaction to a possible hostile aircraft.

The heat from the engines permeated into the control room made the occupants feel a bit uncomfortable, so Hosie ordered the air conditioning unit and some of the overhead electric fans be switched on to counteract it.

After a little while Hosie ordered back to periscope depth again for him to take a look around.

He saw the aircraft way to port of them to witness it make a rectangular loop around the coastline of Australia before it turned to head back towards them.

"Down periscope! 100 feet!" he ordered, turning to Bell saying.

"That was a Jap recce plane taking indecent photos of the place, which means the plot is thickening. We'll have to be careful with our approach to base in case they've got another one on the way." He informed.

"From what Lt Buckle and Captain Griffiths said, the Japs must be up to no good and working on a dastardly plan to come and visit us." Sample replied, regaining control of the periscope again.

Hosie went over to the chart table looking at where they were estimated to be in their transit.

"We're almost at point Kilo. Which means that we appear to be an hour ahead of schedule. That's good going by any standards." He informed, then took a moment to figure out his next transit course.

"Port 10! Steer 165! Go to 100 feet. Down periscope."
The control room crew acted out their orders, reporting the results before Hosie turned back to Bell.

"We'll be on this course for 2 hours before we turn to port again to steer 045. Once on that track then we can go back up to periscope depth for our approach to base. I'll be in the wardroom if you need me." He advised.

"Aye aye sir."

The approach to the small cove where their base was situated, was taken slowly and still submerged until they reached a critical cross-bearing taken from prominent landmarks each side of them, to let them surface at the entrance of the cove and enter the stretch of water leading to their base. Also for the Boom Defence team to open the sea-gates to let them through.

"Stand by to surface. Report main vents. Casing party muster in the control room. W/T raise aerial and let them know we've arrived."

The usual reports received about the main vents being shut added to the hubbub in the control room.

T.S. was standing by with his bridge equipment slung around his body waiting to follow the surfacing officer up the control room tower.

Within moments the W/T office came back with their report. "Captain – W/T. In contact. We're to come alongside port side aft and secure at pontoon 3 behind S62. Passengers will be transferred to a launch and taken ashore for a debriefing at HQ."

"Very good W/T! Stop together. Surface! Open 1,3 & 5 LP Master Blows."

Hosie watched through his periscope to see his boat had simply popped up from the deep and large-as-life almost within the confines of the cove.

"1 clip off. 2 clips off! Upper lid open. Officer on his way up!" T.S. shouted down to the control room.

The helmsman reached up to his left and opening the lower

voice pipe cock, waited until he heard the voice of the officer on the bridge.

The 2nd Cox'n and 5 sailors scrambled up the ladder, going through the fin door to jump gingerly onto the casing of the boat.

T.S. had unfurled his ensign already to put the little chrome 'mast' it was on, into its holder. His horseshoe lifebelt with the Boat's crest on it, along with his new 5inch aldis lamp into their cradles before he got ready with his Bosun's Call, to make the traditional 'pipe' into their a salute between the captains of each RN vessel.

Hosie manoeuvred his boat neatly alongside the wooden pontoon decking for the casing party to secure alongside it. There was no collision, just a gentle bump as the boat touched the fragile landing jetty, which showed anybody who witnessed this, that Hosie was an excellent judge in completing such a manoeuvre.

The casing party had unshipped the gangplank, and assembled it ready to place it onto the wooden pontoon.

The for'ard torpedo-loading hatch had been opened with the access ladder rigged and ready for use.

Hosie left the bridge and having come up through the loading hatch, he crossed over the pontoon making his ascent up the ladder onto the towering ship next to them and boarded it.

T.S. remained on the bridge for a while looking around the base, but saw the escapee passengers emerge to be assembled on the pontoon, whereupon a motor launch arrived to take them on board.

Some of the crew were helping them aboard, then with lots of waves and cheers of goodbye the passengers were taken away to complete their very long journey to safety.

When he finally got back down into the control room, it seemed a very empty place, so decided to go for'ard to see James, to see if he could go and collect the mail.

Lewis had asked him to collect the signals from the Main Signal Office (MSO) as well, and told him that several bags of mail were waiting to be collected.

T.S. climbed up the ladder with his large bag of outgoing mail onto the casing where he met Kendrick, one of the Gunnery ratings on board, who was the duty Trot Sentry.

"Any shore leave for us?"

"Not that I can say Stan. Maybe the Cox'n will pipe that when issuing the rum at 1600, before we are allowed inboard to our mess deck. Anyway, I'm hoping to be back for then, with all that lovely mail I'm going to collect. Whatever the leave is, I'm only glad to be back alongside. "

"Me too, and it'll be nice to get some mail again." Kendrick agreed and assumed his vigil as 'Trot Sentry'.

Chapter III

Inboard

T.S. climbed up the steep ladders onto the upper deck of the Depot ship and made his way for'ard entering the cool interior of the ship, heading to the MSO to gather the signals before he collected his load of mail, and met one of his counterparts from one of the other boats.

"See you Jimmy! Well, it's a Gordon fer me, a Gordon fer me. If yer nae a Gordon yer nae used to me!" T.S. started to sing using his best Scottish accent.

His bad accent and singing produced a salvo of items that got thrown at him, with groans from some of the occupants who were busy at their desks.

"Signalman Gordon Ross no less. What's the Signalman off S60 doing with a bit of inboard time?" T.S asked jovially, catching some of the missiles, throwing them back to whence they came.

"Yeah, our boat got clobbered in the Banda Straits last week and we only just managed to get back here yesterday. Which means that we're the 'Spare Crew' until they patch us up again." Ross replied cheerfully.

"Many casualties Gordon?"

"Yes, 5 badly injured as the boat clobbered good and proper. The skipper had a nice juicy big Jap cruiser lined up, and fired all for'ard tubes at it. The only snag was that they were all duff, which only served to signal to the Japs where we were, to home in onto us. One depth charge must have holed one of our outboard fuel tank, because we were leaving a trail of oil everywhere. The Japs must have spotted it and zeroed in on us. We had to bottom and play possum until they either ran out of depth charges or just gave up hoping that we were sunk anyway."

"Sounds bad!"

"The thing there was, our gun got demolished, our fin blown to pieces, and because we had holes the size of dustbin lids in our ballast tanks, we couldn't surface. Fortunately our main periscope and snort mast managed to survive, as the rest were bent like hairpins. We had to shut down both the fore and after ends pumping h.p. air into them to take the place of the ballast tanks, so that we could at least get up near to be able to surface. But because we still had half our load of torpedoes at both ends, all of which were duff, so we jettisoned them to make us lighter. It was only then that we managed to raise the snort mast to get our engines going., and because it was dark, we were able to snort our way back until we had to dock in that floating dock down there. I tell you what. It's thanks to the Jerry's invention of the Schnorkel system that saved us all."

"Yes I wondered why a boat was down the bottom end of the creek! Bloody hell, that sounds like it was a lucky escape to say the least. It sounds like medals all round. VD and scars possibly."

"Our skipper is in for at least a DSC or whatever, for saving us from being 'Sunk with all hands' as the expression goes."

"Yeah! And I dare say all you boys will get is an extra tot just to go and do it all over again."

"Whatever. Anyway, here're your signals. Mostly weather reports and a few deferred stores signals. But between thee and me, the mess deck buzz has it we're in for something big."

"The last mess deck buzz I heard, had us swanning around Singapore with a couple of those slant-eyed babes bobbing up and down on us." T.S. said sarcastically, and taking his wad of signals, left.

"Hello! Well, if it 'aint Leading Regulator Des Magnes no less! How the devil are you as if I didn't know? Got any mail for me today?" T.S. asked cheerfully, first knocking then entering the mail office

"Bloody Submariners!" Magnes groaned, but allowed T.S. into the compartment.

T.S. looked at the several sacks of mail he was to carry, then dumped his own onto an empty table to be sorted.

"But we've only been away a matter of a few days, and only a week before that. Where the hell has it all come from? Better take this lot first then as I'll need to make a couple of trips, unless you can have it 'sky-hooked' over to the boat."

"It's mostly sea mail which appears to be 'Red Cross' parcels, but you can take the blue 'Airmail' bags away. I'll get it transferred over during the 1st dogwatch like last time." Magnes replied, then had T.S. to sign for the mail he was getting.

T.S. thought for a moment then realised that it would co-incide with 'Tot time'. This being so, any decent letters coming from home would earn him a few extra 'sippers' from the recipients rum glass.

"Yes, that'll be fine. Thanks, and see you in the morning." T.S. stated, grabbing his blue bags and leaving the compartment to return full speed back on board the boat, with extra tot rations on his mind.

"Up spirits!" James announced over the ships intercom, with the usual muffled reply from the crew 'Stand fast the Holy Ghost!

This was the signal for 'happy hour' to commence once more, and for the crew to enjoy the daily tradition of quaffing a glass of rum. On a surface vessel where the fresh water was plenty, the crew got one measure of rum to two measures of water, yet on board a Boat, where water is on a constant rationing, they were given the mixture of one part rum to one part water. That and a couple bottles of ale from the fridge space made for a very jovial time, especially for those who got a precious letter from home to gloat over. But if the letter was a 'Dear John' then there would be very glum faces or even angry outbursts by those unfortunate to get one.

"Cheers to T.S.! Thanks for bringing me good news. My missus dropped her nipper last month! I'm the father of a little girl now, as I've already got a boy." Brannon the Leading Gunner declared ecstatically, and offered T.S a sip of his tot.

"Cheers Tony! Here's another letter for you. Maybe your

missus made a mistake and you've got twins, in which case I'll have another sip." T.S. replied, pretending to take a second sip before he allowed Brannon to rescue his tot glass from him.

"Just wait until she'd drops another one when you're not there!" a disgruntled stoker stated as he entered the for'ard sailors mess with his opened letter in his hands.

"She must have been playing out of school then Stokes. She must have had grease on her bum for her knickers to fall down, or her knicker elastic must have snapped a dozen times." Alan Spencer the Leading 'Fore-endie' said wickedly as he was passing the sailors mess.

T.S. realised that there was going to be some sort of an altercation between the two men and stood between them to prevent one grabbing the other by the throat, but relaxed when the stoker just sloped off back into his own mess deck again.

"Bloody hell Alan, you certainly sailed close to the bloody wind that time. I mean he's a Navy Boxing champ, fer Chris' sake."

"He always gets up my nose, but just put it down to lack of sleep or whatever. Anyway I was only commiserating with him 'cause me missus did that to me last year when I was out in the Med on one of the P boats. We got sunk by an Eyetie destroyer just when the skipper lined up to sink one of their heavy cruisers. Only 5 of us managed to escape from for'ard. When we were finally picked up by a passing minelaying cruiser, the *Apollo* I think she was, and we got back and on survivors leave I turned up out of the blue only to find her playing out of turn. So I gave her a good smacking, but I bloody well nearly killed her fancy Hairy Fairy when I got hold of him, he is still in sickbay as far as I know. I got done for G.B. H. to a Senior Rating, but was offered this draft as a way out it's the only reason why I'm here " Spencer explained angrily.

"Bloody 'ell! No wonder you've been a bit of a bitch since coming on board. I hope when civvy street comes your way, you'll get back to normal again, Japs or Jerry's permitting." T.S.

replied and handed him a letter reeking of 'Woolies' special perfume, which he took delight in sniffing before pocketing it and go into the fore ends.

Fred Gleave, a Leading U.W from the after ends came into the for'ard Sailors mess and asked T.S. if he could take the mail aft for him.

"Thanks Fred! There's a whole sack of it for your boys aft, most of it Red Cross parcels and what looks like a very nice surprise one for you. I won't say anymore, but my ruddy shoulders were sore carrying it on board for you." T.S. said, feigning hurt on his shoulder.

"Oh all right! Come round for a wet, but better bring a few tinnies with you, especially if it's good news for us to celebrate!" Gleave said grudgingly.

"I'll drink to that Fred! Your sack is in the corner by the water tight door in the fore ends."

Gleave came back dragging the heavy sack saying.

"Bloody hell Postie! How did you get this on board? If what you say is true then you can definitely come round."

"Maybe next time you'll appreciate what us Postie's do for a living, besides me flashing at unknown sailors. Perhaps a gulper would do the trick, yes?" T.S. quipped

"Most definitely!" Gleave concluded and groaned about the weight of the sack as T.S. watched him drag the heavy bag along the passageway towards the after ends.

"Those not on duty watch will go inboard. The inboard galley will be flashed up for a meal, make certain you're mustered in the dining hall. Red Watch assume your duties. " the tannoy announcement made by James created a mass exodus from the boat, as the crew went inboard to their accommodation mess deck on the depot ship. All except the 'duty watch' who had to stay behind and clean the boat up.

T.S. grabbed his kit and followed the crowd over the gangway, up the ladder then into the bowels of the depot ship to where they shared a large compartment that was their sleeping quarters.

Once they dumped their belongings, everybody filed up into the galley come dining room where they got fed by the duty chefs. The galley would be open and ready for any returning boat's crew no matter what time night or day. This also applies when the crew are about to board again for another patrol.

After a little while, when the crew had finished eating, they returned to their mess, and as if it was a large magnet, most of them congregated in the bathroom, where they took a well earned shower, taking the opportunity to hand in their dirty dhobying and collect their fresh bundles from the laundry.

This was a daily chore on board a surface vessel, where the men had a galvanised bucket, a large bar of soap, a scrubbing brush if needed, and lots of hot water on tap to wash their clothing. All of this is denied to the submariner due to the lack of fresh water, who can only enjoy such luxuries when they've arrived alongside their depot or host ship. Once done, then there is the long traipse down into the 'drying room' for their dhobying to be collected later when dried. Then having got back into the mess deck, the irons are out for the men to iron any clothing that needs it, before folding them neatly, 'Pusser fashion' into their little steel lockers. On this account, the Submariners and the Depot ship crew now had it easy on that score.

Some of the crew settled down to writing letters in reply to the ones they'd just had, and some just laid in their bunks having a quiet reflective moment with a cigarette or a pipe to draw on.
T.S. reflecting on his missed opportunity with either of the twins due to the boat being under sailing orders last time, hoped he would have the chance to make up for lost time.

The NAAFI canteen 'Damager' on board had opened his shop for anybody wishing to purchase a few cans of beer, extra duty-free tobacco, or some luxury item such as a nicely scented bar of soap, toothpaste, writing material, nutty or chocolate bars, whatever; or go and watch the 'latest' film on the quarterdeck, but for most, it was time for to catch up with their 'sleep time'.

This was the life for any boats crews who came 'alongside' a depot ship, designed to give them as much 'pastoral' time as possible before they sailed on yet another pulse racing patrol where they never knew if they'd come back in one piece again.

The bugle sounded all over the depot ship, which was the 0800 morning signal for the raising of the Ensign, or 'Morning Colours' ceremony, which denotes the start of the working day in the Navy and that it was now opened for business.

T.S. had managed to dodge being up on the main deck where everybody had to stand still, face aft to the quarterdeck of the ship and salute the ensign as it was being raised, even if it was not in sight by that person.

He went into the MSO to see if any signals were to be collected when Ross came onto him, and spoke aside to him.

"We've got a special signal that's just come through for you to take immediately to your skipper." he advised, handling T.S. the signal that was sealed in an envelope.

"Any idea about what it says, given that you've already dealt with it in your Message Handling routine?"

"No! Tony Cheyney our Chief Yeoman did the honours. Better see him before you get it to your skipper a.s.a.p."

"Thanks for the warning Gordon. Better get it off to him now then I'll come back for the rest. I would have been here earlier but nearly got caught on the upper deck chasing arse in a blue suit, as the expression goes." T.S. replied quickly and disappeared on his important errand.

"Chief Yeoman! You did the honours for me with this signal. What's the score on it?" T.S. asked on approaching the man.

"Yes! It is one of many coming through from the Comcen, (Communications centre). Incidentally, you will be advised that we'll be moving into the new underground Comcen facilities, as in future, this place will only be used for routine stuff."

"Cheers for the info Chief! Does that mean we've got to traipse all the way ashore for our daily signals? What about last minute stuff prior to sailing?"

"For the latter part, we'll be manning it for then, but whilst alongside, it's a boat ride ashore, I'm afraid."

"Thank God for that. Anyway, must dash if this is supposed to be a red hot one." T.S. concluded and left in a hurry.

When he got to the wardroom, he found that the P.O. Steward was busy catering for a large group of officers who had been gathered together by the Rear Admiral, from the Melville Island dockyard, with the title of 'Flag Officer Gulf', but was soon known as 'FOGGY'

"What's up George? Some big pow pow?" T.S. asked, as he stood inside the wardroom inconspicuously so that he could hear what was going on.

"I've got a special signal for our skipper. Will you give it to him for me?" T.S. asked.

"Yes, okay." he said, taking the signal from T.S.

"In case you missed it, so far it seems that you're being sent to sea this morning by 1000. I'll tell you the rest when you come back as I need you to go and fetch Leading Steward Brown. He should be somewhere in the wardroom dining room." Faulkner whispered, for T.S. to sneak out of the compartment to obey the senior rate's order.

"Frank! George Faulkner wants you in the meeting room pronto. Something to do with the special pow wow the Admiral is giving." T.S. said urgently.

"On my way. What's the score anyway?" Brown asked, as he finished folding up a pile of table cloths.

"From what George Faulkner has said, something about us putting to sea later this morning. Better we get there and listen to what's occurring." T.S. replied, and retraced his steps, with Brown following closely behind.

When they arrived back T.S. sat quietly next to Brown to listen to what the Admiral had to say, but they were too late, as the meeting had just broken up.

"George! What have we missed?" T.S. whispered.

"Only that one of our best Coast watchers, who according to the list of them is a certain Nick Morris, has reported that those marines you dropped off have managed to stir up most of the ruddy Jap army, and are now desperate to be picked up again.

Two MGBs set off from the base a few days ago to rescue them, but can only reach as far as the Gore Peninsula on the way back, so your boat has been detailed off to take fuel to them. Apparently only a 'Boat' can do this due to the increased Jap Air force activities in that area, also we've lost several long-range reconnaissance planes there during the past few weeks. You'll be loaded with a special fuel tank fore and aft of your fin, but will have water, food and extra ammo for them to make their return trip, but loaded up on both ends. But basically, you'll be playing mother to the gunboats. You'll also be taking Morris's relief, bringing Nick him back from those islands for R&R."

"We were due to sail this evening anyway, so that's no odds. Better get myself back on board and get organised." T.S. muttered, leaving quickly to do the myriad of things his job of being T.S. entailed.

Chapter IV

Matthew 4:19

T.S. stood at the back of the conning-tower bridge and waited until Hosie had come across the narrow gangway and to make his way up to the bridge.

Cdr S/M. was on the pontoon to take his salute from his most senior 'boat' skipper, Lt Cdr Hosie

"Obey telegraphs! Port 10. Half astern port. Let go aft!" Hosie ordered.

"Water moving for'ard port side sir!" T.S. reported, which was the sign that the boat was now moving astern as designed.

"Slow astern together! Let go for'ard." was the swift order, as Hosie slipped his boat away from the depot ship.

The boat went astern for a little while before Hosie judged there was enough water between the pontoon jetty and him to be able to swing around and face out to sea.

"Starboard 10. Slow astern Starboard, half ahead Port." He ordered, which brought the bows of the boat neatly round to become parallel, yet slightly astern of the depot shop.

"Stop together! In both engine clutches." This meant that Hosie had finished his manoeuvring with the battery-powered motors, and was about to engage his main engines.

"Both engine clutches in sir!" James reported from the control room.

"Very good! Slow ahead together. Signalman. Stand by to pipe the side."

T.S. took hold of his Bosun's call, waiting for a suitable moment and in position to make the piped salute as the boat passed slowly by the depot ship. Once the reply was received, T.S. made the customary 'Carry on' pipe, to conclude the ceremony.

The casing party scrambled around the casing, securing all and everything so that nothing would come adrift when the boat dived again.

Hosie was taking various 'fixes' from his bridge gyro compass to be able to order a course for the helmsman to steer by.

T.S. mentally noted that it was a very short time to be alongside, hoping that maybe next time they'd have a longer time if only for him to stretch his legs ashore and burn the W/T office's 'confidential' waste again, and maybe have the chance to meet some pretty WRN, WAAF or soldier girl whilst ashore.

The boat ploughed her way through the Arafu sea, which was thankfully, very calm and benign, making her top speed of 22 knots, for she was in a big rush to get to her r/v position to meet up with the very thirsty petrol engines of the MGBs which had set out days before them. It was a need for speed that was of the essence, which over-rode the need to remain undetected instead of diving and snorkelling to her r/v. The only proviso was that should the boat come under an air attack then she was to dive to continue at her transit, which was less than half of her surface speed.

"T.S. Clear the bridge for diving. Make sure both windows are clean and clear." Hoare ordered

"Aye aye sir." T.S. replied and commenced to remove the Ensign, the Lewis gun and his aldis signalling lamp from the bridge.

The boat arrived during sunset of the following day at the top end of a string of islands just north of the Gore peninsula, which is the nearest to the Tannibar group of Islands at the bottom of the Moluccan Archepelago now occupied by the Japanese.

"OOW – Radar! 3 contacts bearing Red 10, range 15,000 yards. They are moving slowly from left to right. Their projected course will take them behind the island on our port side and pass through our r/v area."

Hosie must have been in the control room at the time for he intercepted the message to take over from the OOW on the bridge.

"OOW! Dive the boat!"

As the boat disappeared under the waves, Hosie looked through his main periscope to see if he could spot these contacts.

"Get our trim right No1!"

"Aye aye sir!"

Looked up at the brass rings, which gave the relative and true bearings of whatever he looked at, he stated that he had managed to see several sets of navigation lights on his port side.

He saw the black shapes of three ships that were silhouetted by the shining rays of the moon and acted as any typical submarine captain would when spotting ships of the enemy in front of him.

"There are 2 merchantmen with an escort destroyer approaching us on the port side. Go to Action stations No1, and to red lighting in the control room."

"Aye aye sir!"

Hosie waited until everybody was settled at their allotted positions whilst he carried on his periscope observations.

"Attack teams close up!" he ordered, which was broadcasted over the intercom.

That order issued was an electrifying moment, causing yet another mad scramble by the crew in their effort to reach their allocated stations as quickly and as quietly as possible.

This was a time for total concentration and alertness by the chosen 'Attack Team', who have been selected for their professionalism and are more than capable of conducting their allotted task. They would remain at their posts until such times their captain completed his 'attack' or was satisfied with his work, enabling him to stand his men down until the next time.

"Attack teams closed up sir!"

"Very good No 1. That was a very swift time I must grant you." Hosie purred as he looked around him to see that the control room was full of very brave men who would do his bidding without even thinking about it.

"Start the plot!"

"Keep 50 feet! Signalman! Stand by to read out relative bearings and ranges."

"Watch your trim No 1."

"I have two large tankers, and an escort destroyer. The first tanker bearing is that! The escort bearing is... that. The second tanker bearing is that!"

"Red 25. Red 27 Red 30! T.S. stated.

"Using the height of the first tankers bridge to sea level, using long range, the range is ...that. From the funnel to the waterline of the escort is ... that! Again from the bridge to the waterline of the second tanker is ...that!"

"First tanker is 9 minutes which is 7,000 yards, the escort is 11 minutes which is 9,000 yards. And the third tanker is 12 minutes, 10,000 yards."•

"T.S.! Identify the escort."

T.S. looked through the periscope and after a moment he referred to his ships recognition and profile book. He was to report details relevant for the captain to use.

"It's an old *Hoko Zen* type destroyer. Two screws. Speed 25 knots, length 300 feet, beam 35 feet, draught 12 feet, and not fitted with depth charges, sir!" T.S reported.
Lower periscope!"

"Periscope lowered"

"It appears that two tankers being escorted by a destroyer are trying to sneak through our area undetected. We should be able to nab all three, seeing as they're all bunched up in close company." He announced to nobody in particular.

"Sonar reports that the cavitation from each tanker is distinct and suggests a speed of 12 knots. There is another multiple screw vessel further away. Suggest a third warship closing fast on them."

"Very good sonar!"

"Okay team, we've got two tankers and their escort coming our way. Navigator, plot their projected course to see where they may be going." Hosie ordered, and went over to the chart table to see.

• Each minute registered on the slide rule was so many yards. These figures are only to demonstrate this, and perhaps be incorrect in real terms.

"Hmm! It looks as if they're going up towards New Guinea. But what are 2 large Jap tankers virtually unescorted doing this side of the Timor Islands? I mean, according to the maps Mrs Richmond brought back, the Japs have designs to take all the islands down as far as New Zealand."

"Maybe they think they're safe in these waters with the knowledge that Oz is virtually unprotected along her northern shores." S/Lt Dave Sample the T.O. opined.

"Well they've got another think coming. Yet again we've come unseen! Group up! Full ahead together. Port 10, steer 320." Hosie ordered, which started a series of orders that commenced his Attack Routine.

"Set for'ard tubes 1,3,5 and 6 to a depth of 15 feet. Set 5&6 ranges of 2,000yards. 1&3 to 1800 yards, and tubes 2&4 to 1500yards, and to a depth of 10 feet."

"Aye aye sir!" Sample replied.

Hosie went over to the perspex screen that was kept as an ongoing plot for him to use when making his swift mental calculations, and to help maintain his 'state of play' during his attack. This was the main attack plot, which was a different one that the navigator kept. The navigator had to keep track of each course and speed they took during their attack. So when it was all over and they were getting the hell out of the area when making their escape, they knew which track to take. This again was a valuable tool for any submarine captain to use, as are his attack team members. Without a well-drilled and disciplined Attack Team a Submarine captain could fail his attacks and perhaps get sunk with 'all hands' into the bargain.

"Raise Attack periscope! Stand by and give true bearings." Hosie ordered, as he opened the handles of the periscope and peered through the lens.

As always, and as an important safety measure, Hosie gave a swift 360 Degree scan around him in case there was something above him that could place his boat into grave danger.

T.S. stood facing opposite the captain and looked up at the bright brass ring that held the bearings

"Stand by! Lead tanker is... that! Escort... that. Rear tanker is... that! Ranges for same are...that...that... and that!"

T.S. gave the readings swiftly then read out the ranges in the same manner.

Hosie peered up to his side of the same brass ring then over to Bell to find out if T.S. had reported the bearings correctly. This was because T.S. had to read a reciprocal bearing then give the true one, as the difference was 180 degrees.

"All correct sir!" Bell confirmed.

Hosie then looked at T.S. and congratulated him on his swift mental arithmetic, before he continued with his observations, then ordered the periscope lowered again.

"The sequence of firing will be:- Tube 6,5,3 4 ,2 then 1. We'll be firing on the swing and will have about 30 seconds to do so. Open bow doors. "

That means, tube 6 will hit the stern of the rear tanker. Tube 5 will go under the escort to hit the bow of the rear tanker, with tube 3 will go under the escort and hit the stern of the lead tanker, Tubes 2 then 4 will hit the stern and the bow of the escort with tube 1 hitting the bows of the lead tanker. Stand by after tubes with a depth of 10 feet. We'll keep the stern tubes on that tail-end Charlie when he starts sniffing around."

"Aye aye sir!" Sample replied and set the configuration into his Torpedo Order Firing Instrument (TOFI), known as the TOFFY machine.

"Sonar! What news of that rogue cavitation reported earlier?"

"A high speed twin propeller vessel approaching from Red 50. Suggest it is another escort destroyer trying to catch up sir!!" the Sonar Room control P.O. reported from his little den a deck below the control room..

"Have P.O. Woods keep a close watch on that one. Whatever it is, it might just decide to come looking for us."

"Aye aye sir!" Hoare responded and relayed the message down

91

to the sonar room via his intercom.

Hosie looked at the control room clock then at his wristwatch before he went over to the chart table.

"What depth of water have we got around here?" he asked civilly.

"This area and all to our port side is 100 plus fathoms. But averaging around 30 fathoms the further East you go towards the Torres Straits." Bell informed him after a few moments.

"What distance is there between our drop off points and our R/V?"

"15 nautical miles ahead and five miles to Starboard of this island." Bell replied and drew a pencil line across the chart to the island, which they were waiting behind.

"Hmm! I think we'll have to sink them all, to prevent the gunboats stumbling onto them. Even a squadron of MGBs are no match against a destroyer." Hosie opined, before going back to the attack periscope ordering it to be raised again.

"Stand by to read off, Signalman! "

T.S. reported each bearing and range in rapid succession, for Hosie to confirm his own mental calculations in order to issue the necessary orders.

"Port 10! Stop together. Set a zero angle on all tubes. Stand by to fire. Open bow caps." Hosie ordered calmly, and kept looking through his periscope.

"Keep me up No 1. I want 50 feet not 54!" Hosie snapped.

"Aye aye sir."

"Stand by ranges! Range is…that, and …that. And …that!"

T.S. gave the answers for Hosie to order the ranges to be given into the 'toffy' machine.

"Stand by firing sequence. Fire on my marks! Slow astern starboard, slow ahead port. Open outer doors." Hosie ordered swiftly, and grabbed his stopwatch from the chart table.

"Mark!" Hosie said aloud, then started his stop watch. The boat quivered and bucked slightly as the first torpedo with 600 lbs of high explosives was sent to its target.

Hose was turning his boat slowly from left to right to complete his firing solutions and timing each of his 'marks'. By the time he gave his 6th mark, there was a loud explosion that told the crew, the first torpedo had hit home. This was followed in rapid succession by 5 more much louder explosions, for Hosie to stop his watch. To hear all six explosions, made their own statement to the fact that the 3 ships had been hit and for Hosie to peer through his little window to see the carnage he had created to yet 3 more unsuspecting victims.

Hosie moved swiftly towards the chart table, giving T.S. the opportunity to take a quick look through the periscope.

A separate and even louder explosion had occurred and he saw the escort disintegrate and sink along with the now capsized tankers that were pouring fuel onto the already burning waters around them.

"Bloody hell!" T.S. muttered, managing to get out of Hosie's way when he returned.

"Good idea signalman. Any person wishing to view what we've done has 10 seconds." Hosie ordered.

The telegraphsman, then Boyall who keeps the attack log followed by Sample also had a quick peep. All remarking on a bloody good job done.

'Well done team! That's our second successful attack in these waters. One all round before we tackle this other contact. Down for'ard periscope. Raise the after periscope. Reload all tubes for'ard." Hosie declared and with an offered cigarette from Sample, sat on his main periscope chair to join the rest of the team for a 5minute cigarette break.

"Contact previously reported is getting louder and has just changed course to Red 20." Woods reported.

"Very good sonar. Okay No1! Settle everybody down again and re-start the attack." Hosie ordered, swinging his periscope round to the reported bearing.

The moon was up and full, which made it much easier for

Hosie to see this strange contact coming his way.

"Signalman. Identify this ship!" Hosie commanded.

T.S. looked through the lens of the powerful periscope for a few moments then flicked through his ships recognition book to find the likeness of what he had seen.

"It's a *Hyusi* class destroyer. 30 knots. Length 360 feet, 45 feet beam, 15 foot draught. 3,000 tons and fitted with broadside depth charge launchers."

"What news from for'ard? Has the TASI (the Underwater Weapons P.O.) loaded up yet?"

"P.O. Hughes reports that they're still loading up sir!" Bell replied.

"Hmm! Looks like a stern attack then. Tell P.O. Anderson to stand by stern tubes 1&2. Starboard 20. Full ahead starboard, half astern port. Open stern doors." Hosie ordered, turning his boat 180 degrees around to meet this new threat.

"Stop together! Stand by bearing and range in high power."

T.S. took up his usual position, facing the periscope with Hosie behind it.

"Bearing is that... Range is. . . that!"

T.S. gave the details for Hosie to give Sample his firing instructions.

"Make the range 1800 yards. Two degrees angle from the stern. Fire both tubes on my mark."

Hosie was waiting for the correct range and had his boat lined up on the same course that the destroyer was taking.

"Open stern caps. Open outer doors! Stand by... Mark!" he ordered, and restarted his stopwatch again.

The boat shook in accompaniment of the whooshing sound as the torpedoes were fired.

Hosie looked at his stop watch counting off the seconds to impact, until two very large bangs and several smaller explosions were heard astern of them.

Hosie looked through his attack periscope for a while to see that the Japanese destroyer had blown up and had 'turned turtle' with just its hull showing and the propellers still turning.

"That's strange! Signalman, what is the reported crew of the destroyer?"

T.S. looked in his book and reported it to be 300.

"It seems as if there's a lot more than that. No1, come and witness this." Hosie ordered, moving aside for Welling to look. When he saw the large amount of bodies floating in the water he declared that there were definitely more men there than just the crew.

"We've got about another hour before the MGBs arrive. So we'll surface and grab some of them as sample specimens to take back with us." Hosie breathed.

"No1. Attack teams secure. Secure from Action Stations. Then stand by to surface. When we have surfaced get a casing party on deck, but armed in case. I want them to bring onboard some of the bodies that're all around us now."

"Aye aye sir!"

The crew reverted to normal diving stations and the casing party were armed and ready to go onto the casing.

Hosie had the boat manoeuvred in among the raft of floating dead Japanese troops before he had the boat surface virtually right under them.

T.S. stood at the back of the bridge with Hoare and Hosie in front of him, both looking over the side telling the 2nd Cox'n which bodies he was to bring onboard. There were already several that had landed on the boat as it rose out of the water, so the casing party brought them onto the gun tower, ready for taking below.

"The signal was right after all, sir! We've become 'fishers of men', and fishing dead men out of the water only to borrow their uniforms as if we've not got one of our own." T.S. muttered to Sample, but got a withering look from Hosie for his troubles.

"Bring 12 on board, strip them and bag up their uniforms. Ditch the bodies overboard once done." Hosie shouted down to Hall.

T.S. was glued to his binoculars scanning the upturned hull of the destroyer looking for any survivors, but with his Lewis gun at the ready.

"There're several men on the upturned hull sir." T.S. reported.

He looked around the floating bodies to see if there was any life showing from them when he heard pinging noises that came from the casing around the after periscope.

He grabbed his Lewis gun, cocked it and sent a full magazine of 9 mm bullets towards the men on the hulk.

Hosie looked through his own binoculars to see that men were falling into the water having been shot by T.S.

"Cease firing! Cease firing!" he ordered swiftly.

"T. S. Who gave you permission to fire?" he asked angrily.

"Those bastards were firing at us sir, and all I did was to return the favour."

"You should have asked permission first." Hosie snapped

"I'm only doing what I was trained to do sir. No bastard slant-eyed Jap is going to shoot at me and get away with it." T.S. replied vehemently.

"Fair comment on the first part Signalman, and I'll forget your outburst on the second part. But you can stow your machine gun away now, as I'm going to drop a couple of torpedoes into their laps. This I can do as your captain, and is the only way to finally despatch their ship so as not to show any traces they had been here or where the ship had been sunk." Hosie stated calmly, then favouring his after tubes so that the fore-ends had the chance to reload a full 6 again, gave his orders via the intercom system to the after-ends for them to fire the 2 remaining after torpedoes.

The two torpedoes struck home in spectacular style, and within a couple of minutes the remains of the destroyer finally slipped below the waves, to replenish Davey Jones' locker once more.

Anderson reported that he'd got a dozen uniforms to bring below but only one of them that would be of great interest.

"Check the lashings on the fuel tanks and the other fuel drums, then have your party come below." Hosie shouted over the side of the conning tower.

"When the casing's clear we'll make for our r/v point now. Remain on the surface. Use main engines and make speed of 20 knots and steer 050. I'll confirm that when I get below." Hosie ordered, and went below to see what these uniforms were.

"Nice bit of shooting signalman. But in future, wait until you're ordered to open fire. You nearly caused the casing party to start shooting back." Sample said sternly.

"They were no sailors sir. And anyway, it was easy as pie because every 6th bullet was a tracer, easy for me to follow across the target area. I managed to shoot tens of the bastards, but those with the guns got it first though." T.S. replied happily.

"How the devil did they manage to get hold of their weapons in the first place, considering the virtual instant sinking of their vessel? But somehow we'll never know, so just keep it that way." Sample remarked, scratching his head in wonderment.

"Well anyway sir, a bit of lead in their diet gives them a lovely white complexion. Makes them a bit heavier to swim mind you." T.S. quipped and carried on with his lookout duties to avoid a rebuff from his officer.

Sample just sighed and let the remark go astray into the now complete silence on the bridge.

Chapter V

Coast Watcher

The boat was now under full power from her two new and very powerful 'straight 8 piston' turbo charged diesel engines, as she raced through the still calm waters in the sub tropics of the southern hemisphere.

She was to meet up with two MGBs to give their fuel tanks a drink of juice for them to carry on back to their base.

It took them less than half an hour to make their designated r/v position and Hosie took his boat slowly in between two small islands, waiting for the MGBs arrival.

It was getting dark now and T.S. was still on the bridge during this time as he was the boat's no 1 lookout, and needed to be on hand to make visual contact with them.

"I've got a small flashing light from the port island sir. It must be our Coast watcher." T.S. reported quietly.

"Sure it's not a marker buoy or something?" Welling the relief O.O.W. queried.

"No sir. Definitely morse code." T.S. stated and read what the flashing light was making.

"He's giving me his recognition code word sir. Permission to reply."

"Do so to establish contact."

"Captain – O.O.W! Made contact with our Coast watcher on the island port side."

"Make to him, I see him. Have relief on board. Getting ready to send him over." Hosie replied.

"Sir! He says that he's made contact with the MGBs on the seaward side of this island. Will send them round to meet us." T.S. reported, showing Welling the message he had just written down.

"Well done Signalman. Acknowledge that, then send our message to him."

T.S. fitted his red filter over his smaller 3-inch aldis lamp and flashing his signal towards the darkness of the small island to the spot where the Coast watcher was.

Welling reported the imminent arrival of the MGBs to Hosie, who had Anderson and his casing party on the after-casing, preparing to transfer the fuel that was lashed well down onto the casing fore and aft of the fin.

T.S. reported the silhouette of the first boat to poke her bows into the little narrow creek, followed closely by the second one.

Welling reported that the boats were now coming along side aft and each side of the boat.

T.S. saw Hosie appear onto the fore casing and stand on the gun sponson waving his cap at the two MGBs that were being tied up alongside.

"I'm Lt Cdr 'Hoppy' Hopkins, RANVR, Commander of FPB 2010 and Leader of the FPB Squadron and this is my buddy and fellow ex Welshman Lt Topsy Turner ex-RN, and Commander of FPB 2012." Hopkins stated as both officers saluted Hosie.

"I'm Lt Cdr Hosie, Captain of S64. Please to meet you both." Hosie responded.

"I've brought you both ten tons of fuel and some supplies for your return."

Hopkins thanked him for getting here when they did, and reported a large warship running up and down and around the islands. Plus the fact that both of them had also run out of food and water.

"You needn't worry now, that vessel is 600 feet below us, which is why I'm slightly late. Bring the Marines on board, as I'll be taking them back for you. I'll have my Cox'n and our chef to provide your crews with some hot food." Hosie replied as he comforted them.

"Get them down the for'ard loading hatch. I'll have my Chief Stoker with his men to refuel you. I'll be down shortly when I've sent the relief Coast watcher ashore and received the returning one." he added, which was the cue for most of their crew to go down into the warmth of the boat.

"I've got a dicky starboard engine. Any chance one of your 'Tiffy's' to lend mine a hand?" Turner asked.

"Certainly. I'll get ERA Ottley to see to your needs." Hosie assured him with a smile, and for them to follow their crews below.

T.S. watched the marines make a slow and seemingly laborious way towards the for'ard loading hatch when he saw most of them were wearing bandages, yet none were carrying side-arms or other equipment that he had seen them take on their way out.

"Bloody hell sir! Those boys look pretty beat up. I've counted them and it seems there's 1 missing, and I can't see their sergeant" T.S. remarked to Welling.

"No doubt that by the time we get back we'll hear all about it signalman. Keep a good lookout astern, in case we get a surprise visit."

T.S. looked over the side to the bullet ridden MGBs and spotted a gunner checking over the heavy machine guns.

"Hello oppo! Looks as if the native moths around here like MGBs for supper judging by the holes you've got everywhere!" he said breezily.

"Yes, Just as we approached the beach where the Marines were hiding, we were ambushed by a load of machine-gun toting Japs who seemed to be waiting for us. Our Chief Gunner, Kelvin Smith over there, put their searchlight out before he hosed the bastards with his twin 20 mm cannon. Our after 40mm cannon gunner got wounded so he rescued him and took over the gun, with fantastic results too. Mowed them down like cutting the grass he did." Evans, one of their gunners replied with relish.

"Yeah! They seemed to drop down from the trees onto the beach like ruddy coconuts. The Marines had run out of ammo and were about to be overrun. We arrived just in the nick of time to sort the bastards out. We reckon on about 150 of them less to worry about now." Smith stated as he had just crossed over the inboard MGB to wait for the others.

"Hurry up and get down into the boat Gareth, and you Kelvin. You can always come back and finish off after your scran.

We've still got a long way to go to get back to base." a voice stated that was coming from the MGB cockpit.

"That's our Cox'n, Robbie Springle. He's our first Aider. Pretty good too as he's just saved the sergeant from bleeding to death." James informed him.

"Well, the sooner you get down into the boat, the sooner you'll have some scran. No doubt our Cox'n will issue a decent tot to swill it all down with." T.S stated, as the gunners climbed up onto the boat's casing and went below.

T.S. scanned all around with his powerful binoculars and managed to spot the off-coming Coast-watcher paddle almost alongside the saddle tanks just aft of the 4inch gun.

"Coast watcher about to board sir!" T.S. reported swiftly.

"Better get down onto the casing and help him." Welling ordered.

"Aye aye sir."

Anderson the P.O. UW in charge of the after-ends when at 'Action Stations', also the 2nd Cox'n, was making sure the FPB's were safely secured alongside.

I've been detailed to stay on the casing Frank, er Scratcher, if you want to go below."

"It's okay now, all is secured, but thanks anyway." He replied and went below.

T.S. was standing on the saddle tanks of the boat and grabbed hold of the rope that the Coast watcher threw to him so that he could come alongside and secure his craft.

"Dr Livingstone I presume!" T.S. joked, helping the man onto the saddle tanks.

"Actually it's Nick Morris! But close enough Cobber!" the man drawled in a broad Australian accent.

"What made you pick such a gawd-awful place to set up a picnic site?" T.S. asked, as he secured the rope to one of the stanchions that formed the gun sponson.

"I was on board an ocean going survey vessel that surveyed

101

these islands and all along the Northern coastline some years ago. These are the two islands that are closest to each other yet on the furthest edge of the mainland. A natural choice in case I had to escape from one to the other should the Japs decide to come ashore. They're all over the place right now, with lots of heavy metal floating by in a great hurry, and aircraft just floating about with nothing else to do except take holiday snapshots of our beaches. Was that you lot that made the skyline shine with fire and smoke a little while ago?"

"Aye. We sunk 2 large tankers and their escort, only to sink another destroyer that was heading your way. The skipper didn't want the patrol boats meeting up with either of them, that's why we had to sink them."

"Was that destroyer a *Hyusi* class? Only it's started to escort troop ships going eastwards, then on the way back, take a close interest on these islands. One thing though and I've got to report it, is that there's an increased activity of fishing boats going eastwards along the coast line. The waters around this part of the world is full of fish, yet they don't seem to catch any. To me that's very fishy, if you pardon my pun." Morris drawled.

"In answer to your question, yes it was a *Hyusi,* and full of soldiers too. Speaking about the fishermen, we came across 3 fishing boats the other day on our way back from dropping these marines off. They had very big and heavy nets on tow, but we managed to get clear of them."

"Maybe the Japs answer to not having minesweepers. The backroom boys back at base will come up with the answers, but in the meanwhile I'm in need of some real tucker." Morris said as he rubbed his belly, and T.S.pointed the way towards the torpedo-loading hatch.

"Just follow your nose, it's chicken a la carte."

"I'm fed up of eating ruddy fish, so I suppose that'll do. I'll definitely have the chicken but you can stuff the ruddy cart, matey." Morris said cheerfully and followed the file of wounded marines down into the boat.

"Looks like you've got a few weeks fishing for your supper then Mr, er, Steve Locke. Better check you've got enough fags with you before you go, or you'll not get your smoked kippers or whatever you catch around these waters." T.S quipped to the relief Coast watcher.

"No worries mate! I'm a non smoker, but as long as I've got a few extra crates of tinnies with me, and a few extra grenades for insurances, then Tojo can take a ruddy jump!" Locke said with a large grin and started to climb into the rubber dinghy.

"Whatever! But keep your head down and one of us will be along to pick you up again next month. All the best!"

Hosie spoke to Lock for a few minutes before shaking his hand and ordered T.S. to help him with his stores into his dinghy.

Lock cast off his little dinghy for T.S. to watch him row the short distance to the shore, and got a farewell wave from Lock when he had finally landed, only to disappear into the dense tropical vegetation.

T.S. was required to remain on the after casing as a lookout, but went to 'keep company' with the stoker detailed off to see to the fuel transfer.

"Pretty powerful stuff to get into your lungs John! Imagine that in the boat, one spark and we'll all be singing soprano and playing a mean tune on a woofter's harp (a lyre)" T.S. commented.

"Yes, too volatile for boats. Better engine performance though. Mind you though, it's not as dangerous as what the Hairy Fairy's use in their aircraft. Kerosene or meths I believe. But I do wish Pusser would invent a better way to get it transferred instead of this bloody stirrup pump contraption." Williams moaned, and stopped for a quick breather, and in time for one of the FPB 'Tiffy's' to come and relieve him.

"Nearly finished the transfer, mate. It's all yours." Williams stated, handing over the pump to his relief and left to go for'ard for a breath of fresh air.

* * *

It was early the following morning for the T.S. to resume his duty as the lookout, to have a chance to speak to the signalman boarding 2010.

"Hey up Bunts! That's a tiddly little Ensign you've got hoisted. Any chance of a swap with mine?" he asked, showing the man his much larger one, still attached to its removable mast.

"Sorry oppo! That's Hoppys, er, the skipper's own personal ensign. It's pure silk and was made by his missus only last week."

"What size do you normally fly astern in harbour? Only I definitely need the next size down from mine."

"A size 1 I think, but your best bet is to speak to Wren Jean Sedgwick in the Base Supply Office. Nice looking piece she is. Tell her Robert Reeves sends his regards!" he replied before the rest of the crew arrived on board, carrying food and other items needed for their return trip.

"Cheers Bob, and I'm T.S. on here. What is your squadron net frequency, in case we've got to rescue you again?"

"We use the spot frequencies 3030 kc's c/w for contact with base, but 2121kc's voice between ourselves. That way I don't spend time tuning up my transmitter. Yours?"

"1050kc's on the net broadcast, but 4340kc's c/w for the main frequency and for Sub Safety. Not sure about the new frequencies now in use down here. How do you get your 'spot frequencies'?"

"My transmitter has those new-fangled things called 'crystals' which somehow matches up the transmitter to the aerial without me tuning it etc. Just switch on and tap away."

"Sounds interesting. Mind you I don't suppose you'd have much time farting about with your set when you're making a run in attack on the enemy."

"Too right! I'm also the bridge gunner for my sins. Got me a very mean belt-fed Vickers machine-gun all to myself. Kelvin Smith our Chief Gunner keeps it in tip-top condition for me. All I do is pull the trigger."

"Yeah me too. I've got one of them and a Lewis gun for good measures. Anyway, Bob, keep your head down and maybe we'll meet ashore at the NAAFI's Armada Club some time." T.S. concluded, allowing Reeves to carry on with his allotted tasks getting ready for sea again, while he made a note of the frequencies Reeves gave him.

Hosie came up onto the casing with the two MGB skippers, talking briefly with them before they waved goodbye and boarded their own vessels.

The powerful engines of the MGBs roared into life, moving swiftly away from the boat. T.S. was one of many to watch the two craft move astern of the boat then turning to go out into the open waters of the Arafu Sea to head their way back to base.

The Marines were being tended to below, the boat got ready to follow on behind these very fast vessels as best as she could.

Hosie couldn't turn his boat around to exit at the same point so decided to move on through the small channel to come out the other end.

No sooner had the bows started to poke itself from its hiding, when one of the MGBS came from around the island, stopping right in front of them.

T.S. was reading their flashing aldis light signal coming from it and reported what was said.

"He says that there's a group of 6 fishing boats approaching about 8,000 yards away and for us to stay hidden until they see them off."

"Make to him. 'Will dive and make our way out of the area using a course of 170. We'll give you 1 hour to catch up'."

T.S flashed his signal over and received the final reply.

He says, "See you again. If not good luck and to mind their nets."

T.S grabbed his little ensign on its chrome staff, waving it over the side as a salute to them, before they disappeared around the back of the island again out of sight.

Soon S64 was also making her way out of the little hideaway, moving out into the open waters.

"Clear the bridge. Stop together. Go to diving stations." Hosie ordered quickly then went below to take charge whilst T.S. and the O.O.W. completed their orders.

Bridge cleared. Shutting upper voice pipe cock." Welling reported then ordered T.S. below.

"Upper lid shut! Clip on. Both clips on. Officer coming below!" T.S reported as he stood looking up into the control room tower, Welling climbed down the ladder entering the control room.

"What depth of water have we got?" Hosie asked, as Welling went to take up his position behind the two planes men who were sitting at their positions waiting for the boat to dive.

"10 fathoms below us now but deepens rapidly to 50 within 2 nautical miles."

"Very good! Dive the boat No1."

Scarlett known as 'Red the Wrecker' by the crew, sprang into action, pulling the main vent levers, which received the reports back that 1,3 & 5 main vents were seen to be open.

"Group up. Full ahead together. Take us down to periscope depth. I'll be able to get a fix before we swing round onto our return course." Hosie ordered.

"Stand by bearings!" Hosie snapped, which prompted T.S. to get into position to do so.

"Promontory on port side is...that! Peak of starboard Island is... that." Hosie stated, giving a bearing that where the lines crossed on the chart, was the exact position to where they were.

Port 15 Steer 170" he ordered to cause the boat to swing on its reciprocal course, as the one given to the commander of the MGB.

Hosie looked astern of his boat to see that the 2 MGBS were slaughtering the occupants of the fishing boats each with their several twin barrelled 20 mm machine guns whilst sinking the craft with each of their two twin 40mm cannons.

Hosie stood for quite a while looking at this sight giving a commentary on what he saw, until he saw the MGBS break off and start to race towards him.

"Take us up to 30 feet so that they can see us. Signalman! Use the after periscope to make the following signal to them. 'Well done! We can all go home now.' Make sure they reply."

T.S got his torch and flashed the message to them, observing their reply, before they sped away from them at a good 40 knots, leaving the boat to plod on at around 8 knots.

"We've got a tiger in our tanks now. Thanks and be good."

The noise from the high speed propellers of the MGB.s roared close by each side of them before they finally were heard no more.

"Return to periscope depth. Secure from diving stations! Go to watch dived No1. We'll clear this area. I intend to snort in 2 hours so we can get back in a decent time. Remain on this course until then."

"Aye aye sir. White watch, Watch dived."

Chapter VI

Going Dutch

The boat was tied up, nestling port side for'ard on no 1 pontoon of her mother ship referred to as 'Trot 1', with everybody back into their mess decks again.

T.S. found himself duty again doing his 2 hour stint as the duty 'Trot Sentry'.

Scarlett came up on deck to ask T.S. about the bullets that pierced the casing of the after periscope and snorkel mast.

"I didn't know any had Red. There're quite a few holes in the side of the fin just below where I stand on the bridge, if that's any good to you."

"Well something is letting water into it. You've told me your glasses need de-humidifying so that might be it." He said and left to go below again, when an officer whose wavy lines of gold bars on his epaulettes denoted that he was a Merchant Navy Engineer Officer coming over the narrow gangway.

T.S. saluted him as he reached the end of the gangway and stepped onto the casing.

"Good afternoon sir, can I help you?" he asked politely.

"Yes, good afternoon. I'm Engineer Officer Nick Baxter from the Ship Repair Yard down there." he replied, pointing to the 2 floating docks.

"I need to contact your Engineer Officer." Baxter spoke in a Lancastrian accent, whilst returning the obligatory salute. His accent surprised T.S. considering that most of those he met from ashore so far, apart from the boat's crews, had Aussie accents.

"We don't have an engineer officer now, but we have a Chief Engine Room Artificer by the name of Bill Clutterbuck, but unfortunately he's just gone inboard, sir." T.S explained politely.

"Oh dear. Maybe when he comes back you can tell him to meet me in the depot ship wardroom. " Baxter stated, turning to retrace his steps over the gangway again.

"I can always get you another Engineer sir if you care to come back on board." T.S. responded quickly.

"S'okay Signalman. I'll deal with this." Scarlett offered as he retraced his steps and made his way to the gangway.

"I'm ERA Scarlett, the boat's Outside ERA. Our Chief Engine Room Artificer Bill Clutterbuck has gone inboard to get some engineering drawings he needs. Maybe I can help you in some way?" Scarlett asked politely.

"Well, actually you can. Your boats seem to suffer from excess internal condensation, which will eventually corrode any metalwork not easily accessible. The Squadron Engineer Officer has requested that I look into it and assess your needs for a full air conditioning unit system. (A.C.U.)."

"Yes, that is the standard situation on board submarines, sir. Cramped and inaccessible on both accounts. I think ERA Dave Ottley will probably be your man for the job but I am available to assist as and when, as I have other tasks on board to conduct. He's also on board at the moment, so if you care to follow me down sir, I'll escort you to our wardroom where you can meet our duty officer. In the meantime I'll get ERA Ottley for you." Scarlett offered, and Baxter followed him down the for'ard torpedo hatch into the boat.

"OOW – Gangway. Engineer Officer Baxter coming below, and escorted by ERA Scarlett." T.S. announced through his gangway microphone, which was connected up to the boat's intercom. A muffled reply was his response from the control room.

Several ratings had come and gone over the gangway before Clutterbuck finally came on board, just as the T.S. was about to be relieved by the next trot sentry.

"Chief! There's a Merchant Navy Chief Engineer Officer by the name of Baxter, who is down in the wardroom, but is being seen to by the Outside Wrecker. The officer is from the ship Repair Yard coming to see about some a.c.u's." T.S. informed him.

"Ah! Just the very officer I wanted to see. I've been told to expect him. I need him to take a shuftie at our Port engine clutch."

Clutterbuck replied cheerfully then went below.

It was 1000 the following morning when T.S. who was standing on the top of the depot ship's gangway ladder, coming back with the mail and another ream of signals, saw a boat come slowly into the base, through the boom defence gates.

He only just recognised the boat as S63, as she looked almost a floating wreck, with her Ensign draped over her gun tower as the fin was virtually non-existent.

He watched as the boat was manoeuvred alongside 'Trot 3' astern of S64, and the berthing party secured her alongside.

A single file of ratings carried stretchers and black bags down onto the pontoon, the boat's skipper with a few of the men came scrambling up out of both the gun tower hatch and the engine-room hatch, which was a rare sight on it's own.

T.S. made his way to the top of No3 ladder waiting to see their Signalman as his opposite number arrive up on deck, to perhaps get a quick word as to what had happened.

T.S. saluted the skipper, then 2 of his officers as they arrived to be met by Cdr S/M, then saw some of the bleary-eyed crew stagger onto the deck, followed by the walking wounded, but not their Signalman. He managed to recognise the boat's Leading Telegraphist and took him to one side.

"Bloody hell, is that you Ken Long?" T.S. asked, offering him a lit cigarette.

Long took the cigarette, drawing deeply from it as if it was his first one for a long time, before he spoke.

"Cheers Oppo! Hasn't had a fag in days. In face none of us have."

"What the bloody happened to you? Must have been one hell of a patrol!" T.S. said gently, stuffing his fag packet into the top pocket of Long's shirt.

"We were sent on a photo reconnaissance mission off the northern coast of Java. On our way back and just when we thought we'd be out of range from land based aircraft, we started to snort to charge our batteries, we were spotted by then got set upon by a couple of Jap fighter bombers who must have come from some unseen carrier or whatever. Within one hour there were several of them onto us, kept us pinned down until their corvettes with depth charges came along, giving us a right pasting. No matter where we went, they managed to find us, I suppose mainly because the water depths were shallow to about 100 feet and we couldn't find deeper water let alone a thermal layer to duck under. In fact we somehow got wedged in between some rocks and couldn't move for fear of rupturing our ballast tanks. The constant detonations of the depth charges must have blasted the rocks away for us to finally move away. As you can see, our gun, sonar dome and most of the fin have been ripped to shreds. Our masts bent like hairpins. Lucky when you think of it because those rocks saved us from total annihilation. Thank God our for'ard group of h.p air bottles survived for us to surface again as our gun tower hatch was still operable. The skipper had to use the gun tower as our bridge when we did get away. Dave Fagg our outside wrecker took several hours to free, then managed to crank the external snort mast up a fair way so that we could use the engines without creating a wind tunnel in the control room. At least we were able to surface before we had no1 battery tank blow up that set fire to the accommodation space. The thing is, our skipper thinks the reason for us to be followed and nailed, is that we're painted black, which means that we may well be seen from the air to around that depth especially in clear blue waters. Maybe if we changed our colour scheme to something Hank the Yank has on their boats, then we might stand a chance. I mean, a black painted boat is fair enough out in the Atlantic but definitely not in the clear blue waters off these islands. I think our boat is too damaged to be repaired, which means that with luck we will end up as 'Spare Crew and perhaps enjoy a few days ashore before attempting the next mystery trip." Long said wearily.

"If there's something you need that I can get you? What about the rest of the Sparkers, as I haven't seen your signalman yet?"

"Better go and see the Sin Bosun about him."

"Thanks for the info Ken! Get inboard and enjoy a few days survivors leave. See you later on in the mess deck." T.S. concluded and gently patted Long on his shoulder.

"Cheers for the fags! Maybe once we've got ourselves sorted out inboard, especially after some scran and a bloody good dhobying, I'll catch up with you later. But one thing is for certain, Pusser needs to sort out our décor for us to survive this bloody lot." He concluded and left T.S.

He watched the stretcher cases and 6 black body bags being brought on board, then decided that he should get on board to spread the word among all those who were on the casing watching the spectacle of one very damaged boat unloading her dead and wounded.

"Look at the damage to her! She's only fit for scrapping now." Hughes the P.O. U/W and duty P.O. declared, pointing down to the boat as he and T.S. arrived on board together.

"6 dead, 8 in a bad way and a further 10 injured. Apparently the skipper is blaming it all on the colour scheme, Doug. Says if the boat was a different colour to black." T.S. said slowly.

"Yeah! Who told you that?" Hughes asked in disbelief.

"I've just had a word with Long, the Killick Sparker on board, who told me. My opposite number is missing." T.S. replied curtly and related to him what Long had said.

"If that's the case, then the Scratcher will be having us paint the boat in God knows what fancy colour."

"Let's put it this way, unless something is done about it and bloody well soon, we won't have a squadron left."

"I suppose there's something in what you say, and perhaps is the answer to the reason why they were clobbered. We might come unseen, but look out when we're discovered and located. That's when the proverbial shit hits the fan and all that when we start dodging the showers of depth charges they like to throw at us." Hughes concluded, as both men climbed down the for'ard torpedo-loading hatch and into the cool of the boat.

T.S. had spread the news about the state of S63 with the general conclusion being drawn about the black painted hull. The same conclusion must have been reached by Cdr S/M, who by the end of the forenoon, issued the order for all boats to be painted a matt 'Teal' colour, for the Scratcher to have all hands turned to, to paint the boat overall right down to the water line.

The stink of paint mingling with white spirit permeated right through the boat with angry exchanges from those who had to walk across the freshly painted casing to leave the boat or those who came on board unaware of the 'Wet Paynte' notices stuck around the upper deck.

This was out of routine to a normal day, as on an ordinary day the boat's crew secured for the day at 1300 and the duty watch took over. This was called 'Tropical Routine' which meant that everybody started work at 0700 and able to work on deck before it got too hot. But as an operational squadron of boats, any work needed to be done would be carried out virtually there and then, but with luck, they would have the rest of the time off to do something else.

By 1600 on the following day the boat had been painted from stem to stern, and because of the hot weather, the paint was quick to dry, with the crew getting ready to go inboard to enjoy a nice cool shower after spending the afternoon in the scorching sun, with plenty mugs of cold 'Harry Limers' to quaff to help slake their thirsts.

For the next three days, S64 enjoyed a period alongside whilst the boat was fitted with an a.c.u. in each mess, much to the relief of all on board. Instead of sweating in the hot humid conditions both up on deck or below reaching 90 degrees, they enjoyed a much cooler temperature of 60degrees. The cool air contrast was like stepping out into a furnace once you left the boat, for the crew to wish they also had 'air conditioned streets' ashore.

The fore hatch was fitted with a special wooden frame with little glass panelled double doors on it to keep the boat cool helping prevent the a.c.u's from overloading. As each boat came off patrol then so they got fitted out, making the depot ship's company complain until they too finally had theirs fitted throughout the ship. Soon Engineer Officer Nick Baxter was in charge of a creeping fitting out of the entire base, including the village with a.c.u's, or even electric fans hanging from ceilings, by a veritable army of electricians, engineers and plumbers all working flat out to provide and complete the work. When it was all done in record time, Baxter was congratulated, becoming, for a while, the toast of the entire base.

It was also the time when news came in from Chief of the General Staff HQ in Sydney that the Japanese military codes had been broken, that all the little pieces of evidence previously gathered by Mrs Helena Richmond, the different uniforms brought back by S64, the patient building of evidence by the Coast watchers were now adding up for the allied forces to make sense of it all.

From now on, the base would start to perform its primary role to conduct an all out war against the bad neighbours who were only a couple of hundred miles of sea away, threatening to come their way.

"Boat ready for sea Cox'n?" Welling asked down the conning tower voice pipe to James who was sitting at the helm.

"3 passengers entered into the Next of Kin book sir. T.S. has taken it inboard and brought two Mackenzie Charts back, they're now with the N.O. sir."

"Very good Cox'n." Welling responded before looking over the side of the conning tower, turning his attention to Hall who was taking charge of the casing party.

"Single up 2nd Cox'n. Stand by to remove the gangway. The captain will be along shortly." he ordered.

"Aye aye sir." Anderson responded.

"Permission for Leading Stoker Morgan to come onto the bridge sir?" James shouted to attract Hoare's attention.

"Permission granted, but quick about it." Was the swift reply. T.S. was waiting at the back of the bridge to help Morgan up with his bucket of cleaning material.

"Well if it ain't our illustrious windows man, Tony Morgan." he greeted, taking the bucket so Morgan could climb up onto the bridge to clean the glasses and filters of both periscopes.

Morgan bathed the glasses with metholated spirits then wiped the excess liquid off with a clean muslin cloth before they were polished by a sheet of specially soft paper nicknamed 'periscope paper'.

"Any chance of a few sheets of that paper Tony? Only my Bino's are getting too grubby for me to see through." T.S asked softly.

Morgan nodded, then gave him a couple of pieces off his roll that were the size of a standard sheet of toilet paper, saying.

"Use it sparingly as it's like gold dust at the moment." He advised.

"Cheers Tony! Come and have a wet off me next time around." T.S. replied, starting to clean the lens and the eyepieces of his binoculars.

Morgan reported that he had completed his task then went below again.

Hosie arrived onto the bridge to be greeted by Welling, with the standard report that the boat was ready for sea.

"Very good No1! Obey telegraphs! Group up! Let go for'ard! Port 20! Slow ahead Starboard!" Hosie ordered in rapid succession, watching the results of his orders, as the boat started swing away from the pontoon by her bows, before he judged there was enough clearance for him to let go aft.

"Let go aft. Mid ships!" he ordered, waiting until the boat was completely clear of the pontoon.

"Stop Port! Starboard 20! Slow astern Starboard, half ahead Port!" he ordered to bring the boat round the bows of the depot ship, lining himself up for his left turn to approach the gorge.

"Stand by to pipe! Pipe!" he ordered, as T.S 'piped the still' and waited until they had passed the Flagstaff pier, then having received is return salute, piped 'the carry on'.

The boom defence team had already opened the 'Sea Gates' to let them through, once through and about to clear the cove, they were shut again.

"In engine clutches!" he ordered, then waited until the report came back that the order had been completed.

"Full ahead together! Make speed for 20 knots! Port 20 and steer 325!" he ordered, taking the boat out into the Gulf with her powerful diesel engines roaring into life to propel her swiftly through the water.

He took a few compass bearings from the land behind him and had them plotted by the navigator in the control room below him.

"Okay No1. Fall out Harbour Stations. We're in safe waters but go to Patrol Routine. Keep on this course for 3 hours, I'm going below."

"Aye aye sir!"

The boat's casing had been cleared away for sea, with the casing party safely below before there was a change of voice from the voice pipe to indicate the change of helmsman, for T.S. to realise that it was his watch that was nominated as the first watch on patrol.

"Looks as if I'm duty eagle again sir!" T.S. commented, as Welling was about to be relieved by the new oncoming O.O.W.

"Never mind signalman, practice makes perfect and all that!" Welling replied with a smile then related to Sample as his relief, the current course and speed as ordered by the captain.

The boat was riding through the almost wave-less sea, yet gently dipping her bows down and up over the gentle swell, with the sun beating down on their now capless heads.

"Nice day for a cruise sir!" T.S. quipped, feeling the bracing air filling his lungs to making him feel almost glad to be back at sea again.

"Yes, it is. Air conditioning is one thing, but you can't beat the cool sea air." Sample responded with equal appreciation of the moment.

"Where are we going this time sir?"

"Musn't tell, 'cause there's a war on you know. Tittle-tattle loses battles. Loose lips sink ships and all that jazz." Sample smiled wickedly as if to tease T.S.

"Fair enough sir! But we're at sea now, all in the same proverbial boat."

Sample chuckled, surprised at the response.

"Let's call it a mystery trip. Maybe you can guess as to where?"

Well let's see. We normally turn right from the cove and head north on a 140 sort of course, but we've turned left, going the wrong way for that, especially on this course of 325. Therefore we'll be going down into the gulf to say hello to the sharks and other fishes. Yep that's my answer!" T.S said with satisfaction.

Now which blabber-mouth told you that Signalman? He is right of course, and yes we're going to check out a few, er, holes in the sea bed in this part of the oggin." Sample agreed amiably.

Don't forget sir you're talking to T.S." T.S. quipped, as he scanned the horizon with his powerful binoculars.

Sample chuckled again at the T.S then lapsed into the respectful silence between lookout and OOW.

It is times like that when on a one-to-one basis, without any other person present, all the trappings of rank gets left behind, two men can enjoy a natural conversation, man to man, to help foster a mutual bonding between them, given that each is reliant on the other to survive during dangerous times. This is not because of lack of discipline, but mainly because in Submarines, discipline is implied not implicit. The bubble gets burst when another person joins them, or an order is given, for them to revert to rank/surnames.

Sir! There's what looks like a Dutch Cruiser. I can tell by the almost clipper like bows they have. She's a medium heavy cruiser that's supposed to have 2 twin 9inch gun turrets for'ard and aft sir, but one of them for'ard seems to be missing, along with one of her smoke stacks and her after mast. From the pennant numbers of what looks like 2 Dutch destroyers towing her, with one lashed each side of her. They are probably their 'H' class destroyers akin to our 'V' class, bearing Green 140."

Sample turned round taking a good look with his own binoculars before reporting the sighting to Hosie, who responded by raising the after periscope to have his own look.

T.S kept looking astern to see that the boat's wake had a distinct curve to starboard, so guessed that Hosie had ordered a change of course, which indicated that they had been turned towards the sighting,

"OOW- Captain. I have altered course to 140. Get the signalman onto the bridge to identify who they are!" he ordered.

"T.S. is already on the bridge. He reported the sighting sir! He says that the cruiser looks to be the *Den Helder*, but would need to get closer to identify the destroyers."

"Very good! Make visual contact with him to let him know we're British, in case they think we're otherwise."

"You heard that signalman. They can probably see us anyway."

T.S. flashed the double letters AA to them which asked who they were, then followed it up with his own international callsign MVBR. A few moments later he had the reply back with their call sign VHEL which he reported to the W/T office to check the ship's name.

"Royal Netherlands Navy, 9 inch, medium cruiser and confirmed as the *Den Helder*. Suggest if the escorting destroyers are of the 'H' class, then as there's only 4 of them they'll be the *Hilversund*, *Hoogven*, *Helmond* and *Haarlem*." came the swift reply from them.

"Well done signalman!" Sample stated then asked Hosie if he needed to get in radio contact.

"Good idea. Make it so signalman." Hosie ordered over the control room mike.

T.S. made a brief exchange with the cruiser, followed closely by the destroyer astern of the group.

"Message passed sir! The cruiser says to contact them on 3663kc's, and the port for'ard destroyer is asking us to contact them on 2050kcs voice."

Sample had now been joined by Hosie who wanted to have a good look at the group and ordered the radio contact.

"Going below to the W/T office. Stay with them on this course but do not close to more than 2000yards." Hosie ordered then disappeared below again.

"Bloody hell sir! Now that we're close up to that cruiser, she looks as if she's been hit with several large sledgehammers." T.S. whistled, as he was able to get a clearer view of the ship due to the rapidly closing range between them.

"Judging by the destroyer nearest us and the ones lashed to her, they don't look too clever either. Must have been one hell of a scrap. Let's hope they don't end up as that, as we'll probably need every last one of them before long. But where would they be patched up. Melville Island Naval dockyard?"

"Yes, they certainly have been in the wars, and yes you're right. FOGGY has a dry docking facility there as ours would be too small for them." Sample said as both men gazed at the battered ships for some time and watching them making their slow but sure way through the water.

"OOW – Captain. Let the procession pass, then turn to port to steer north on 150. Raise the radar mast and make a 2 minute sweep of the area."

"Aye aye sir!"

T.S. was able to take another good look at the disappearing battered ships before the boat headed the other way into nothingness again. He also noticed that the radar dish had stopped revolving, and knew that if anything was out there it would be ahead of them.

"OOW – Radar! Completed the scan. One small contact on Red 5, range 17,000 yards. The cruiser's being towed at an approx speed of 8 knots, whereas this contact is closing at approx 14 knots!"

"OOW – Captain! Clear the bridge and get ready to dive. Radar, make another sweep on that vector for further 1 minute." Hosie ordered from the control room.

Sample and T.S. carried out their orders then vacated the bridge for the control room.

"Go to diving Stations! Lower the radar mast." was the order when the upper lid was reported shut and secured with both clips.

"No1! Commodore Van Du Kuyper of the *Den Helder* told me that he thinks they've been shadowed by an unidentified vessel astern of him, and have asked us to go and investigate it. So I intend tracking the reverse course of the cruiser to see what is what. Let's 'go Dutch' for now." Hosie informed, before issuing the sequence of orders that brought the boat down to periscope depth.

"Sonar! Keep a good ear out ahead of us on a vector of 30 degrees either side of our main course."

"Aye aye sir" Woods responded from the sonar room which is below the deck plating of the control room.

"I have a nasty feeling about this, so go to Action stations No1 and be quiet about it. Leading Seaman Hemmings! What was the last bearing and range of that contact?"

"Bearing 145, 13,000 yards. Suggest speed approx 15 knots. Sir!" Hemmings reported from his little cubby-hole next to the control room chart table that was the Radar Office

"Okay No 1, keep me at periscope depth. The Attack Team will be closed up shortly but be quiet about it. We've been practicing all types of attacks on our way out here, especially this one against a boat, so now is our chance to see if our system works." Hosie stated, then added

"In fact, go to Silent Routine No1."

"Aye aye sir." Welling replied then carried out those orders.

This is a time where all unnecessary machinery, activities or anything else that might contribute towards the general noise of the boat, gets stopped. Everybody settles down, only moves when necessary. Conversations are kept to a minimum and even all orders are spoken in whispers, or relayed down the line of messengers to the recipient.

"Sonar reports a twin cavitation consistent of a warship on a course showing 325." Hoare whispered

Hosie was looking ahead of the boat for most of the time but gave an all round sweep just in case another vessel appeared from nowhere.

"Yes I see him! It looks like a submarine on the surface but not quite sure which type or who it belongs to. Dig out the submarine recognition book for me and let me have a look-see."

The book was produced then put onto the chart table for Hosie to refer to. After he made his identification of the vessel he ordered the Attack Team to close up.

T.S. managed to sneak a good look through the main periscope at the boat coming their way, but it took him a few moments to recognise it.

"We have a Yank Gato class boat on the surface trying to catch up with our Dutch friends. I wonder why?" Hosie stated almost to himself, returning to the periscope.

T.S moved swiftly over to the chart table, grabbing hold of the recognition book, flicked through it until he saw what he was looking for.

"Captain! I saw her pennant number of 173 and looks like a Jap type K7. Also, a Yank Gato class has two twin gun-turrets fore and aft of the fin, 1 is a 5 inch with the other probably 20mm AA. Whereas this one has only got one twin turret for'ard and one smaller single one aft, sir. On top of that, the Yanks are fitted with a radar mast like us, whereas this one doesn't seem to have one. Maybe because of the lack of radar she's probably not picked us up on screen, for her to remain on the surface, sir!" T.S. stated boldly, daring to invoke the wrath of his captain. Hosie grabbed hold of the book to look at the different pictures then at the real thing above them, as if to countermand and shoot down both T.S.'s theory and his discovery.

Hosie looked very carefully at the evidence for several seconds before agreeing with T.S.

"In that case Signalman, we've got a Jap boat trying to catch up to do them more mischief, and yes your assumption appears to be right. Given that if they had detected us or even if they'd seen us, they would have dived to get out of our way." Hosie admitted graciously.

"Start the attack! Stand by for readings! Bearing …that! Range in high power …that! Down periscope!"

T.S read out the bearings, working out the ranges on his magic ruler for Hosie to formulate his plan of approach.

"We're now 15 degrees on his port bow, so I want to be around 45 degrees." He mumbled then turned to Sample.

"Okay T.O! I will fire tubes 1&3. Set tube 1 at 20 feet and tube 3 at 10. I don't want to give him time to dive if he sees our fish, so I will let him close me to 500 yards. Make that range to target."

Hosie looked at the Perspex screen for a few moments to see Mike North the R.P. plotting several items of information onto it, and marvelled as to how the man was able to write not only backwards but also from right to left, then looked at his watch as if to make further calculations.

"Slow ahead together! Watch your course helmsman. Keep 45 feet! Up for'ard periscope slowly!" Hosie ordered, and almost lay down onto the deck grabbed the handles of the periscope as it rose out of the periscope well, which pulled him up almost into a crouched position

"Well!" he whispered, when he was satisfied at the angle

"Stand by to read off! Bearing is …that! Range is… that! Down periscope!"

"Stand by for'ard tubes. Open bow caps! Open outer doors. Fire both tubes on my mark! Flood 'Q'. Have the camera set up on the after periscope to record the attack." he ordered, taking out his stopwatch and starting it ticking.

After what seemed an eternity he ordered the for'ard periscope raised in the same manner and T.S. sounding out the readings given.

Hosie mumbled his hasty calculations then returned to the periscope to make his final check on the target.

"Stand by! Mark... Mark! Starboard 20 come round to steer 320. Full ahead port. Full astern Starboard. Go to 150 feet! Raise the after periscope." Hosie whispered, then looked at his watch to count the seconds.

The boat was still turning away from her attack position to try to get as much distance from the expected impulse of a double explosion. When the explosions happened, the force of the underwater shock waves made the boat rattle and shake as the torpedoes found their mark. This told the crew that they had hit their target once more. Hosie ordered the for'ard periscope to be lowered as he raced to the after periscope and took the pictures of a Japanese submarine being blown sky high.

Hosie was feeling pleased with himself as it's a rare occasion for one submarine to get the chance to sink another.

"We've certainly lived up to our motto and at the same time earned our King's shilling today No1. That's one Jap boat who won't be giving our boys grief anymore. Well done team! All our hard work on our 'shake down' cruise out here has paid off." He breezed, first rubbing then clapping his hands together in a show of appreciation.

His show of appreciation met with a silence and there were glum faces around the control room as each man realised that those were Submariners just like them, but Welling dared to voice that feeling.

"A noble sentiment No1! In normal circumstances I would feel the same. But think of it this way, it's kill or be killed. It's us or them. You can't harbour such sentiments in this game No1. There's a bloody great war up top, with men, women and children being killed or dying in their millions at the hands of the enemy. The object is for us to try our best to reduce the odds against us by reducing the enemy numbers to a decent size for us to win the damn thing. The Jap Navy may have lost one boat with say 70 men on board, whereas we could have lost 1 cruiser, possibly four destroyers totalling about 2,500 men on board, be they Dutch, Yank, Aussie or our boys. If it makes you better, we'll surface and see if there're any survivors. In fact you can even have the privilege to get onto the casing and haul each one on board just by yourself." Hosie chided abruptly, which forced Welling to nod his acceptance of his captain's admonition.

"Oh well! Perhaps we can all get aloft again to enjoy a bit of sunshine now sir!" James chirped from his after planes seat position, as he looked up at Hosie and grinned.

This quip seemed to lance the state of tension felt by the attack team, for everybody to relax again.

"Quite Cox'n! Fall out Attack team No1. Prepare to surface. W/T contact the *Dan Helder*. Make to them. 'Your shadow was a Jap boat, now being mustered in the big locker below us. Good luck." Hosie ordered in quick succession, as the control room lost most of its occupants, and for those remaining to relax to undertake a more mundane task of surfacing the boat.

"Surface! Who's the OOW?"

"Me sir!" Hoare stated, as he put his binoculars around his neck.

"Steer 240, speed 18 knots and get the echo sounder running. Patrol routine. I want 2 lookouts, 1 armed." Hosie said evenly as he issued his string of orders.

"Aye aye sir!"

The boat rose up out of the depths, shaking off the last vestige of water from her casing to bathe herself in the warmth of the subtropical sunlight.

Soon her powerful engines gave a throaty growl as she raced through the blue water, to join in with the steady 'dik-dik-dik' sound of the echo sounder that was tracing the depths below her.

The boat conducted her mini survey of the hitherto uncharted waters in a certain patch of the Gulf, before she was allowed home again.

As this was a relatively quiet time the boat was able to almost saunter back into base again, and for the crew look forward to the hectic 'shore life' of barbies, dances and dancing with bodies wearing skirts, excluding any Scotsmen amongst them that is, which one would normally associate with a sleepy inlet base far from the madding crowd.

Part Three

Chapters

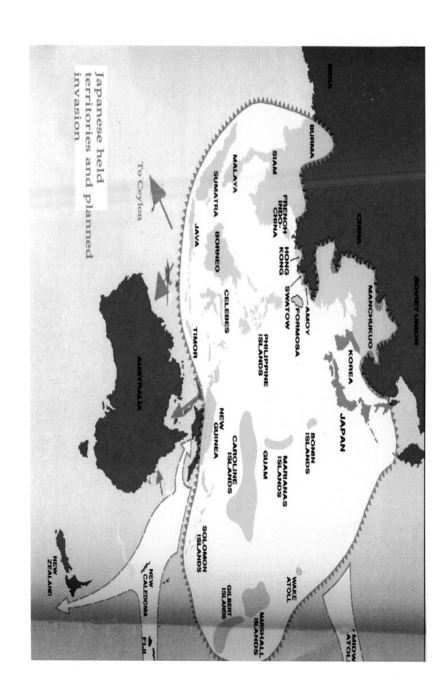

Japanese held territories and planned invasion

To Ceylon

INDIA
BURMA
SIAM
MALAYA
SUMATRA
JAVA
BORNEO
FRENCH INDO-CHINA
HONG KONG
SWATOW
AMOY
FORMOSA
CELEBES
TIMOR
PHILIPPINE ISLANDS
AUSTRALIA
NEW GUINEA
CHINA
MANCHUKUO
KOREA
JAPAN
SOVIET UNION
BONIN ISLANDS
MARIANAS ISLANDS
GUAM
CAROLINE ISLANDS
SOLOMON ISLANDS
NEW CALEDONIA
NEW ZEALAND
FIJI
GILBERT ISLANDS
MARSHALL ISLANDS
WAKE ATOLL
MIDWAY ATOLL

128

Fiendish Plans

Since the breaking of the Japanese Military code, the intelligence teamwork of several Allied units were risking their lives trying to glean as much information as possible, which would help to piece together the network of military orders and political rhetoric spewing out of the Japanese High Command.

Admiral Yamamoto approved a plan submitted to him for an attack on the Midway Islands as the springboard for their final approach to the Hawaiis to complete their so far undoubted superiority and dominance in the Pacific.

At the same time Admiral Ugaki along with his chief of staff Kurishima, argued that it would be better to direct the main Asian Battle Fleet south and west in a double pronged attack. To go west and destroy the British Indian Ocean Fleet then invade Ceylon, go up through India to link up with the Axis forces. The southern prong would send the main force of their Battle Fleet to smash the American and what's left of the British naval forces in the Coral Sea then invade New Guinea using their troops amassing on New Britain.

It was considered that as Australia was reported to have only 8 million occupants, and had already committed the main bulk of her forces against the Axis forces, she would be defenceless especially on her northern coastline. The manpower needed to overcome such an unprotected island continent, was considered as a mere 8 divisions, which would then consolidate their southern territorial borders.

The line taken by Ugaki was called the 'Australian School' was give much consideration, especially the detailed invasion plan. Their main invasion force of Australia would consist of 95 – 120,000 men from their 31st Army, most of them landing at the bottom end of the Gulf of Carpentaria, at the same time the main battle fleet would engage in the annihilation of whatever the American and allied could throw at them, given that most of the Allied fleet was sunk in the Battles of the Java and Banda Seas.

The final overall decision was made by Admirals Yamamoto and Nagumo, to engage the Americans in the Coral Sea then invade New Guinea using their 25th Army, taking over Port Moresby and the rest of New Guinea currently occupied by the Americans, at the same time send a carrier force to take over the Midway Islands. The Australian and the Ceylon invasions therefore would be of a secondary consideration.

This then was the master plan of the Imperial Japanese Forces, and like the Germans, the Japanese were sweeping all before them, taking all islands or countries at will, with the belief that all they had to do was turn up and accept the conquered opponents 'Unconditional Surrender' allowing them to continue their murdering, raping, pillaging ways at their will.

Unfortunately for them, it was their self- belief of being invincible which set the rot of complacency. This bolstered by their enormous dose of 'Victory' sickness, would eventually prove to be their undoing.

For the only big advantage the Allies had over the Japanese Naval forces at that time was the superior numbers of quality long-range Submarines and their crews. Which meant that a certain amount of unwashed bodies living in the depths of the seas, were popping up unexpectedly, seemingly anywhere and everywhere, making the lives of the Japanese a lot less happier than they were getting accustomed to.

Chapter I

Scrap Job

T.S. was relaxing in his bunk down in the accommodation space of the depot ship when he heard the 'pipe' announcing the muster of all S64's crew back on board. He looked at his wrist watch thinking that 2300 was a strange time to be mustered considering they were due to store up in the morning and sail later that evening.

"What's the buzz Cox'n" T.S. asked when he entered the control room, but didn't have to wait for his answer, as Hosie arrived straight from the wardroom wearing his 'Officers evening dress'.

"Everybody on board Cox'n?" he asked.

"All mess decks reported correct sir!" James replied, giving Hosie his mandatory salute.

Hosie reached up for the control room mike then tested it for usage.

"Do you hear there! Our sailing time's been brought forward to 0900 tomorrow so we'll commence re-storing up as of now. Chief Stoker will supervise the fuel barge due to come alongside aft. The T.A.S.I will take charge of loading up from a T.L.V. coming alongside for'ard with torpedoes. The after ends will be loaded up from inboard. The Gunnery P.O. and his team will see to the stowing of more ammunition. All others, not involved with these activities will be required to store the boat as and when the duty inboard crane driver starts up. The sooner we get stored up, the sooner we can get turned in again. All other Senior Rates will assist in this as directed by the Cox'n." Hosie commanded, then concluded by saying.

"The Cox'n will make a special rum issue on completion, with an allowance of 2 cans per man. That is all!"

The groans of working virtually all of the night were swiftly overtaken by a cheer when the men heard of the extra tot and free cans.

131

"See Cox'n. An extra glass of rum always does the trick. I've got some of the inboard crew to help out, so 0200 should be about the time to secure, but make sure the boat is cleaned up before they disappear." Hosie said with a grin and went into the wardroom where his officers were waiting for him.

T.S. was talking to Brown who was busy making coffee for the officers.

"Shame about those lads on S63. According to their Killick Sparker Ken Long; my opposite number copped it trying to secure the upper lid. The lower lid got jammed in the open position and the upper lid was leaking badly. Apparently one of the clips on the upper lid snapped off, so he rushed up into the tower to try and shut the lid with a spare one. As there was too much water coming down he managed to free the lower lid and standing on it he wedged it shut. He tried to shelter in the skipper's cabin but found the breathing apparatus was duff. He reported this to the control room via the skipper's cabin intercom then told them that he would attempt a free escape from the tower, they realised that the tower would be completely flooded. His last words before escaping were lost in the exploding depth charges, according to Ken. He probably got torn to pieces from the blasts as he headed up to the surface. The Japs must have seen the debris coming from the boat and his body, so they must have thought that the boat had finally been destroyed. This was borne out by the fact the Japs stopped depth charging and buggered off. They waited for a couple of hours before their skipper got them away into deeper waters and go deep, for them to finally escape and able to return." T.S. said quietly.

"Yes that's the official record as what their skipper had given to Cdr S/M and the Admiral will probably recommend him for a posthumous V.C." Brown stated almost in a trance as if he was living the same nightmare.

"Looks like a long dockyard job maybe a scrap job?" T.S. asked with incredulity.

"Yes! The boat's internal state is almost bad enough for the

132

boat to been considered as a write-off by Harry Harley and the boss Admiral 'Spam' is asking for a couple of replacements, let alone a couple more to bolster the squadron up. By the by, I think our squadron will be confined to these northern waters especially around of the Gulf area because of it. Perhaps it's due to having 2 boats out of commission, is the reason why we're putting to sea for an eight week patrol, I heard mentioned." Brown volunteered.

"An 8 week patrol means just a few extra stores let alone fuel and the like, so just imagine a 20 weeker like what the Yanks do on a regular basis. Any so-called passengers this time? I mean, are we taking Marines on board? T.S. asked.

"Maybe that's what the captain is discussing with the officers right now."

"This is a tad bit short notice Frank. If that's the case, then I'll be expecting a full sack of mail going off in the morning."

"Just think of all the lovely Red Cross parcels we'll be getting when we get back. As for me, I've already got the latest edition of the 'Reveille' which has gone up to 6d now. But I managed to barter a hell of a lot of fags for one special edition of the Scandawegian magazine 'Health and Efficiency' from Barrie Morris's NAAFI shop inboard. I'll be charging gulpers for the Reveille, but 6d or 5 fags a time to look at my H&E. It's guaranteed to give the lads a few sweet, if not dirty and very rude dreams." Brown said with a grin.

"And here's me thinking you'd lend me them for nowt."

"You should know that nowt is for nowt these days! And in case you haven't noticed, there's a war on you know! Anyway, must get these to them before they go cold, see you later." Brown concluded, leaving T.S. to go to his for'ard mess deck where the sailors lived.

The boat got stored and the crew turned back in again when T.S found that the watches were changed and he had the next watch, which was 2 to 5 am.

133

It was all nice and quiet for him to enjoy the peace of the early morning, lazing by the gun sponson enjoying his luxurious duty-free cigarette with nobody about to bother him.

He gazed through the darkness of the inlet and was able to recognise various features around him despite no light or any indication as to what was what or even where.

No sooner had he flicked the remains of his cigarette overboard and looked towards the entrance of the inlet when he saw a small red light flashing at him, coming from the blackness of the water.

He grabbed his binoculars dangling from around his neck and focussed onto this strange phenomena. To his surprise he watched as two divers popped up from the deep almost and seemingly within reaching distance of him, yet in fact were several hundred yards away. He suddenly remembered the signal about clearance divers on night manoeuvres, then watched them climb into their little rubber dinghy to disappear into the darkness again. He was distracted by this spooky scene when he turned his attention back to the entrance of the inlet, discovering another little red light above the profile and outline of a boat he recognised as S62 that was about to glide past him. This was mainly because she had an external snort mast whereas S64 and S65 were the only two with the new-fangled internal masts. He watched her complete her downward track and turn to make her way round to the starboard side of the depot ship where there would be a berthing party waiting to secure her alongside. The boat seemed to glide past him in total silence before she turned round to make her final approach. She, like the rest of the boats in the squadron were operating independently from each other, with their own set of orders to perform. Unlike a squadron of surface vessels, seldom would a squadron of boats act whilst at sea under the command of just one captain, because each captain would have his own separate orders to interpret then expedite them as he saw prudent to do so.

His ringside seat to watch the boat enter the base with that little red light above it, gave him an insight as to what his boat would look like in the same circumstances.

There were no navigation lights showing, only the little red light, then put it out of his mind as a 'one off' experience.

His time was up and he was anxious for his relief to come up onto the casing, but he allowed himself another cigarette enjoying the last of the fresh air, when he saw the shape of his relief Roy Sedgwick coming up from the fore hatch, scratching himself before donning his hat.

"All quiet up here Roy. S62 has just come back off patrol looking a bit battered and bent. It must be getting hectic out there, and we're next."

"We've had our gun modified so let's hope we get the chance to use it otherwise it's just another piece of junk." Sedgwick stated, patting the short 4 inch gun barrel.

"Speaking of which Roy. The ready-use ammo clips on the front of the gun tower have still not been topped up."

"Bloody hell! I knew there was something I had to do before secure." He replied

"Hang on though! Our fresh supply of ammo has not been taken on board yet from the ammo lighter. Probably after brekkers and before we sail!" Sedgwick added with relief.

"Okay then Roy, I'm going below now, but keep an eye on the water level around the fore-hatch. You might have to get one of the stokers to flash up the L.P. blower for a while.

"See you!" T.S. advised, then went below to rid himself of a few 'Z's hanging around his eyes.

Chapter II

GNATs

S64 was fully loaded up and sleeping peacefully alongside her 'trot' waiting for her crew to man and take her out on her next patrol.

T.S. was on the bridge early, ensuring his 'part of ship' was ready for sea taking a last look around the base with his binoculars, when he was joined by Welling who was the OOW, followed by the Captain shortly afterwards.

He had the bridge ensign fluttering in the morning breeze as the main ensign and its flagpole had been removed in readiness for sailing.

The morning was a bright one with a few clouds scudding by to indicate that it was still the 'monsoon season'. To him it meant that there could be some roughers waiting for them once they got out into the open waters of the Gulf.

"Morning sir! Next of kin book ashore and all signals collected from inboard!" TS. reported to Welling as he arrived onto the conning tower.

"Morning Signalman! We've got a short delay as the Captain's being given some last minute briefing. You've got the bridge cleared already, well done." Welling replied in a business manner.

"Any idea where we're going sir? Maybe a banyan up in Jap land, at least judging by all the stores stowed below?"

"I think I'll let our Captain do the honours as your guess would be just as good as mine!"

"I know! Maybe the Japs have taken a make-and-mend for the day, for us to keep the new paintwork dry. Perhaps they won't see us coming now so we can sneak up to them to shove our 30 fish up their arses. They don't like it up them apparently. Something to do with them being a bunch of dwarfs, I'm told." T.S. quipped, which made Welling chuckle at the very thought, but refrained to reply.

Lt. Cdr Hosie arrived onto the bridge and returned the salute from Welling who reported that the boat was in all respects ready for sea.

"Very good No1. We've got a very important patrol ahead of us, so let's go to it." Hosie responded, then commenced to issue his orders to the casing party, whilst giving manoeuvring instructions to Welling who relayed them down to the control room.

T.S. piped the side as the protocol for the salute between one C.O. to another was exchanged, Hosie got on with the business of swinging his boat right round getting ready to make his dived exit from the base.

The usual sequence of commands were given for the boat to sink in a flurry of air and water as she disappeared out of sight, with only her periscope sticking up to make a small crease in the water as the boat was propelled along.

The final bearings were taken from the land features then plotted onto the sea chart, for Hosie to start his first transit course taking him on his long patrol into enemy waters.

"Secure from Diving Stations No1. Go to watch dived. Keep on this course at a depth of 70 feet." Hosie ordered then taking hold of the control room mike made an announcement to the ships company.

"Do you hear there! In about an hour or so we've got a friendly GNAT aircraft coming out to look for us on this course to see if our new paintwork does its stuff. If he spots us he'll drop a grenade on us to let us know, if not then we can consider ourselves invisible to the enemy but not necessarily invincible. That's all!" Hosie informed, then left the control room and went into the wardroom which is a small area attached to the control room compartment, yet sealed off enough to keep a degree of quietness within it.

"Blue watch, watch dived. Up spirits." Welling ordered before being relieved of his Diving Officer duties by a fresh OOW.

The crew settled down for a relatively quiet transit, thankful that the sea was still relatively calm, offering a gentle roll coming from the beam just to remind them they were out in King Neptune's backyard again. Yet through it all, they kept alert listening out for a grenade explosion above them

Time was ticking itself away on the control room clock, with anxious eyes glancing its way when the time allowed was nigh. The suspense in the boat was such that everybody adopted the 'silent routine' so that they could hear that telltale bang even from several miles away.

As time slipped well beyond what Hosie had given, with no sound from above, he made the announcement from the control room that they were now invisible, which was received by a loud cheer from all quarters of the boat.

"Sonar! Any contacts ?" he asked before ordering to go up to periscope depth.

"Faint cavitation starboard side. Suggest a fishing boat." Came the reply.

Hosie had the main periscope raised for him to take a peek and see what was what.

"Can't see anything. Raise the radar mast, make a 1minute sweep then lower it and report."

The small radar dish was raised up to poke itself just above the waves on its own little telescopic mast and then lowered back down again as ordered.

"Have 6 craft spaced out equidistant from each other at a range of 17,000 yards, with another fast moving one. Suggest it's an aircraft that has passed through them and appears to have has stopped only 7000 yards ahead of us on a bearing of 045 sir." Hemmings reported via his intercom.

Hosie turned his periscope to that bearing and seeing that it was a seaplane, called for T.S. to muster in the control room to recognise it properly for him.

T.S looked at the aircraft for various recognition pointers.

"It's a GNAT, sir. He looks in a bad way too…" T.S. started to report, then stopped Hosie from taking over the periscope by saying.

"He's spotted us sir and is signalling to us. Says he's in shit street and needs rescuing." T.S stated after he had read the flashing lamp.

The fact that they had been sighted produced a groan from the control room as they realised that after going through all that trouble they had still been spotted.

"Go to Action Stations. Stand by to surface. We're going up to help them." Hosie ordered swiftly, which galvanised the sleepy boats crew into an alert hive of hectic activities.

T.S. arrived swiftly onto the bridge behind Welling, followed by Hosie who ordered T.S. to signal them.

T.S asked them what was wrong and what assistance did they need.

The GNAT signaller flashed his message slowly for T.S. to read aloud what was being said.

"They were out on patrol looking for you but discovered 6 Jap fishing boats approaching territorial waters some 15 nautical miles away. Investigation proves that they're heavily armed Jap fishing boats towing a large array of netting behind them. Suggest a squadron of Jap minesweepers. They clobbered us good and proper for us to ditch. Says, glad you boys came along. Have vital films to get back a.s.a.p."

Hosie looking through his binoculars saw that the small seaplane had been riddled with bullets looking almost ready for sinking.

"Ask him if they can taxi over to us to cut the time delay."

"Says will try, but fuel tank shot full of holes."

"Get a casing party on deck. Have them stand by to help them in case of casualties." Hosie ordered quietly to Welling, as T.S. watched the stricken seaplane move slowly over the undulating swell of the sea.

"Just as well it's calm sir, they're only just about moving through the swell as it is. Half of their starboard ski float is missing.

139

From what I can see, there're 3 of them with one who appears to be covered in blood." T.S. reported.

The boat seemed to almost fly across the distance between them and the plane, for them to go astern for a few minutes in case they collided with it. The plane bumped gently against the ballast tanks, letting the 2nd Cox'n and his men assist the Airmen onto the boat.

"2nd! Have them brought down into the boat, then prepare to scuttle the plane." Hosie shouted down to Hall, who raised an arm as an acknowledgement to the order.

"Can't we just leave it there for these Japs to take a peek sir. I mean, we can always put a dummy on board, then booby trap it just to give them something to think about as they get blown up?" T.S. suggested whilst he watched the Signaller climb up onto the casing from the ballast tanks.

"Would love to Signalman, but we've got to get out of sight before the Jap vessels start to show on our horizon. I'm going below No1, but once the casing party has got below, dive the boat and come to periscope depth."

T.S. made his usual report about the upper lid being secure, before Hosie ordered the radar mast be raised having another 2 minute sweep before lowering it once more.

T.S. had taken the Airman Signaller for'ard to the 'Seamen's mess offering him a quick cigarette whilst his wounded pilot was being seen to by the Cox'n and the Observer to be questioned by Hosie.

The GNAT Signaller introduced himself as Signalman Farquhar to T.S. explaining that whilst he was the Signaller, he was also the gunner. But because his machine gun only pointed skyward he was not able to return any of the fire coming up at them.

T.S. asked him how the boat got spotted, considering it has been given a new camouflage coat of paint.

"We didn't see you at all despite flying up and down your course we were given. What gave you away was the fact that the sun reflected off the glass on your periscope, and I happened to spot it in time, otherwise we'd be food for the sharks when the Japs got hold of us. Yes, the sun shining off your scope was like a lighthouse in the night, the way it was twinkling in the water." Farquhar replied in a broad Scottish Accent.

"That sounds interesting Jock! Maybe our skipper will think that too." T.S. said quietly, casting his thoughts immediately to the little red light he had seen during his 'middle watch' thinking how similar they were, perhaps offering an answer to the proverbial mystery as to why the boats got found to be clobbered good and proper.

"These vessels must be the Jap answer to our minesweepers, so they must be up to something that the brass hats are not letting on about. I mean, we've already met a few of them on our last patrol."

"Our squadrons of GNATs and the Fast Minelayer vessels of the coastal forces have been sowing mine fields in strategic positions along the territorial waters of the northern sea board that is not covered by land forces or an air base. The Japs have been probing the coastline dragging nets to clear any minefields they find. As fast as we're dropping them, the bastards seem to know for them to come back to sweep them up. Either they can't make their own or are collecting them for themselves to start up a scrap merchant company." Farquhar stated.

"Anyway where are you boys headed, or need I ask?" he added "Don't know Jock. But you sure can't come with us, as we're not allowed stowaways, or non-paying passengers. We'll probably drop you off on some island then whistle up one of your lot to come and fetch you. Your very own private plane if you like." T.S. replied with a grin.

"An' me without my cossie! Still, a few days off with pay won't go amiss. Just as long as those Japs don't come and spoil the beach party. Hope you've got a doc on board as my skipper Ted Lewis is in a bad way. Got shrapnel in his legs he has." Farquhar replied unabashed, and started to smoke yet another cigarette from the pack T.S. had given him.

"Our Cox'n James is our Doc, so your skipper will be in good hands. He'll be dancing like a good 'un before you smoke that packet of fags I've given you, no doubt."

"Yes thanks Sparks. I'll just help myself to a glass of orange juice from your fridge if that's okay."

"Help yourself. John Gourdie, our 'Baby Chef' here will look after you now as I've got to go." T.S. said with a smile as he introduced Gourdie to Farquhar, wondering just how a big 'roughie toughie' ex Paratrooper to boot, managed to be given such a name.

"Aye, leave him with me. Maybe a 'Herrings in' sarnie and a good cuppa instead?" Gourdie offered, and was thanked by Farquhar for the offer.

T.S. was summoned back to the control room where he should have been and had to explain that he was only taking care of the Signaller. His explanation went a long way to alleviate the bollocking he got from Welling for him leaving without permission. 'Absent from place of duty' was the expression used. Hosie must have been in the wardroom talking to the two pilot officers, as he returned and took hold of the control room mike to make an announcement.

"We have a delay in carrying out our orders, as we have to make a detour to get our passengers ashore with some vital films they need delivering a.s.a.p. In the meantime we've got a double barrier of Jap sweep nets to dodge." Hosie stated then paused to issue more orders.

"W/T! Raise the whip aerial. Contact the GNAT base to come and r/v with us. Also contact the FAIREY Bomber squadron and give them the co-ordinates of these Jap minesweepers to get rid of them. Get the details from the N.O. then report when done so. Flight Lt Lewis will assist you. Radar! Raise your mast. Keep a vector sweep to cover these vessels, but give a random all round sweep until you pick up the friendly aircraft. Flight courses etc will be given you by the W/T." he ordered then returned the mike back into its cradle.

"Excuse me sir. The Base Comcen will have all the different frequencies in use. Maybe their Signaller can give us their 'emergency frequency' just like the one we've got." T.S. suggested to Sample rather than direct to the Captain.

Sample relayed what T.S. had suggested and it was agreed that it was a good one for the W/T office to make an immediate response.

"Starboard 20 Steer 125. Fall out Diving Stations, go to watch Snorting No 1. Tell engine room to make revs for 10 knots. That should keep us ahead of those Jap fishing boats and for so we can keep tabs on them for when the fly boys show up."

"Thanks to this strange event it's solved the mystery of those Jap vessels. Maybe they've not got proper minesweepers down this far yet sir." Welling opined.

"Yes! We now know what to expect from that quarter but we've still to solve our colour scheme problem." Hosie said slowly as he stepped away from the main periscope indicating to Bell the oncoming OOW to take over.

T.S. overheard that remark and took the brave chance to speak to his captain direct, before he left the control room.

"Actually sir! Farquhar, their Signaller told me that we could not be seen, despite their search. There is something I have to report that you might wish to shout at me for." He ventured.

"Well, go on Signalman!" Hosie urged gruffly.

T.S. related the incident he witnessed as 'Trot Sentry' and what Farquhar had said about the periscope glinting in the sun, so Hosie called for Farquhar speak to him.

"Is what my Signalman telling me, true?" Hosie asked more civilly than he spoke to T.S.

"Yes, it is. Only your 'scope' glinting away like a sparkler is what I saw to pin-point your location. That's why we landed near to where you were hoping that you'd be one of ours to rescue us. Hank the Yank have some sort of filters over theirs like what you get with sunglasses."

Hosie looked at his periscope then at the two signallers as if weighing up his answer, then called for Leading Stoker Morgan to come to the control room.

Morgan entered the control room cautiously to see what it was he was summoned for.

"Ah Morgan! It appears that I have two very sharp eyed Signalmen here with a tale to tell, and I need you to create a solution to the problem." Hosie stated, telling Morgan what T.S and Farquhar had reported.

"I'll get onto it right away sir. The red eye from the periscope can be solved immediately by placing a small cardboard type of cup or a cover to place over the eyepieces when you're not actually looking through them, sir. But leave me to the other one and I'll have it ready a.s.a.p." Morgan insisted.

Hosie first grunted then nodded his approval then dismissed the 3 of them with a wave of his arm.

"Your pilot will be told of your report which might get you promoted, Jock!" T.S. whispered aside to Farquhar.

"What for? All I did was see you advertising your position!" Farquhar said with a shake of his head.

"It's precisely that, that's been our problem, maybe this will be a less expensive way to cut down our discovery rate somewhat. Whereas mine was by sheer good luck to spot a small piece of red light in an otherwise very dark void where you couldn't make out what was sky and what was sea."

"Oh well! That should make you promoted as well as me then."

"Not me Jock. All I'll get is probably an extra tot ration issued by the hand of our Cdr S/M. when we get back again. Anyway, must off! I'm next on watch." T.S. concluded then went for'ard to have five minutes for a smoke and a cuppa.

144

Chapter III

Gun Action

"**C**aptain – Radar!   Have 4 aircraft approaching the fishermen, with a 5th one coming towards us." the on watch R.P. reported.

Hosie went swiftly to the small radar booth, where he was shown the fast moving blips on the radar screen, which he deduced were the aircraft about to merge into the much slower blips that indicated the fishing vessels. Also noticing one coming from a different angle and onto their position.

"W/T. Raise your aerial.   Get in touch with the aircraft to find out which one is for us." Hosie ordered.

By the time Hosie had stopped the snort, he got the boat at 'diving stations' the W/T came back with their report.

"Captain – W/T!   In contact with WALRUS 30 who has requested we surface for him to meet alongside us."   The on watch Sparker announced.

"Take us up No1.   Have the casing party ready to transfer our passengers over to the aircraft." Hosie ordered swiftly as he kept peering through his main periscope.

Welling and T.S. arrived onto the bridge with his signal lamp with Hosie coming up immediately behind them, to see a large biplane with two propeller engines stuck on top of the upper wing.   It had two large ski floats, which were attached to the underside of the lower wing, taxi-ing slowly towards them.

T.S. saw a door in the side of the plane open and a person flashing a signal lamp at them.

"He says that we're well away from the air raid on the fishing vessels but they need to be up and away sooner rather than later." T.S. reported, having read the morse sent to him.

"Make to him.   'Have 3 passengers, one needing urgent treatment'" Hosie ordered, which T.S. did immediately.

"He says that he'll be coming starboard side to." T.S. reported, acknowledging the signal.

"Lt. Lewis. You're being given a lift on one of your Search and Rescue seaplanes. It'll be alongside in a moment. So better get yourself ready for your transfer." Hosie informed Lewis.

"Yes thank you captain! I've been bleeding like a ruddy stuffed pig, but your Cox'n has fixed me up good now. Thanks for the ride and good luck!" Lewis replied and was helped onto the casing by Farquhar.

"So long Jock! Hope you get your promotion." T.S. shouted down to Farquhar, who smiled and nodded his reply.

The plane's wings were almost touching the fin when it finally stopped. A small rubber dinghy with 2 men in it was rowed the short distance between them, climbed onto the casing. The 2nd Cox'n had the 3 off-going passengers sent back in the dinghy, thus completing the transfer, for the casing party to get below again.

As the boat dived again, Hosie watched the ancient but still perfectly operational sea-plane take off then gradually disappear from sight.

"Go to watch snorting until we clear this area. Use this transit course and snort for 2 hours. Take the usual measures if you see any aircraft in the area." Hosie ordered then left the control room and his very capable crew to their own devices.

"Snort completed sir, batteries are at full capacity." Hoare reported as Hosie came strolling into the control room.

"Very good. Standby to surface, and lets get some mileage behind us. Once on the surface you'll steer 300, speed 20 knots. Keep a 5 minute radar scan in every 30 until dusk. I want to use this relatively safe part of the sea for my transit.

T.S. was at the helm with Gunner Guard as the control room log recorder cum messenger, when the voice of ERA Dave Fagg who was one of three men on loan from Spare Crew, spoke to the OOW, requesting permission to reduce revs and speed.

There was a noticeable vibration being felt throughout the

boat, which indicated there was trouble in the engine room for the on watch ERA to express his deep concern.

"Engine room- Captain! What's the problem?"

"Starboard engine has developed a problem. It's not firing properly, so I've sent for the Chief ERA to confirm my diagnosis." Fagg reported.

"Very good! Keep me informed." Hosie responded.

With that, Bill Clutterbuck came swiftly through the control room and disappeared into the engine room compartment. Within minutes he had confirmed Fagg's diagnosis, reporting it to Hosie.

"Need to shut down the Starboard engine sir! With luck we'll have it running in the hour."

"Very good Chief! Inform me when you've completed and tested it for operational usage again."

"Blimey, it's not going too well for the skipper on this mystery trip, Dave. Let's hope you boys can still use your peashooter by the time we've finished dunking it in seaweed filled oggin." T.S. said quietly, as Guard recorded the telegraph and other orders given for the boat to run on just the one engine.

Then to record the engine had been fixed again allowing them to return to normal and resume their transit speed..

"OOW – Radar! Possible aircraft bearing Red 20 range 18,000 yards." North reported from the little radar shack at the after end of the control room.

"What is it doing? Going away or approaching?" came the swift response.

"Seems to be going away sir, and very fast too!"

"Radar-Captain! Use a 5 minute sweep every 15 until dusk."

"Aye aye sir!"

All incidents, and orders issued, are recorded by entering into the control room log, which is the general one. The Attack Log however is much more complex, recording all the boats operational orders issued during an attack. The Captain scrutinises these at his leisure, analysing his attack skills and tactics.

The boat had now been at sea for nearly 2 days and was fortunate to be able to transit the 900 miles on the surface in relative safety. But crucially and more to the point, without being detected by the Japanese aircraft or ships whose numbers seemed more abundant, with each mile they had sailed to reach their area of 'intent'.

"OOW – Navigator! We've reached 115Degrees E, 8Degrees S, the start area of our mission."

"Very good! Coming down!" Hosie replied, climbing down from his little cabin in the control room tower, to prepare himself for his next series of orders.

T.S. was on the bridge as the Port lookout when Hosie emerged up through the little square aperture that allowed access onto the conning tower bridge.

"Morning sir!" Sample greeted.

"Morning T.O! looks like a nice sunrise we're going to have." Hosie said as he took a deep breath, looking looked around the immediate area with his own set of binoculars, which T.S. keeps in tip-top condition at all times.

"Hmmm! No sign of our neighbours! Right, lets get a fix on some prominent points. Tell the control room to stand by for fix. Have them relayed to the navigator.

"High point bearing 300. Some sort of fishing village bearing 350. Promontory piece of land bearing 005, and another bearing 020." He observed.

"Okay, lets get below, out of sight in case some Jap 'Kate' aircraft comes and bounces us just like S63. Clear the bridge and go to Diving stations." Hosie concluded, handing T.S. his binoculars to bring below for him.

Hosie watched the boat disappear below the waves then ordered an echo sounder recording to check the depth of water beneath his keel.

"2000 fathoms, decreasing sharpishly to 150 fathoms and steady on that, sir. Suggest we've cleared the Java Trench!"

"Very good. Let's take a bathy dip No1. Take me down to 600 feet and back up again to see if Mother Nature is kind enough to give us some decent thermal layers. When we get back up we can check our trim."

"Aye aye sir". Welling responded, reporting each 20 foot depth they had reached until the boat reached the 600foot as ordered.

"No 1, get ERA's Fagg and Ottley to check the boat for leaks then report back when done. ERA Scarlett! What is our telemotor and air group state?

"Aye aye sir" Welling replied.

"4,200 and 3,900 lbs as normal sir. Full telemotor pressure." Scarlett reported evenly.

The boat came back up to 300 feet and Hosie made sure his boat was in tip-top shape before he attempted to pass through the notorious Lombok Strait and go round the back end of the Bali Island to reach his special mission r/v point.

"What has sonar got?" Hosie asked Hoare, who after a brief consultation with the sonar room beneath him replied.

"Two twin screw cavitations approaching from Green 10, speed approx 20 knots, suggest destroyers. Another slower one, with a single cavitation coming up behind us on Red 175, speed approx 10 knots, suggest a merchant ship. Several faint cavitations on Red 45, suggest fishing vessels."

"Very good sonar. Nobody is expecting us at this time of the morning, so just keep a check on those fishermen as the warships will probably just pass over us without a second look." Hosie concluded, going over to the navigation chart.

Fagg and Ottley came back to report that only 2 minor leaks were found, now fixed.

"Good! Remind me to try 700 feet next time and see what this boat can really go to. After all they're brand new and of the latest design." Hosie grinned wickedly as he saw a shadow of concern on the faces of two very able 'Tiffy's'.

"Okay Pilot! What's our transit length, width and the mean depth of the Strait, before we enter it?"

"Only 25 miles before we bump into a sea mount which according to this McKenzie Chart is an active underwater volcano, especially at this depth, sir, about the same distance between Gib and Morocco, erm, about 8 miles across."

"Hmmm! No wonder we've got an abundance of sea layers coming down through it." Hosie stated, rubbing his chin, looking at the control room clock.

"Okay, we'll come up to 100 feet and go starboard side of the sea mount at that point. How far to r/v?"

Bell used his dividers over the chart then reported that it was only 10 miles, also that the depth of water had gone back down to the 70 fathom mark.

"Sounds good to me! No 1! Go to watch dived until 1000, then go to Action Stations as this might just turn out to be one hectic shopping trip."

Hosie, by dead reckoning had arrived at his r/v point, was deciding on his next move.

"What depth is this area Pilot?" Hosie asked as he came over to the chart table again.

"50 fathoms sir."

"It looks like a sandy cum pebble floor below us No1. We'll go in nearer to the shoreline and bottom. Take me to periscope depth for me to take a look-see. Keep 52 feet."

"Aye aye sir."

"Up periscope. Slowly, slowly! " Hosie ordered as he crouched near the deck allowing the periscope raise him up to shoulder height.

"Hmmm! There's a dense jungle right up almost to the water line. I see a small cove to my right, I'd say around the 2,000 yard mark away." He muttered.

"Okay No1. Down periscope! Stop together then take us down gently onto the bottom. It's a lovely sunny day up top, with sunset in about 5 hours time. So we'll wait here until sunset before we pop up again."

Welling read off the increasing depth until everybody felt the boat come to a gentle rest some 300 feet down at the bottom of the sea.

"We might as well relax now No1. Fall out Action stations. Go to a Reduced 'Watch Dived' and at Silent Routine in case some nosey Jap pokes his sonar device our way. We've got until sunset before we go up top again" Hosie enthused, clapping his hands as if to conclude his little performance in the control room.

It was only when they had arrived that the crew cottoned on as to what was about, and their Captain to explain what was required, what to anticipate and be ready to act at a given moment or situation.

As the boat was on the bottom, settling herself down for a few hours of peaceful slumber, so it was for the crew. This was a time to relax, have some food, maybe catch up with some sleep before the next curtain raiser.

The 5 hour interval came to an end with the boat reverting to 'Watch Dived' then onto 'Action Stations', with everybody eagerly awaiting the possibility of the main hatch being opened, so they could get some fresh air into their lungs again.

"Blow a 5 second guff into No 3 ballast tank." Hosie ordered, which lifted the boat off the bottom for the propellers to be free to move.

"Group down! Slow ahead together. Come to Periscope depth. Assume red lighting in the control room. Up for'ard periscope."

"Stand by to read off bearings!"

"Aye aye sir" T.S. responded.

"Cove ahead! Left hand point...that! Right hand point ..that! I see a small red light in the bushes on the shore-line. Come and read it Signalman."

T.S. peered through the powerful lens reading what the flashing light was telling him.

"Says there's 4 of them. Have a rubber dinghy and will row

out to you. Keep your periscope exactly where it is. Better hurry as there's a patrol boat due round the cove in about 20 minutes.

"Tell him we'll come in as far as we can. As soon as you see our gun break water, you get yourself onto it."

T.S flashed the signal, watching as the darkened shapes began to approach them.

"We can go to 35 feet to clear the gun tower, any shallower and we'll ground ourselves. So keep a close eye on the depth No1." Hosie ordered, as he took over the periscope again.

"Gun breaking the water! Stand by to open the gun tower hatch." Hosie ordered, as he watched his boat come slowly out of the water like some monster of the deep. He looked at the depth gauge then down over his fore casing to see a rubber dinghy on the casing with 4 bodies clambering out of it, trying to climb onto the top of the gun tower.

"Open the gun tower lid and get these men down. Be quick about it." Hosie ordered.

Within moments 4 very wet men arrived into the control room, for the dinghy to be stowed on board and the gun tower hatch shut, for the boat to reverse and sink below the waves again, to become unseen once more.

"Welcome aboard gentlemen. We arrived some 5 hours ago but had to wait until dark before we could come and get you. My name is Lt Cdr Hosie, captain of this boat, S64." Hosie commenced, as he kept looking through his periscope until he was satisfied it all was safe for him to lower it and get away from the area.

The men were looking like native refugees, yet spoke in perfect English, when they introduced themselves.

"Yes, I know who you are Captain. I'm Major Tudor Price of the British Counter Espionage Unit from London, and am returning from a mission to make my in-depth report and debriefing. Apparently there're a couple of well placed spies in the Australian and Yank War Ministry who need to be eliminated to prevent any further damage to our war effort." Price said, as he introduced himself.

"I'm Ormond Sanderson, a Dutch South African formerly from the Dutch Embassy in Palembang. I'm a cipher and linguistic expert for my sins. I was captured by the Japs and used as one of their top linguists/interpreter which meant that I was shuffled from Sumatra right down to Timor.

Major Price and a troop of his guerrilla fighters managed to retrieve me in Surabaya for processing by the escape network team. I have several manuscripts, dictates and proclamation from the Japanese High command, notably from Admiral Yamamoto and General Tojo to all his forces in the Southern Pacific. As you can se, this bag is stuffed full of them that should be handed over to our Authorities. You will know that they contain information which will affect the decisions to be made as far as London, Washington, let alone Delhi, Canberra and Wellington." Sanderson explained, showing just a few of the documents he fetched out of the large sack.

"I'm Sergeant Major Ronnie Sinclair, Delta Company 1st battalion of the Gordon Highlanders, Sah!" Sinclair stated with a smart flourish of his right hand in salute to Hosie.

"What's a Scottish Regiment doing down this way Sarn't Major?" Hosie asked with surprise, yet with an automatic response in returning the salute.

"I'm an explosives and weapons expert and head of the Java Sabotage Group, with most of the lads from my Company as their so called 'Advisors'. But I'm returning from a mission involving Major Price." Sinclair said slowly, removing the top of his 'native' disguise to expose his British 'I.D.' tag that all Allied servicemen wear in times of war.

"I'm Terence O'Brien, an ex-British pat working for the Dutch East Indies Company as a Geologist and a Mining Engineer Consultant, but I own a few mines along the chain of islands, until the Japs took over that is. Major Price and I ran an escape route all the way down from Borneo to Bali and Timor using my Bali mine as their exit point. My wife is a native girl who was the co-ordinator for all the escapees coming to this point,

153

until she and the children got rounded up and sent to a labour camp. Unfortunately for most of the escapees they were found and recaptured, then they had the mines sealed off. All except this one shaft that is only 100 yards from the beach, that only I know of due to it being a disused vent shaft anyway. The escape route had now been shut down and we're the last to use it, although Price and Sinclair will still be able to use it to come and go as they please." O'Brien explained at length.

"Yes, we helped hundreds to escape from here, and as there's no more coming through the pipeline we're probably the last to come out alive, so to speak. But I'm hoping to use it as a trap door into the Japs back door, as I've got several 'special Ops' plans being developed that could use this excellent facility, for extra curricular activities, shall we say." Price added.

"As a matter of fact, only recently we were sent to pick up a load of escapees only a couple of hundred miles from here.

They'd escaped from Singapore on a ship as far as Surabaya, and tried to fly to Port Moresby, but came unstuck and got shot down at Bali." Hosie informed them.

"Yes Captain! You dropped off 2 units of Marines for an assignment. I had two of our local units waiting to guide them to their targets. Did a nice job on the Jap oil and ammo dumps too, but had a spot of bother on their exit, but 2 MGBs turned up and rescued them." Sinclair stated.

"Yes that's right! We had to come and meet up with them due to them running out of petrol some 300 miles from the base. But how the hell were you able to contact us to come and get you?" Hosie asked in amazement.

"As stated I'm part of a counter espionage unit, operating with several groups of guerrilla warfare units in place to give the Japs a bit of a hard time. We used O'Brien's powerful radio on a special frequency, and got in touch with somebody called FOGGY. I guessed it was something to do with the Military so made arrangements for you or somebody to come along and pick us up. We were told when to expect our pick up and who would be

154

in charge." Price revealed.

"Well here we are! But don't relax just yet, as it's one thing getting here, quite another getting back." Hosie commented, which made the four men look in bewilderment, so he explained his comment.

"The thing is gentlemen, this boat plus a squadron of them have been on station for a little while now, which the Japs, and perhaps dare I say even the Yanks don't know about, or even know what we look like, let alone some of our trigger happy soldier boys ashore. Sunk by 'friendly fire' springs to mind, as the Yanks are bloody good at that. My orders state that we must bring you back to our base, unless you have a direct line with Winston Churchill to state otherwise?"

"We've been told Darwin, then fly south to Canberra from there. But the Japs are flying air raids over that area so I suppose it's your place this time, certainly not ours." O'Brien informed.

"Well here we are on our way back to base so if you'd be kind enough to see our steward here he'll look after you and tend your needs." Hosie concluded, then asked them to leave the control room.

The boat had managed to race through the dark and very dangerous Lombok straits on the surface, turned left to head on her reciprocal course until it was nearly sunrise again, before they were forced to dive deep and very quickly too.

The radar office had picked up several aircraft coming their way, followed by a formation of ships indicating that one looked as big as a carrier with a couple of escorts.

The aircraft had disappeared starboard side of them, which meant that they were heading for Australia, but they didn't know they were Yank bombers returning home from yet another 'Dolittle' raid, or a squadron of Jap Aichi Dive Bombers on another bother mission dishing out grief over Darwin, who had already sunk several ships in the harbour there on a previous visit.

Hosie decided that as his boat's batteries were pretty well near its capacity, thanks to the running charge he had done to them, he would turn and face this threat, if only to remind the Japs that the British were still around, even though the Yanks would get the blame for any ships lost.

"Sonar reports that there are 2 ships pronounced cavitations, with some sort of slapping noises coming from astern of us, on Green 175. Hoare reported

"Very good! Up for'ard periscope! Let's see what we've got! Stand by to read off!"

Hose gave a quick sweep all round to ensure that nothing was approaching him since his last look.

T.S. stood on the opposite side of the periscope ready to read off each bearing and/or periscope ranges. He had his little magic ruler, which, with a deft flick of his wrists he would use to calculate the ranges as given.

"Okay let's see. Bloody hell! We've got two ocean going tugs towing a large dry dock with what looks like a destroyer on it. The floating dock looks like one they've taken from us, AFD 39 it reads. What do you suppose the Japs are trying to do bringing this slow moving vessel on this side of the Java mainland?" Hosie cooed, then called for Price to come to the control room.

Price arrived quietly alongside Hosie and for him to ask what the problem was.

"Major! We've discovered that the Japs have towed one of our own Dry docks that was last seen in Singapore, yet here it is sailing along nicely along the coast of Java not in the Java Sea but here in the Arafu Sea. What is going on?" Hosie asked, inviting Price to take a look through the periscope.

"So that's what it looks like. Looking out of a periscope that is." Price murmured, taking a few moments to offer his opinion.

"I would guess that our enemy is trying to muster as much naval power capability Eastward, to prepare for some big assault on New Guinea and even Australia. The Yanks have all but destroyed any docking facility available to the Japs, so presumably this large floating dock would be a Godsend, certainly for the repair of their destroyers and escort ships. I dare say Mr Sanderson could give you a clearer picture." Price offered.

"Thanks for your considered opinion Major, I intend that they will be denied not only the dry dock but also the destroyer on it. But first I must take care of the two tugs, as without them the dock goes nowhere fast." Hosie said with a grin and a gleam in his eyes.

"It seems that you relish a good scrap too, Captain. Better get out of your way then. I'll tell your passengers to fasten their safety belts or whatever you fasten on board a submarine." Price chuckled, leaving the control room for Hosie to give the order 'Attack Teams close up'.

"Attack teams closed up sir!" Welling informed, as Hosie slowly pirouetted around with the for'ard periscope seemingly stuck to his eyebrows.

"Very good No1. I intend using only 1for'ard torpedo to sink each of the tugs but will surface usinge a gun action to sink this dry dock floating along merrily as you please. Hosie stated, offering Welling a quick look out to see what he was about to do.

"But that's one of our AFD's! Won't the Admiralty court martial us for the loss of, erm, company property' so to speak?" Welling asked.

"Not when they know there's a Jap destroyer in its cradle taking a cruise around the place." Hosie chuckled, taking over the periscope again.

"Stand by to read off! Left hand tug bearing... that! Range... that! Right hand tug bearing...that! Range... that!" Hosie stated quickly and T.S. reported the bearings and ranges.

"T.O! Open bow caps. Use tubes 1 & 2. Set the torpedo range of 1200 yards, using a depth of 8 feet. The tugs are deep-sea ocean going ones with their sterns deep in the water so we should be okay. No1. Have the gun Captain muster in the control room."

"Aye aye sir" both officers responded quickly.

P.O. Hall reported to the control room to be informed of his gun action task, for Hosie to let him take a look at his target.

"2,000 yards using 6 armour piercing shells? Piece of cake! Or would you like us to board it and just pull the plug out sir?" Hall opined with a smile on his face, knowing there would be return fire this time.

Hosie looked at Hall and grinned.

"Actually that's not a bad idea Guns! But we'd still have to put a few holes in the destroyer to make sure she sinks with the rest of it." Hosie declared with excitement, then carried on with his periscope observations for a few moments before giving his decision.

"Sorry Guns, but that destroyer might have some of its crew on board that might be armed. I'm licensed to kill not thrill, so I'm afraid it's back to plan A"

"Spoil-sport!" Hall muttered but Hosie heard what he said, and laughed.

"Sorry to be such a killjoy Guns, but I'll be needing you again, not just for today. 6 rounds to start off with I think."

"About time somebody wanted him sir!" Welling quipped, which made everybody laugh despite the need for total concentration at all times during an attack situation.

"Open outer doors! Stand by for a final check." Hosie ordered, taking a final check of his bearings to target and the ranges.

"Set an angle of 3 degrees each side of the bow. Stand by… fire 1 & 2." Hosie commanded, which resulted in the boat giving a shiver and a shake as the powerful air launch of the torpedoes left the boat, before the trip lever on the tube tripped the switch to start the onboard motor of the torpedo as it left, speeding their way at some 30knots towards 2 unsuspecting ships.

Two large explosions told of the targets being hit, for Hosie to order the boat to surface and start his gun action.

T.S. was always the person in behind the surfacing officer to arrive on the bridge, standing by with his machine gun in case of small arms fire directed at them.

Hosie arrived onto the bridge shouting down to Hall who was standing on the gun tower directing the gun crew.

"Set gun angle of Green 90. Use an elevation angle of 5 degrees. Set range of 2,000 yards, Load with A.P. Stand by to fire on the down roll. " Hall ordered before asking Hosie's permission to fire.

"Send 4 rounds into her waterline then fire at will guns!" Hosie ordered.

Hall gauged the roll of the boat until it was at the optimum firing point, before he ordered the gun to be fired.

The report from the gun was almost deafening for those on the bridge, with each shot being observed by Hall, using his binoculars, to gauge where to place his next shot.

Somewhere a machine gun started firing from the top of the dock, with the bullets arcing towards the gun crew, with several whizzing over the heads of those on the bridge.

"Well don't just stand there Signalman! Return their fire or we'll have a few dead gunners on our hands." Hosie screamed, ducking as another bullet ricocheted off the gyro compass stand.

"At least I've got permission this time!" T.S. muttered, returning the gunfire with his Lewis gun.

Hall must have seen the machine gun nest and sent a shell their way.

Thus the little gunfight was short lived as T.S.'s aim, helped by the 4 inch shell that landed nearby, put paid to the enemy gunners resistance.

Hosie who was also observing the shoot with his binoculars, declared that there were enough holes in the waterline for Hall to shift his target to the sides of the floating dock, using high explosives. No sooner had several holes appeared into the upright hull of the dock when it started to sink slowly towards them.

"Guns! It must be pretty warm cooped up in that ship. Let's be neighbourly and give them some ventilation. Maybe the holes we give them might help to make it sink easier. Load up with A.P. again and shoot at the destroyer." Hosie directed with glee as the destroyer's weight shifted over to the side thus giving a big momentum towards the capsizing of the dock.

T.S. stopped firing then commenced his lookout duties to maintain vigilance again.

He saw the debris floating in the water astern of him, which marked the end of the two tugs. By the time he looked around at the floating dock, it was disappearing below the surface in a cauldron of bubbles.

"Cease firing! Cease firing!" Hosie shouted with glee.

"Aye aye sir!"

Hall had his crew cease-fire and return the gun to its stowage position again.

"Permission to go below sir?" Hall called up to the bridge.

"Well done Guns! You've done a grand job in waste disposal management. Get your men below and secure the hatch." Hosie replied with a large grin on his face, before he ordered the bridge be cleared and the boat dived again.

Once everybody was below in the control room again, with the boat at periscope depth, Hosie had the Attack Team secure for the boat revert to watch dived.

Before the team 'fell out' from actions stations, Hosie congratulated everybody on a good 'exercise' saying that it's not very often a boat sinks a heavily armed destroyer, and a floating dock with a mere 4 inch pop gun.   And that the last time a warship was sunk in that manner was during WW1. Everybody knew he had discounted the two measly ocean going tugs, as icing on their cake.

The 'Jolly Roger' flag would be flying high once more when they arrived back into the base, and yet a few more 'dits 'to swap with the other boat's crews over a pint or few in the NAAFI club.

Chapter IV

Shopping List

S64 had an uninterrupted and safe transit back to base, with the crew getting to know about some of the hieroglyphics painted on the pieces of parchment paper as narrated and interpreted by Sanderson. So being more or less forewarned as to the future prospects dished out by the Japanese, the crew resolved to enjoy inboard or ashore time more whilst they could before being called before the mast again. As for their passengers, they seemed to melt away like their previous ones had, and the base somehow took on a more demanding role both on board and ashore.

T.S. and his fellow Sparkers were making their way through the canteen flat towards the dining hall for scran when Brown spotted a large poster advertising the next entertainments night, scheduled for that Saturday night:

'Our Base Entertainments Officer Lt Evonne Broad is delighted to announce the arrival of a Troupe that has come all the way from Melbourne to entertain us. Starring the 'Master of Comedy' the very popular 'David Tollerton and his Mincing Matelots'. Followed by our very own Flight Lieutenant Brian Nolan and his hilarious troupe of Airmen, with Brian's adaptation of Snow White, called 'The Hairy Fairy and his 7 dirty little short-arsed gits.' Seats only, so get in early so as not to be disappointed. Tickets now on sale at the Base Supply Office or at any NAAFI shop: Priced at only 1/-, 1/9d and 2/6d.' He read out aloud for their benefit.

"That sounds a good night lads! Let's get some tickets!" Brown said full of enthusiasm.

"Saturday? Who's got the duty watch?" Boyall asked thoughtfully, then discovered Brown and Underwood chuckling to themselves and pointing towards T.S.

161

"Well bastardin' 'ell! Just my luck! And here's me hoping to take out one of the comcen girls I've just lined up." T.S. moaned.

"Never mind! We'll take her out for you old son!" Underwood said, putting his long arm around T.S as if to console him.

"Yes! Plenty more fish in the sea and all that dear boy! Who's the lucky girl, do we know her? " Boyal scoffed at T.S's bad luck.

"Well thanks for nothing! And no I'm not telling. I am prepared to offer a couple of days tot and 20 fags to whoever stands in for me too." T.S. offered.

There was a sharp intake of breath from the others when a 2 days tot forfeit was offered.

"Now if you were to say 7 days plus a tin of 50 fags, I'd just about take you on! "Brown said with a wink towards the others, but T.S. spotted the gradual wind up he was getting.

T.S. merely grinned and bore the bad news so left him in peace, entering the dining room for their meal.

After they had their duty free fag, Boyall told T.S. that Dave Lewis was going to give a 'Departmental' briefing in the morning but that he was excused on account that he had the camel trek into the village to get the mail.

"I should be issued with a Posties' bike for all the walking I do to get there." T.S. moaned.

"There again, if you see the Sin Bosun (Naval Chaplain), for an issue of Jesus Boots then you'll be able to take the short cut across the water instead of going all the way round by land." Brown quipped.

"Har-de-flippin-Har! Mind you, it means I get to have a wander around the big NAAFI complex there. You never know what 'Submarine Comforts' I might come across to bring back. Now, I fancy some of that 'woofters' powder, Cusson's Lather I think it's called. Apparently all you've got to do is just get a handful of it and whilst you stand under one of the overhead fans, chuck it all up into the air, then stand under it and wait to get a real 'Submariner's shower. After that, you can become a woofter from the 'Brown Hatters Brigade' for as long as you like." T.S. said wickedly, as he saw his chance to get back at his messmates.

"Hmmm! Maybe you'd bring us back some postage stamps as well?" Brown asked.

"Yeah! Maybe some of that fancy soap that Barrie Morris is short of, em, Lifeboat or buoy soap, or whatever. It's the one that's supposed to stops you from keeling over under the smell of your armpits or other hairy places!" Underwood suggested.

"Nah! I'll only get my own, sorry and all that. T.S. teased.

"Et-tu-Brutus! Boyall said laughingly, realising that T.S. was just getting his own back on them.

T.S. took the rail shuttle ride through several area gates, noticing the changes since his last trip. His big surprise was seeing S60 still in one of the floating docks with the other one empty, until he saw that S63 had been beached and was being carved up as spare parts for the others.

"We're still 2 short of a full squadron, but I don't suppose anybody will notice considering that there seems to be no more than 2 alongside at any one time." he muttered, then suddenly realised he was approaching the railway station in the middle of the sprawling village.

He walked down a small side lane to the ever-increasing size of the Mail Sorting Office cum Post Office building and entering it from the Post Office end, saw the place empty of customers yet busy with counter staff behind a lattice work grill.

"Morning! Can I help you?" a pleasant voice asked from behind him, turning, he saw a slim woman standing there.

"Yes, I wish to speak to the Post Master about the shortage of certain stamp denominations that I need to sort out." T.S. replied

"My name is Doreen Roberts, the Post Mistress here. Maybe you can give me a list of what you need whilst you take your sack to the sorting office. What ship are you off?" she asked failing to see the distinctive cap-tally declaring to the world that he was in H.M. SUBMARINES.

"I'm the Postie off S64. I normally get my mail from Leading Regulator Magnes off our Depot ship but he suggested I came to see you."

"There's been a change of routine lately. My husband Ken Roberts is the Censorship Control Officer, handling all outgoing mail, so he will take yours for processing. You'll find him in the Sorting office when you go there."

"Oh that's nothing to worry about Mrs Roberts. We censor our own mail and stamped as such by Magnes as I've said. Anyway, here's my immediate requirements list, but what I would really appreciate is if I can have them stamped and franked here as and when I bring it along. The postal charges will be paid each time so as not to run up a tally, so to speak."

"I don't see why not, as it'll give my staff something to do during the slack times you men are away at sea or wherever."

T.S. thanked her then left to go into the back room to collect his incoming mail.

"What ho Des! How's the missus and kids coping with all this heat?" T.S. greeted as he threw his sack onto a sorting table.

"She loves this weather, so do the kids. They're always to be found in the swimming pool or up by the waterfall, like a pair of dolphins they are. There's a new routine here now so you'd better go see Ken Roberts with your outgoing stuff, as that's his job from now on." Magnes replied cheerfully.

"Yes, so em, Doreen Roberts the Postmistress has just told me. She's going to fix me up with some stamps for now, but will be looking into the possibility of us being able to stamp and frank up here instead of on board. Says it'll give the counter staff something to do during the slack times."

"Hope so, as it'll save me a great deal too. If I wasn't R.A. (Ration allowance paid to married personnel living ashore with their families.) I'd offer you a wet of my tot next time I get one."

"Much mail for me? Only I'd like to nip around to the NAAFI complex to get some 'home comforts' in case I'm not back again for another while."

"Just the one so far, but be back in 20 minutes, as I've got a different time schedule to keep now."

"Roger that Des!" T.S. said quickly, leaving the room to go on his errands.

"I should have written it all down as I'm bound to get in a muckin' fuddle as to who wanted what. Let's see now. Foo foo! (talc), fags, lighter fuel, er, hand soap, dhoby dust, (soap powder) some decent nutty but I can't remember what, toothpaste, a soft bog roll, maybe a tin of Koo plum jam and some posh biscuits. Oh! mustn't forget some razor blades, Oxo cubes and a decent writing stick either. Sod it! Now what else was it? Hmm, I hope I've got enough Aussie money on me." He muttered as he went through his mental shopping list.

Whilst he was waiting in the queue to pay, he made a quick tally of the amount and saw that in fact he didn't have enough. Fortunately he spotted a C. P.O. Writer wandering around the self-service shop and went to see him.

"Excuse me Chief! I'm T.S. on board S64. I notice that you're a Scribe so maybe you can help me out of a spot. I'm due back on board but don't seem to have enough Aussie money to pay for my shopping, even though I've got plenty of Sterling on me."

"Hmmm! A tricky one that. Wait for me to finish my shopping then I'll come and vouch for you. T.S off S64? Ah yes, I remember you as I've seen you with your Cox'n, er, James, yes that's him, come into my office on the Depot ship for items needed on board." the Chief said, as he recognised him.

T.S. managed to recognise the Chief to remember his name relaxed, as here was somebody known who would help out.

"Yes, you're Ken Matthews, er sorry, Chief Scribes Ken Matthews. That will be great only I'm due back to the Mail Depot, shortly." T.S. said, looking anxiously at his watch.

"I won't be long. Just a simple matter of on the spot, authorised money exchange, that's all. In fact you've just given me an idea about all that. Maybe I'll tell you some time when

165

next you're in my office." Matthews answered with a wink, then carried on with his shopping whilst T.S. waited for him.

The deed was done and T.S. thanked Matthews for his help, promising to tell his Cox'n about it before rushing back to collect his mail and other things from Mrs Roberts.

On his way back to the boat, with 2 sacks of mail with another one doubling up as a grocery bag, he recognised a woman sitting on a seat opposite him.

"Erm, excuse me, but aren't you Mrs Richmond?" he asked politely.

"Yes I am, but who are you?" she asked.

"I'm T.S. off S64. We're the boat that rescued you along with several others a few weeks ago. We didn't know what had happened to you all when we arrived. Tell me, are the children okay now?"

"Oh yes, I remember. Yes, you sailors were truly our saviours, and yes all the children are well now, all of them going to the village school. In fact we all decided to stay at the Base as we've nowhere else to go. Besides, the Base has been sealed off with nobody allowed out with very few allowed in without very expressed permission. Those documents I brought back certainly caused a panic, but from what I'm told there's an even bigger panic caused by the latest lot your boys brought back from, shall we say, a recent shopping trip."

"Oh! Panic as in 'don't panic! Women and children first? Or a panic as in 'for God sake hurry up and pass me more ammo'?"

"Can't say, and won't, but I think that what you will observe around the place will speak for itself." She said, nodding to one of the extra machine gun posts they'd just passed.

"So what are you doing with your free time then?" T.S. asked, to change the subject.

"I'm part of the 'Think Tank' that's full of backroom boys and girls' if you like, whereas my husband is now the Base's Chief of Police due to his long and distinguished service record with the Singapore Police Training School."

166

"He's what we refer to on board as 'the Marshal' with our Cox'n being his 'Sheriff', but congratulations. Let's hope all the others settle in just as well. Anyway Mrs Richmond, here's my stop, so tell everybody we on board S64 send our regards to our former passengers, especially the children. It was nice to have met you again." T.S. replied, shaking her hand in goodbye then staggered off the railway carriage with his sacks of mail and shopping to catch his next duty launch out to the Depot ship.

There were lots of odd jobs to do on the boat to prepare her for their next patrol, not least some T.S. had to complete.

He was on the bridge trying out his new pennant holder fitted with the new sized ensign when he saw smoke coming from the outboard side, making him look over to see what was what.

He saw Leading Stoker Banks welding some new hand railing that went along the length of the fin.

"Didn't know you could weld Dave? I thought that would be a dockyard or an inboard job." T.S. commented.

"Bill Guyan detailed me off as the boat's welder due to the fact I was one in civvy street before joining up. Or to be more precise, almost press-ganged into joining boats." Banks admitted.

"Actually Dave, I could do with another sleeve bracket to slot my machine gun into, as this one is getting a bit dodgy. I don't want it to come adrift when I'm hammering the Japs with hot lead or the bullets might go through our tanks instead of them."

"Better see Bill, or put a chit in for that, as I've got several other welding jobs to see to before we sail. Alternatively, if you've got a length of piping suitable and available by secure time, I'll nip up here and do it for you."

"Cheers Dave! I know of a nice piece of tubing, but you'll have to lend me a hack saw to get it off its present location." T.S. said with a grin.

"Oh! From where are you going to, shall we say, rescue it? No, never mind, I don't want to know, but come and see me at tot time then!" Banks concluded, hiding his face behind his welders' mask.

167

That sort of exchange between the two of them typifies the resourcefulness from time immemorial of a British Servicemen, and long may it continue.

He climbed down the vertical ladder from the bridge to go onto the casing via the fin door access, landing next to Roy Sedgwick who was sitting on the casing with a grease gun in his hand.

He looked down to see that Sedgwick was pumping like mad, trying to get more grease into the barrel of the gun with the flexible hose dunked into a large tub of grease.

"Fishing in a grease barrel? I've heard of oily fish but that's ridiculous!" T.S. chortled, tapping Sedgwick on his shoulder.

"Bloody hell Signalman! Didn't know it was this hard to get grease back into the gun again. I've been pumping for ages now and nothing to show for it. Look!" Sedgwick moaned, showing T.S. the open grease gun barrel that was very empty.

T.S. managed to stop laughing to ask him how long he'd been a Gunner, and when was the last time he used a grease gun.

"Never used one before. I've always been the loader or manning the elevation handle, er No 4 or 3 to you. Why?"

T.S. took the grease gun off him and with a hand full of grease he rammed into the open end of the grease gun barrel, before handing it back to him, saying.

"That's the way to do it!" in a Punch and Judy style voice, then took a rag and wiped his hands clean.

Sedgwick looked at the flexible lead end and at the now half full barrel.

"But the grease comes out of the end of the flexitube so that was where I thought it was the way it would be put back." Sedgwick stated and copied T.S. to refill the barrel up again before replacing the cap onto it.

"I won't tell a soul Roy, but I feel you owe me at least a gulper, considering I've saved you hours of pumping the gun and getting nowhere."

Sedgwick started to laugh at the implications but blamed it all on not knowing what to do in the first place.

"Just as well you're one of our red hot gunners, and the best gun crew in the squadron then Roy, or Brian Hall would shove the gun right up your arse if he ever knew."

"Fair enough! Anyway, I'm wrapping up now for stand easy."

"Before you go Roy there's something that you might be interested in. There's a good looking Aussie Jack Dusty Wren in the B.S.O who I happen to know, and before you say anything, her name was given me by one of the FPB Sparkers I also happen to know."

"Oh! Why me?" Sedgwick asked with interest.

"Well the thing is, her name is Jean Sedgwick who shares the same name as you, and even spelt the same as yours. It's a typically British name to find all this way some 10,000 miles away, and I'm wondering if she might be belonging to you, perhaps from way back. She could have been deported for some misdemeanour from way back as I've said, but from what I've seen she's not wearing the proverbial ball and chain, but definitely sports a decent, dare I say, a very healthy 'May West'. Maybe next time you should get ashore you could go and definitely look her up as I certainly did the other day." T.S said, making a 'coca cola bottle' shape with his hands, and flicking his eyebrows.

"Hmmm! If what you say is true, then it's worth a try. Maybe get to take her out to the Base entertainment night on Saturday if all goes well. Thanks for the info. For that you can definitely come round a couple of times." Sedgwick concluded, and T.S. went below into the cool of the boat.

Part Four

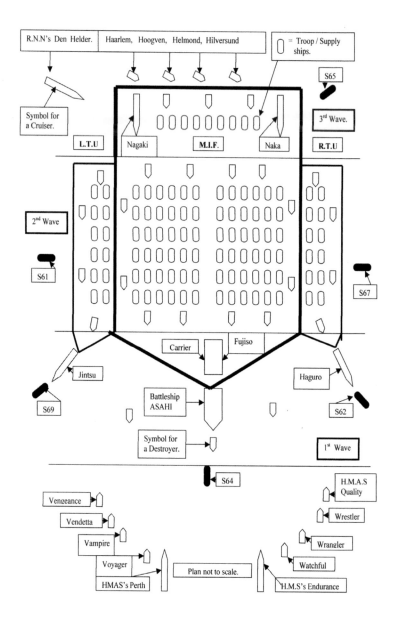

R.N.N's Den Helder. | Haarlem, Hoogven, Helmond, Hilversund

〇 = Troop / Supply ships.

S65

Symbol for a Cruiser.

3rd Wave.

L.T.U | Nagaki | M.I.F. | Naka | R.T.U

2nd Wave

S61

S67

Carrier | Fujiso

Jintsu

Haguro

S69 | Battleship ASAHI

S62

Symbol for a Destroyer.

1st Wave

S64

H.M.A.S Quality

Vengeance

Wrestler

Vendetta

Wrangler

Vampire

Voyager | Plan not to scale. | Watchful

HMAS's Perth | H.M.S's Endurance

172

The Battle of Oz

The plans and documents that were spirited away into the hands of the Allied Intelligence Agencies, (as depicted in Part Three) showed that Japan had not only formulated their plans for a 3 pronged invasion of New Guinea, Australia and Ceylon, but crucially, planned a fourth, much bolder attack on Midway. The Japanese Generals with their armies, their Admirals and their Fleets were allocated with the provisional details as to what was to happen, depicted on a diagram plan.

The fortunate interception and discovery of these plans plus the absolutely vital fact that the Americans had long since cracked the Japanese codes enabled them to anticipate or at least re-inforce themselves wherever the Japanese might decide to strike next.

As America took on the apron of protecting New Zealand and Australia, they had decided that only they would fight the Japanese for New Guinea, and with luck stop them completely.

Thus the Australian forces would have to make their own defence preparations, as the British would for Ceylon.

This last part explains the Japanese Invasion plan and details that could have been conducted on the assault and invasion of Australia, with the main thrust of their plans being directed through the seemingly undefended back door, hoping to gain at least a decent foothold and beach-head deep into the heart of Australia, with little or no resistance from the considered 'much depleted or non-existent' Australian forces.

Despite their pincer movement to create a diversion on the Western and Eastern coastline, their main target earmarked was the Gulf of Carpentaria, for their main Invasion Force to start off from.

Unfortunately for the Japanese High command, their intelligence gathering facility fell far short of that of the Allies, and failed to uncover a special Australian base, which was also the home of a squadron of the Royal Navy's latest type of long range Submarines.

The detailed manuscripts and documents that were brought back onboard S64 was like a bombshell to the various High Commands issuing the orders for their patch of the globe.

The ripples of orders from the strategic planners went out to only those who had a crucial role to play, including F.O.N.A.C. and FOGGY, where not only the fate of the military personnel was at stake but also that of the entire Australian population.

This then sets the scenario for a massive invasion and the forthcoming battle called 'The Battle of Oz' and where the story as narrated by T.S. continues.

Chapter I

Ploy Boys

S64 had just crossed the wide-open mouth of the Carpetarian Gulf, when Hosie decided to surface to make his final lap towards the base.

"Anything on Sonar?" Hosie asked, as he revolved around the periscope on his little electric drive seat.

"Two sets of cavitations. One bearing Red 30 and the other on Green 50. Suggest fishing boats, sir." Hoare announced.

Hosie looked directly at the two bearings and confirmed that they were friendly minelayers, but T.S to see and give their recognition.

"They're the Fast Minelayers from our base. The pennant number on the nearest one to us is ML 1660 their Squadron Leader, sir." T.S. reported.

"Let's surface next to them and speak to them, only I'm not too keen on wandering into an uncharted minefield, No1."

"Standby to surface. Report main vents. Open 1,3 and 5 LP master blows." Welling ordered in response to Hosie's.

"Signalman! Make sure you show them our Ensign before they start shooting at us. Stop together. In both engine clutches. Surface No1."

"Blow 1, 3 & 5 main ballast." Welling commanded as he acted upon his Captain's word 'surface'.

Once the boat was fully surfaced, the OOW followed very closely by T.S. was on the bridge, the voice cock to the control room was opened and the L.P. blower running to complete the air top up in the ballast tanks.

Hosie appeared onto the bridge and found T.S. was waving his ensign vigorously on both sides of the bridge, before he commenced flashing up the minelayers with his aldis.

"Hello sailor! Coming up for a spot of sun tan then?" T.S. reported as he read out the opening signal from ML1660.

Hosie laughed at the cheeky greetings, then revealed that the last time he surfaced in the middle of a gaggle of coastal forces vessels he was nearly shot to pieces.

"So now you understand the value of waving the flag Signalman. Make the reply. 'Nice eggs you're laying, duckie! Then ask him to close on me for a shout."

T.S. flashed the required signals and the ML moved slowly towards the boat that had now stopped, wallowing gently in the slight sea swell.

Once both vessels were almost touching one another, both captains exchanged recognition code words before having a brief chat about what was going on.

Both Captains exchanged greetings and introduced each other, using first names to be able to have their chat.

"We planted a wreck off the coast of Timor two weeks ago with a sea chart showing where we'll be sowing our minefields. Then recently, one of our patrol aircraft spotted a squadron of Jap minesweepers along the coast, going across the Gulf. By now they have discovered that what they picked up were in fact dummies, meaning that any they come across from now on will be ignored. But we're the Ploy Boys who will perform our magic and interlace them with real ones. The dummies can be detected by radar because of the bits of metal we put on them, will show up in a neat pattern on the radar screen. What we're doing is interlacing the dummies with real ones that have been given rubber coats so they won't show on the radar, pretty much what you boys have on your 'scopes and snorkel mast heads. Therefore, when they choose to ignore the dummies or even decide to steam through the 'holes' marked on the screen they'll hit one of these beauties. Guaranteed to blow a nice big hole through at least 3 inches of armour plating, they will. They took the bait for the air patrol to spot them checking out the details. 'Reading the small print' as we'd say." Lt Reynolds informed Hosie at length.

"Any chance of giving me a spare copy of your activities, or am I getting one from the big boss when I get back Harry?" Hosie asked.

"I only have my own matrix laid out on the chart, but I dare say all will be revealed when the Admiral starts his series of lectures on tactics or whatever. That will be very soon as we're expecting the balloon to go up within the next few days or so, at least according to the listening posts and recce reports coming back from the GNAT patrols."

"No peace for the wicked then! Hope to see you soon back at base. Must dash now as I'm late to check in with my boss before they'll let me back into the base." Hosie concluded.

Reynolds waved his cap as a salute, to which Hosie responded in kind, before he ordered the boat to continue on.

"Full ahead together. Make revs for 20 knots. Keep on this course and speed No1. Any sign of aircraft, get us down. I'm going below now." Hosie ordered.

"Aye aye sir!" Welling responded, then issued his own command.

"Control room! Go to Patrol Routine, and have the 2nd Cox'n to get the gash ditched via the fin door."

"Aye aye sir!" the helmsman responded, relaying the orders to the duty control room P.O.

T.S. was relieved off the bridge with the change of watches, making his way through the watertight door between the control room and the accommodation space when he saw the cleavage of a hairy bum sticking out of a dirty blue pair of shorts.

"I recognise that hairy arse as none other than our 'Scouser' Leading Amp Tramp Dave Roberts. If you're praying to Allah then you're pointing the wrong way!" T.S. teased, yet knowing full well he was taking a 'battery dip' and waited until he was finished.

"Hmm! Looks lower than it should be, better tell POLTO. Which means that we're going to charge to the 2nd reduction. Better tell the lads, as the 'no smoking' boards will be on soon." Roberts informed, then replaced the metal disc that was the battery cover back over the 'test battery cell' hole.

"That'll make it the second time on this trip. Battery ok?"

"Let's hope so as Doug Hughes will be slapping in a 'Stores Req' for a new cell or three." Roberts revealed, standing up and went aft to the motor room.

This would be the time when the battery cells in the boat were charged up to a gassing point, which meant that due to the hydrogen gas fumes given off, it would be foolish to smoke in case it ignited causing a massive explosion with fatal results not only for all on board, but also to the boat.

For those that smoked which was almost everybody on board, it also meant that they had either to go up onto the bridge, or onto the casing, sea swell permitting, or even up into the fin to have their one '5 minute' smoke, as it would take several hours to clear the boat from the gas. Once the 'no smoking 'lights were switched off then it was 'as you were' again.

It was early the following morning just before sunrise when S64 tied up alongside her usual 'trot' for the first time since the boats arrived into the base the 'trots' were full again.

"Looks like a full house sir!" T.S. commented to Welling, after Hosie had left the bridge to go inboard.

"Yes indeed Signalman. No doubt there'll be other surprises in store for us when get inboard." Welling agreed for both of them to make their way back down into the control room again. James made the announcement as to who was on duty, informing them that the galley was open for early breakfast, but that everybody had to return back on board for a full muster at 0800.

"What do you suppose is going on then?" Ward, one of the Leading Stokers asked T.S. as they climbed up the steep ladders leading onto the depot ship.

"Reading between the lines and from certain signals we got, CDR S/M thinks it's about time we started to earn our 'King's shilling', Roy. But then what the bleedin' 'ell does he think we've been doing since we arrived here?" T.S replied glumly

"Yeah! Well, I think I'll slap in for a swop draft then, or wangle a 'spare Crew billet' if what we've gone through so far has

178

been 'for exercise'." Ward gasped as they finally reached the top of the ladders.

"Can't do that Roy, think of the extra money you'll lose as our 'Ship's Diver'. I'm cleared for 30 feet yet you're a Part 3 'free flood head' wallah! (Deep sea Diver.)"

"Yeah I suppose you're right." Ward concluded as they reached the boat's mess deck to go to their own separate little mess.

Due to 4 boats being alongside, it felt a bit crowded in the mess deck again, but it was the chance for each boats crew to renew their re-acquaintance with each other, and for the combined comradeship of the squadron to be whole again. This ambience was overshadowed with the gut feeling that the war was about to come to them instead of the other way round. For when they are inboard, it is a time to reflect on what is to come, for each man to make his own private preparations in the event they should not return again. For a Submariner, whilst he is able to come unseen, the moment his boat is and comes under a depth-charge attack from a surface vessel, his chances of survival already slim, are virtually nil.

T.S. and all the Sparkers from each boat were able to learn and appreciate certain details due to the signals being received on board, was unknown to the rest of their crews. So it was when they all mustered on board boat at 0800, James told them that the Captain would be reading the 'Articles of War' to them, even though they had been at war for some time now.

"Do you hear there, this is your Captain speaking!" Hosie started then commenced to read the 'Articles of War' with each mess reporting that everybody had heard him.

He then went on to announce that as of 0900 they'd be fully stored for war and putting to sea by 0300 tomorrow, so that if everybody put their back into it, the sooner they finished the more time off.

179

"The Base has been sealed off by a Battalion of Marines, with air patrols stepped up to keep us informed of the Jap movements. All heads of departments are to muster in the control room in 15 minutes for a briefing. The Attack Team is to muster at 1030 on the quarterdeck of the depot ship to join the other attack teams for transporting by launch to the Flagstaff offices ashore, to attend a briefing by Cdr S/M. All officers will be required to attend the Admiral's briefing at 1500. Once the boat was fully stored and ready for sea, the boat can secure with the 'Spare Crew' taking over the duty watches until we sail. That will be all!" Hosie concluded, switching off the control room 'mike'.

This announcement was received with the stoic fortitude, typical of any British serviceman who was about to 'stand to' and face the enemy, even though they had been doing that from day one. The knowledge that they had a few hours grace to indulge themselves was like a tonic to them all, somehow acting as the sweetener to the bitter truth of the reason why they were sent all the way to Australia. To defend our Commonwealth peoples with all their might, from the enemy that was about to knock on their door, even if it does cost them their lives.

Chapter II

Tactics

"**R**ight settle in everybody." Cdr S/M Harry Harley ordered, then unfurling a large scale map of the Gulf with several details put on it, and went through each one.

"As you can see from the chart, the Japanese are currently in the formation of 3 separate waves shown thus. The whole invasion force is split yet again, into 3 columns, with the centre one being the largest therefore the main thrust of their attack, after they expect to smash FOGGY's base on Melville Island. Maybe that's why it has the battleship and the carrier in the lead.

The two outer 'prongs' will peel off making landings estimated to be 50 miles each side the main landing between Burketown and Normanton. The Japs will be allowed to reach this point, where we will be positioned." He stated, pointing to an 'X' on the chart.

"The reason is, that the shaded area shown is the large pear shaped basin roughly 50miles into the Gulf and of about 70 square nautical miles, reaching a reasonable depth of around 300 feet. We have been given the privilege of starting the attack on these, shall we say, unwanted visitors, but I'm not detailing that here, only at the Officers muster this afternoon.

From the diagram, you'll see the position of each boat, and the reason why you're here listening to me.

We have been ordered to take out the first wave of warships before we start getting into the meat of the sandwich of sinking as many assault and troop ships as possible. This tactic has been agonised over, but we hope that the Japanese will adopt their 'protect the invasion fleet' rather than spend their time chasing our boats and ships around the place.

S64 as the senior boat Commander, the most experienced one in the squadron, will be at the bottom of the funnel to take on the battleship and the carrier. She will be flanked by S69 on the left, with S62 on the right to take on the cruisers. S61 and S67 will be on the outer wing of the funnel to take on the flanking escorts before attacking the ships in that column. S60 will not be ready for sea and will be kept back in reserve. S65 will meet up with the Dutch cruiser and her destroyer squadron to come in behind to carry out a pincer movement on wave 3. Again, be bloody well smart to get away from the ammo ships when they blow, as they can devastate anything within a 6000yard radius of them. Once we've stopped and hopefully sunk the first wave thus completing Phase1, expect FOGGY's forces coming up from the south, to start Phase 2. The F.A.A. will be launching their air attack starting Phase 3 on the main bulk of the invasion fleet, while a squadron from the RAAF will be around to take care of any enemy fighters. You are warned to take particular note of these friendly forces, so stick to the areas allocated to you. We don't want to be attacked by our own men to suffer the ignomy of being sunk by the Yank disease of 'friendly fire' let alone crushed under a sinking vessel from somebody else's attack. Don't forget they'll be in close formation so for God's sake watch where you go. If you need to reload, then get out from under and return to base to do so. But as you'll have a full load of 30 fish each, the maths dictate that there should be no need to do so. On that note, watch out for the FPB's and the fleet of fishing boats armed with machine gunners who will be going around mopping up taking care of any Jap survivors to see that they never set foot on our soil, alive that is."

The briefing went on for a little while before Harley asked for any questions.

"Yes sir! Given that this is supposed to be a large invasion force; How many ships and men involved with the invasion, and why are they sending it, from what you've shown us, virtually unprotected. I mean, I would expect at least three times as many, something in the region of say 3 battleships 2 heavy or medium cruisers, 6 light cruisers, 3 carriers, about 25 escort destroyers plus say at least 4 boats?" T.S. asked.

"A good question. From the previous map, as you can see, the Japanese are committing themselves to a massive expansion to encompass the whole of the Pacific, at the same time pushing westwards towards Ceylon to start a link up with the Germans.

This being so, according to intelligence they will do it with a major assault or invasion on 4 areas. New Guinea above us, Ceylon out to the west, with possibly Midway, way out in the east and us right here." Harley stated, pointing to the large arrows indicating the Japanese forces and their destinations.

"We calculate that most of their battleships and cruisers will be used up in 3 of them, especially against the Americans in the Coral Sea and against us in the Indian Ocean, with maybe a carrier led strike force against Midway.

Be that as it may, we are only concerned with their intentions to invade of Australia, as the large map indicates. Their attack here at Port Hedland with the left prong to cut off the Northern Territory; Here at Rockhampton, as their right diversionary invasion force which is expected to meet up with the right prong to cut off Northern Queensland, with us here at the top as their main landing beaches, they are expected to make the main march right down the middle to take over the southern half of the continent. The diversionary invasion forces are designed with enough heavy metal to protect about 2 divisions and a couple of brigades each of around 70,000 assault troops to force us to spread our fleets in those directions thus making us the unprotected back door for them to sneak through. An unprotected back door as you can see, and hence their reason for a virtually unprotected invasion force.

As far as we who are based here in the gulf of Carpentaria is concerned there will be some 90 to 110 troop ships carrying, according to the intelligence boys, 4 divisions for the main prong, with around 2 Brigades for each of the outer prongs, totalling approx 120,000 men, or in other words almost half an entire army. If these do get ashore to establish a good beachhead, then you can rest assured at least the equivalent of a full army will be

183

sent in after them." Harley explained, which drew a gasp from the audience, before giving his opinion and his explanation as to why the unprotected invasion fleet.

"Our enemy has become complacent, over confident and arrogant in their attitude towards us and the Americans, with what we label 'victory sickness'. They have the superiority in ship numbers this side of the Pacific who can more or less please themselves, as indeed their so far 'air superiority' over us. Therefore its not surprising that they think they can annihilate or conquer anything thrown at them with their belief of being invincible. The thing is men, they already know that the northern coastline is virtually unprotected with only 3 clapped out, battered cruisers in these waters to offer any token of resistance. Also the fact that almost a third of the Australian population have taken up arms, but were sent over to defend the United Kingdom against the Axis forces, with terrible losses defending Malaya, Borneo, and the Dutch East Indies. As mentioned, they have the attitude that we British and our Allies of course, have been beaten virtually out of sight, especially taking the Battle of the Java Sea and Banda Sea into consideration. Your captains will be briefed as to the tactics I intend to use, but I hope that all goes well with you. This will be Australia's finest hours that will go down in the history books as 'THE BATTLE OF OZ!'" Harley stated, receiving a rapturous applause from the attack teams, who were suitably stirred to do whatever was necessary to stop the murdering Japanese troops from landing on the shores of this island continent.

"Our Ace trump card if you like, which will produce the biggest surprise for them, is that as stated earlier, they still do not know of our base here. So it's up to your expertise in helping your captains to prevent even just one Japanese soldier landing on our shores. Our squadron of just 6 boats will be the weapon to slay these Japanese invaders, and by God make every torpedo count. In doing so you will have lived up to and kept the tradition of being a British Submariner, sweaty and smelly bodies, hairy arses, warts and all. In the meanwhile enjoy the last few hours you have to make peace with your consciences and hope that we all can come out of this alive to tell this story to our future generations." Harley concluded, receiving a roar of approval from the teams, with their respective skippers looking on with pride towards their men.

T.S. and the rest of his fellow attack team members arrived back on board into the hectic preparations of storing for war. Each boat had a Torpedo Loading vessel hoisting torpedoes by their belly bands onto them, they disappeared first down the for'ard torpedo loading hatch then the after one, like putting bullets into the magazine of a gun. Each boat had a fuel lighter alongside transferring the diesel, then when they left they were replaced by ammo barges loading up with 4 inch rounds and machine gun bullets. When the TLVs left, the depot ship cranes were used to send food and other stores down through the fore hatches.

He found himself on the bridge, looking around at the base, saw a procession of FPBs coming alongside the ammo jetty to load up their 18 inch torpedoes as opposed to his boat's 21 inch, taking on board several tons of ammo, before moving over to the fuel jetty to take on board their petrol as opposed to the boat's diesel. He also saw that the GNATs were making shuttle runs in and out of the base, loading up with yet another net full of 'real' mines to take from the ammo jetty to the FMLs who were already out in the Gulf to laying them. Then completed their task by taxiing alongside the fuel jetty to take on board their avgas (aviation fuel). Thus at around 1700 on a warm Friday afternoon, the boat and FPB squadrons were loaded up and fully stored for war before it all came to an end and a loud silence fell over the base as everybody went to prepare themselves for the onslaught of acting as butchers to several thousand Japanese troops.

"Good enough for the bastards." was the consensus of opinion of every service person there, except a few religious nuts going around the village and the camps with placards declaring that 'The end of the world was nigh', until the Shore Patrol got

hold of them massaging their heads with oversized truncheons
before taking them away to be locked up.

Chapter III

The Trap

"Boat ready for sea! We have 2 extra gunners and a War correspondent complete with his camera on board, with the changes entered into the N.O.K. book which has just been handed ashore, sir!" Welling reported, as Hosie arrived onto the bridge.

"Very good No1. Obey the helm and telegraphs. Single up! We won't be piping the side this time Signalman." Hosie ordered, then issued helm and telegraph orders, shouting over the side with instructions to the casing party.

It was part of T.S.'s duty to look over the side and observe white water coming from the propellers as the boat moved astern through it, then report it to the captain as an aid for him to continue his manoeuvre of casting off. Once the captain had his vessel free and clear from the berth and in position to use his main engines, he stopped using his battery power.

"In both engine clutches!" he ordered, waiting a few moments for them to be engaged.

"Okay No1. Let's go and do our duty. Starboard 10 slow ahead together." Hosie said evenly then turned to wave his cap at the shore party as a parting wave from him and his crew.

T.S. looked up at the full moon in a cloudless sky, then at his watch to note that it was only 0100 in the morning and they had only a few hours to get into their allocated position. He looked astern to see there was that 'daisy chain' again, formed by the other 5 boats snaking their way through the boom defence system to pass the now very empty beaches of the cove before entering the open waters of the Gulf.

He scanned the horizon slowly to see if he could spot a light or detect a movement on the water or even in the air, as did Guard on the other side.

"All seems quiet, nothing sighted sir!" both lookouts reported, which satisfied Hosie who went below leaving Welling and the lookouts to themselves.

"Do you know those extra gunners Dave? Are they the ones to operate that swivel gun on the after casing?" T.S. whispered as if not to break the silence on the bridge.

"No! All I know so far is that one is a volunteer from the Marines, the other a diver just like Roy Ward. They'll be manning the gun tucked into the back of the fin. Dave Banks did a good job of welding to provide an access hatch at the back end of the fin to house the gun. Let's hope it's fully seaworthy, as I don't fancy firing a gun with its barrels loaded up with fish or seaweed, for it will give you a nasty headache if it blows up in your face." Guard, the starboard lookout replied

"Hmmm! Presumably that's for any future gun actions. Which means that my little machine guns are now not required. Oh well, less for me to tote up the ladder onto the bridge." T.S. breathed.

"No such luck! It just means we have extra firepower we needed the last time we had a gun action. You were bloody lucky we stuck a 4 inch shell in their mush otherwise you'd be playing merrily with your woofters guitar long before now."

"Oy! I was zeroed into those bastards." T.S. argued.

"Silence on the bridge you two. You're supposed to be lookouts not apple women gossiping over the garden fence." Welling ordered then got relieved by the next OOW

"Morning sir!" T.S. greeted.

"Morning signalman. Anything in sight?" Hoare asked, taking time to get his night vision sorted.

"All quiet, nothing in sight, not even a ruddy shite hawk, sir." he reported, then asked a leading question to try and get some info from him.

"How did your pep talk go sir?"

"Very well actually. Once we get to our area we can settle down to wait for our guests to arrive. It should be a piece of cake, as long as we keep our heads and out of trouble." Hoare said quietly.

"We've been told of the basic plan but how far are we going down the gulf. Erm, how far to our allocated spot sir."

"The length of the gulf is approx 420 miles from our base to the bottom, with approx the same across, designated as 'the range'. We'll be about a third of the way down range."

T.S. asked a few more leading questions making Hoare chuckle at T.S.'s probing questions, but merely stated that they would be transiting to their position, arriving in time for breakfast.

"Let's hope the skipper, er, the captain I mean, lets us brush our teeth and comb our hair before we dive. We must make ourselves presentable for our guests and all that sir!"

"Yes quite Signalman." Hoare responded with another chuckle at the typical British indomitable spirit.

"Permission to come onto the bridge sir" Morgan asked, handing T.S. his little bucket to climb up onto the deck.

"Yes Morgan. Incidentally, how did you resolve our flashing periscopes?"

"Easy sir. I made little eyepieces to fit over the lower end to stop any light shining up through when there're no eyeballs in the way. Then I stuck some tinted glass over these top windows, so now the captain's got his very own long-range sunglasses to use. I'm here to make sure the windows are clean and that the glasses are still in position. The thing is sir, the captain won't be able to see very clearly at night with the tinted glasses unless he switches to high power. He understands and is quite happy about it." Morgan stated, and carried on cleaning the periscope lens, asking permission to leave when he was finished

"I've just been relieved sir, permission to go below as well?" T.S. said shortly, handing a pair of binoculars over to his relief, as only he and the captain had personal ones that were more powerful than the ordinary run-of-the-mill Barr & Stroud issue.

"OOW – Captain! Clear the bridge and dive the boat."

"Aye aye sir!" was the instant report. Within seconds the

189

harsh, raucous noise of the klaxon sounded twice for the crew to galvanise themselves into action and have the boat sink safely beneath the waves.

Hosie looked through the main periscope to see the sea was like a millpond, with a few wisps of sea -mist swirling around, yet nothing in site for him to feel satisfied everything up top was quiet and nothing to disturb them.

"W/T – Captain. Are you finished with your schedule yet?"

"Not yet sir! Several signals coming through via the broadcast, and one from FOGGY sir." Lewis reported, getting a smile from Hosie at the nickname for the F.O.G. was stuck with and even used by the Admiral who himself was given the odd name of 'Spam'.

"Very good. Let me know then lower the whip aerial. Radar! Raise your aerial then make a 2 minute sweep with a vector of 45 degrees from the ship's head."

"Aye aye sir!" came the response from both offices.

"No1. It's sunrise up top now. Once the wireless office lowers their mast, take us down for a bathy. We've got 300 feet to play with so no lower than 280 in case we're over a small sea mount. I'm going to the wireless office." Hosie ordered smoothly

"Aye aye sir!"

"What have you got for us Lewis?" Hosie asked, sitting down next to the P.O.Tel.

"Just received 2 flash signals, but have 2 'Ops, 3 'Priorities' from F.O.N.A.C. and 1 Ops signal from FOGGY sir. Boyall here is deciphering the 'P's and I've just finished with the 'O's. But here are the 2 'flash signals." Lewis stated, handing over the signals for Hosie to read.

"Hmmm! Have you got our diving signal off yet?"

"On 4340kc's as normal sir, and we're lowering the mast now."

"It appears that there's a scouting party of minesweepers way ahead of the main invasion forces, which means that we're all to keep our heads down when the F.A.A. come to deal with them. The other one states that the enemy is about to enter the gulf, some 2 hours ahead of what we were expecting. Also that the Japs have added more protection to their invasion force than previously reported. That'll be your last transmission for a while Lewis, but keep a listening watch every time we come up to periscope depth. It seems as if our guests are proving once more that they are unpredictable and can't be relied upon to stick to their plans or etiquette for visiting the neighbours." Hosie commented, scanning through the other signals as they came available to him.

"Okay then Lewis, when Boyall is finished bring the signals to me." Hosie concluded and went the few feet back into the control room again.

"How's the trim No1? Must have a decent trim before we hit the basement floor." Hosie asked, rubbing his hands as if in a good mood.

"Bit heavy overall sir, but more so for'ard, with a 2 degree after bubble."

"Yes, we've got a full load of fish and extra ammo for'ard. Pump out the bilges and sanitary tanks then flood 200 gallons aft, that should do the trick." Hosie ordered, watching as the bubble on the after planes spirit level evened itself to adopt that crucial 'zero bubble' which meant that the boat was level with both ends balancing from the middle like a see-saw.

"Stream the bathy! Take us down to 280 feet. Radar! Make your report!" Hosie commanded softly, watching the depth gauge pointer take them down to the ordered depth.

"1 air contact, range 18,000 yards, was joined by 2 more before the first one disappeared. Perhaps it was a Jap recce plane being shot down by the RAAF. Also a line of 6 surface contacts appeared on the outer range of 20,000 yards." Hemmings reported.

"Sonar! Any contacts?"

"Just one faint one astern of us. Suggest a fishing boat. And some faint ones ahead some way off. P.O Woods suggests the noises come from minesweepers, sir!"

"Hmm! Probably those minesweepers mentioned on the

191

signal. Take us back up to periscope depth No1. I want to see what it is coming our way, considering our guests were not due to arrive for another few hours or so."

"Aye aye sir!"

The boat came back to periscope depth for Hosie to check on those radar and sonar contacts to discover that there were several F.A.A's Fairey Bombers winging their way to intercept those minesweepers.

"Tell sonar there will be lots of bangs and underwater explosions very soon but not to worry. Those contacts P.O. Woods spoke about are the enemy minesweeper about to be blown to bits by our Hairy Fairy's." Hosie ordered with a grin, leaving the periscope to go over to the chart table.

The muffled noise created by the bombers on their targets reached them a few moments later to prove what their captain had just told them.

"Just clearing the decks and getting rid of the spies in the closet No1. It seems as if FONAC wants our guests to have the red carpet down for them, so we can shut up shop for a while." Hosie grinned.

"Take us down to the bottom very slowly after 280 feet. Down periscope. Stop together. We'll remain in position on the bottom, then go to 'Silent Routine'."

Welling reported each 10 feet down until the 280 mark then counted out the depth every 5 feet until there was a slight bump letting everybody know they'd reached the seabed, with the depth gauge stopped at 305 feet.

"Not bad No1. You'll make a good C.O. one day." Hosie said with a smile.

"Silent routine. Get the galley to rustle up sarnies for later as it's going to be a very long day ahead of us. Switch off all unnecessary lighting. Go to a reduced 'Watch dived'. Open the lower lid and rig the ladder, I'll be in my cabin if you need me." Hosie said quietly and waited for the vertical ladder to be rigged, then climbed up into his little specially built cabin just above the control room.

"We only have about 4 hours now to rest up No1 so make the most of it. Carry on!" Hosie stated before disappearing up unto his cabin.

Before T.S. also left the control room, he looked at the chart and noticed that each boat's position had been plotted in a funnel shape with S64 at the bottom just as Harry Harley had ordered, then at the arrow shaped formation the Japanese invasion force had formed, again as had been predicted.

The distance from the outermost boat forming the funnel was no more that 20,000 yards which made him think of how close together those troop ships must be, and just how the skipper was able to get in between two ships to sink them without being run over.

"Very interesting, but the trap is now set." he mumbled, then went for'ard to his mess to have a cup of tea and relax in his bunk for a while.

Chapter IV

Trap Shut!

T.S. was sitting in the cool, quiet, dimly lit control room on his
duty of being the control room logger cum messenger, but as
it was quiet he was reading through the Japanese Naval section of
his book of fighting ships, which gave the details and profiles to
assist him in 'ships recognition'. He was refreshing his memory
of the different enemy warships that may be coming his way,
especially from the battleship and cruiser section, as he knew
there would be no Jap boats, only British.

Brawn poked his head up from the aperture of the AMS
(auxiliary machine space) and whispering loudly to him.

"Do us a favour and get Slinger Woods down here, I think
we've got the company of a herd of elephants coming our way
judging by the faint asdic transmissions ahead of us."

"On my way Dave!" T.S. responded and went to fetch Woods,
who after a few moments came back up from the sonar room
and 'knocking' on the wardroom curtain acting as the door, spoke
to Hoare.

"Sir we've got several sonar transmissions coming from R10
to Green 10, with several cavitations intermingled with them.
One heavy one in particular that is on our reciprocal course."

Within moments Hoare went up into the conning tower to
Hosie's cabin to make the report, then both came down the
ladder hurriedly.

"Go to diving stations. Remain in silent routine." Hosie
ordered.

T.S. went to the wireless office, and stowing his book away
told Underwood, the on watch Sparker what had happened.

"The shit is about to hit the fan, better tell Chris and then
POTS before we hit the roof." Underwood suggested.

Within minutes, the control room was full of bodies again,
closed up at their 'diving station' with the 'Amp Tramps' standing

by to make with their 'white man's magic' by getting the motors running and lift them off the seabed to rise up back to the roof again.

"No1! Take us up to periscope depth. Radar, stand by for a 1minute sweep. Sonar! What news of that contact on our reciprocal course?" Hosie whispered aloud.

The boat rose up gently and quietly to periscope depth so Hosie could take a look around him and for the radar mast to spin around taking a screen picture of what was coming their way.

"Captain – W/T! Just received a flash signal. It says that the enemy is in a box 10 nautical miles wide by 14 nautical miles long, and is now consisting of 115 ships, and seemingly much heavily armed, now estimated to be 100 miles down range. Be in position. The code-words of TRAP SHUT, and BADDIES have been used, sir." Lewis reported on entering the control room.

"Very good Lewis! Radar make your report!" Hosie chuckled at the choice of code words.

"There is a 'V' formation of ships in front of the first Japanese wave, range 10,000 yards. The first main wave range is 16,000 yards, the next on 20,000, but can't see the 3^{rd,} one, probably off screen and on it's way sir. There are a few contacts that appear to be stationary, suggest fishing vessels sir. We have marked all contacts along with the Jap forces matrix onto the screen, they are being transferred onto tracing paper ready for plotting, sir!" Hemmings said, poking his head out through the door of his little radar office.

Hosie scanned all around him to see and identify a couple of fishing boats each side of him, yet some distance away for him to comment on them.

"We are the 'BADDIES', and they're our ploy boys, acting as innocent fishermen. They've got pretend radar on board to mask any of our transmissions. They will report the enemy fleet's exact composition and progress, also to give us a marker as to how far down range they have reached. Which means that we have about

45 minutes before contact. Get A/B North to set up the attack screen with all ships positions clearly marked, and make another one onto the chart. No1. It looks as if we've got a long day at the office today, so have the galley provide sandwiches and a hot drink for us, with everything stowed securely away in 20 minutes, then go to action stations. Remain in silent routine." He added, still scanning the world above him.

Soon the pings of the enemy active sonar arrays became louder, seeming to cut through the ever-increasing roar of ships propeller cavitations and other noises, which escape through metal out into the 'amplifying' nature of the water.

Hosie went over to the chart and started to examine the trace reading of the bathy dip to find out the best depth, but more importantly the thickest thermal layer for him to hide under and from the probing sonar transmissions.

"There's a screen of 3 destroyers ahead of the first wave. Keep 150 feet. Stop together." He ordered quietly.

'Inng doch! Inng doch! (as in loch) Ping doooch. Ping doooch!' Came the sound of the various sonar pulses, until the sound of a fast pinga li li li li li ling noise was heard, which meant that the sonar transmission had struck the thermals but not detected the boat hiding under it, otherwise it would sound a distinctive 'Inng Chii'.

This was the time for the crew to eat their sandwiches and drink their tea in peace as they heard the roar of the destroyers pass over them until they faded away.

They knew that the heavy cavitation that seemed to drown all the other lesser ones, was getting ever nearer, and closer to the time for when 'England expects every man will do his duty, and God help Australia to be saved from the murderous hordes that were about to descend upon them.'

Chapter V

The 'DEAD' Sea

"**A**ttack teams close up, remain in silent routine. Group up slow ahead together. Come to periscope depth then keep 52 feet. Stand by to give a 1minute sweep from the radar. Up after periscope!" Hosie ordered, having his periscope raised so that he could see the instant it broke the surface of the water. The radar dish spun quickly before disappearing below the waves again, and waited for Hemmings to make his report.

"Got the full matrix of the enemy invasion force now sir. The bigger the trace the bigger the ship." Hemmings reported, handing the tracing over for Hosie to look at.

"Well well well! Not only have they gone and given us a nice clear aisleway right down the middle behind this large ship, presumably their carrier, and one between the flanking prongs, they've also spaced themselves a good 1,000 yards in line astern. We can't do much with the 500 yards separation in line abreast though. Hmmm! That gives me an idea." Hosie said in amazement, striding over to the chart table to lay the tracing over the neat matrix Bell had plotted onto the special chart he had stuck down next to the main sea chart then confirmed his last remark.

"The outer prongs have a column of 2 ships 500 yards apart, keeping 1,000 yards in line astern, which means that any one wishing to swerve out of the way from the one in front would collide with the next one over. More importantly we've got a 3000 yard separation from the lead ship, which presumably is the battleship, and the carrier astern of her. Maybe to give her aircraft take-off clearance room!" he said with glee, rubbing his hands together.

"Thank God for radar! Our sonar boys are having their ears bashed by all that infernal racket to make them virtually useless." Hosie said to nobody in particular.

"Right then men! This is the day we've all been training for. We've come all this way out here to do just this, and give the Japs a dose of Admiralty Mark 12 torpedoes.. So be on your toes, pay attention to detail and with luck we'll all come out of it alive. Good luck men!" Hosie announced over the internal tannoy sytem, knowing full well the noise from the Japanese ships would drown his transmission from the sonar screening escorts.

"Start the attack! Here comes the BADDIES! Up for'ard periscope and stand by to read off!" he said quickly, clapping his hands as if to entice the attack teams to sharpen up.

The adrenalin was now flowing rapidly through the veins of each man, as they geared themselves up mentally for what was about to take place.

"Battleship that looks like an Asahi class, bearing that! Range from her bridge to the waterline in full power is .. that! An escort carrier astern of it, looks like a Fuji class, bearing that... Range from flight deck to waterline... that! Down periscope! Full ahead together, Starboard 10, steer 320." Hosie directed.

T.S. read out the bearings and the ranges, but Hosie looked at the Perspex screen to check his own bearings relative to the targets he had been commanded to attack. He knew that he had the first strike at the enemy fleet, starting the ball rolling to commence an all out attack on the enemy by all the forces at the command of F.O.N.A.C, not forgetting FOGGY, such as they were.

Due to the combined forces of the British, Australian and Dutch fleets, FOGGY nicknamed them the 'BADDIES'

The ambush set by the boats would be Phase 1to start off the attack. The MGBs and the fishing fleet would be taking care of the survivors (making sure none got ashore alive) the MTBs and the Swordfish to chase after any fleeing ship trying to get away. They would carry out their last order by ensuring no Japanese ships or troops got out of the Gulf alive. This then what is called unrestricted warfare with no quarter given.

"T.O! I'm 10 degrees on his starboard bow and will be coming onto his reciprocal course.

"Have you got your book Signalman? Find out the exact details for an ASAHI class battleship, I want to know what hull armament she's got. Look for two triple barrelled 15inch gun turrets and what looks like a twin 6inch turret for'ard and 1 triple barrelled 15 inch and a 6inch twin gun turret aft. She's got what looks like a square bridge with a round tower on a main mast just abaft of her bridge" Hosie described swiftly.

"Yes sir! She's an old ship of 39,000 tons with a speed of only 25 knots. Her length is 700 feet, and a beam of 90 feet. Her hull is a solid cast moulding made out of 6 inches of steel, with a further 12 inch girdle from the waterline right down to her bilge keels sir. Her draught is 30 feet, triple screwed with a 5 blade 8 foot diameter propellers, with twin rudders only 3 feet up from her keel. In fact she has deck armour of 10 inches with 14 inches on her guns and around her bridge and control tower sir." T.S. reported, showing Hosie the picture and the details so he could confirm what he saw.

"Yes, that's her. She's going to take some stopping let alone sinking. You'd need a bloody great sledgehammer to crack open that nut. No wonder she was chosen for this job." Hosie opined, stroking his chin, looking at 'Asahi profile and pictorial drawings of her for a moment.

"Ahah! It seems as I've just found her 'Achillies heel', Pilot! Look, the only 'soft target on her are her propellers and rudders that stick out of the thick armour plating!" Hosie exclaimed, and showed Bell the area on the drawings, then added.

"Okay that's that, now plot the invasion fleet's positional matrix, then get T.S. to check out the aircraft carrier and give a description of the screen destroyers."

"The carrier is one of their new fleet carriers, bristling with guns but only 2 inches of steel hull, with 5 propellers, 3 rudders, top speed of 30 knots. She is 650 feet long, with a beam of 90 feet, draught of 28 feet and capable of carrying 120 aircraft." T.S. reported then started to report on the destroyers but was told to stop, yet thanked for his information.

Hosie looked at his watch then ordered the for'ard periscope raised again for another look at his intended targets.

Hosie had ducked under the escorts, lining himself up for his kill, but blurted out the fact that the planned tactics of Cdr S/M would be almost useless against the mountain of metal that was coming directly at him.

"Sonar! The battleship is my first target and I need you to try and track her course and speed." Hosie ordered then looked over to the plastic screen, which told him exactly what the up to the second 'state of play' was.

"T.O. I want all tubes set up in the following order. Set the for'ard tubes 4, 5 & 6 to a depth of 20 feet, the remainder at 8 feet. Set stern tubes 7 & 9 to a depth of 20 feet, then 8&10 on a depth of 25 feet   Set stern tube ranges to 1000 yards, with the for'ard ones at 1800."

"Aye aye sir!"

"Up periscope! Stand by to read off!" Hosie ordered then took a second fix on the targets to gauge their speeds to see if they were on constant courses.

"She's coming at me nicely on our reciprocal course. Tell sonar to check the course and speed of the carrier." he stated before he had the periscope lowered, getting the reply from the sonar room.

"Both steady on course, speed approx 12 knots sir." Hoare reported.

Hosie looked at his watch again then ordered the for'ard periscope up again.

"Signalman, give me the range of the battle ship when I say 'now'."

T.S. needn't reply, merely took his magic ruler out ready to give an instant report.

"Now!"

"1700 yards"

"Down periscope! Flood 'Q' Full ahead together, go to 120 feet." He ordered quickly then gave a brief explanation to his attack team about what he was about to do, so everybody knew they were heading for a collision with a dirty great big battleship about to steamroller them.

"I intend ducking under the battleship, so tell the sonar room to put their earmuffs on and for everybody else stuff a fag end or whatever in their ears to protect them when the battleship passes over them. As soon as she's passed over us we'll return to periscope depth shooting both the battleship and the carrier in one go. The tactics I'm using are called, 'Up the kilt' for the battleship as I intend not to sink her but blow her propellers and rudders off her with our stern torpedoes to stop her, with a very dodgy shot against the carrier. So be at your sharpest until we get from under them."

The mental activity by Hosie was so phenomenal it would grace any decent modern computerised system. He had to calculate the combined closing speed of his boat and the target; the velocity rate of the torpedo and the time taken to hit the target; the turn and diving speed of the boat as it dived whilst turning away in evasive action; the rise and fall of the target going though the water so that he could hit it under any armour belts; the detonation and concussion on the boat; the time taken to line up his for'ard torpedoes and fire into the targets. The list was endless. This was one special tactic that only the bravest dared to take on.

Such a tactic was used by only one Submarine captain, who had developed it into a fine art for keeping him alive while lesser captains got themselves killed and their boats sunk by trying to emulate him.

That captain was none other than Hosie, while the tactic was called a 'DOWN THE THROAT' shot. Just one slip up, and the boat would be crushed to bits as the steamroller above them came right over where they had been only a mere few seconds earlier.

"Stop together! Blow 'Q'   Stand by to come back up to periscope depth No1."

201

The noise of the engines and the swishing of the battleship's propellers was almost ear splitting, as it passed only a few fathoms above them as Hosie judged the timing for him to be able to come up again without being chopped to pieces by the propellers of the battleship.

T.S. managed to hear him count down the seconds and saw that everybody was ready to anticipate their captain's next string of orders.

"Open bow and stern caps. Full ahead together, come to 52 feet. Stand by to read off." Hosie shouted over the receding noise of the battleships cavitations. Raise the for'ard periscope.

"T.O. When I give the ranges have all tube outer doors opened. I intend firing the after ones first before I let go with the for'ard ones."

Hosie waited until the water had cleared from his lens and gave a quick look at the stern of the battleship to make sure he was still 'in line' with it, before he turned his attention to the carrier.

"Range of battleship is... That!"

"1000 yards"

"Fire all stern tubes." Hosie commanded.

The *whump* noises coming from the after end told of each torpedo being fired as Hosie got his stop watch out to time the explosions.

He looked astern quickly to see that the rear of the battleship had lifted several feet out of the water in a loud explosion and smiled. Then turned his attention to his next victim.

"Carrier Range... that!"

"1400 yards"

"FLOOD 'Q' stand by to fire the for'ard tubes on my mark. Set 1300 yards"

"Keep me up No1. I want to see their eyes not their bollocks." Hosie shouted.

"Mark! Reverse your planes! Full ahead together. Starboard 20. Come round and steer 350. Take me down to 100 feet No1. I don't want to go below and not be able to come back up again with all these ships milling around the place!"

Hosie ordered in rapid-fire manner. He was in full control of his attack just like a Maestro conducting a full orchestra as they obeyed every nod, shake of his baton, expression of face and other nuances the Maestro would use to get the best sound from each professional musical instrument player.

Hosie waited until the boat shook 3 times but dared not wait to see what the outcome was, even though he knew exactly what it would be.

The attack team were quietly counting the seconds to impact, and were rewarded with an ear shattering explosion making the boat give such a lurch to starboard that the helmsman fell off his seat, and the rest grabbed onto whatever was nearest in case they too went flying across the control room deck.

The boat managed to right herself and Hosie calmed everybody down again then came back up to periscope depth again.

He looked out of the periscope calling several of the team including the news reporter John Lacey to look at the destruction they had caused.

The battleship was stopped dead in the water with smoke pouring out of her two funnels, whilst the carrier had capsized to starboard, shedding aircraft and bodies into the water like rain, before finally sinking rapidly into the water until disappearing onto the seabed.

"Well done team! We'll let the Baddies come along and take care of the battleship. We've got other fish to post all the way to Japan." Hosie said almost gloatingly.

"One all round, No1. There's nothing much we can do for the moment until we're fully loaded up again." Hosie said, but was interrupted by a report from Hoare.

"We cant hear much due to the explosions but we think there's a fast moving contact bearing green 5 range about 5,000 yards. 2 screws suggest destroyer with a nasty problem with her engines."

"Is there now! Probably an escort destroyer coming to pick up some survivors. Up for'ard periscope and stand by to read off!"

"Destroyer bearing... that! Range... that! Down periscope."

"Escort destroyer bearing right down on me. Stand by for'ard tubes 1&3"

"T.O. We're about 3 degrees on his starboard bow but he's coming straight at us. Set for'ard tubes 1 & 3 to 8 feet and the range of 1400 yards. Use a 2 degree angle each side of the bow. Open outer doors stand by to fire. Up periscope!"

"Range that...that 1400 yards!"

"Fire!" Hosie shouted over the noise filled control room.

Hosie looked at the oncoming destroyer steaming full speed towards him, all the while filling his periscope with the ship. He was about to conduct yet another textbook example of the very dangerous 'down the throat ' attack. Perhaps the only thing on the destroyer Captain's mind was to try and rescue as many of the several hundred bodies floating in the water from the sunken carrier as possible but what he got was two 12 foot Admiralty Mk 8 torpedoes, each filled with 600lbs of high explosives streaking at 30 knots towards him which blew the bows off his ship, so he too sank rapidly to join the carrier.

He kept his periscope up to observe the sinking and commented on what else he saw.

"It looks like our counterparts have succeeded in sinking the other two cruisers which you've probably heard through all the noise. Yet look at the bloody Jap ship! They're still coming on like lemmings about to jump off a cliff. It's as if nothing has happened and they're prepared to press on despite having their heavy mob destroyed right in front of them." He said with astonishment.

"According to one of our passengers, they've got a death wish attitude and shout 'BANZAI' or is it 'TORA TORA TORA' Some historians liken it to our 'Charge of the Light Brigade'. But they'd rather die in trying to press home their attack than retreat." Welling stated, and took up the invitation from Hosie for him to look through the periscope.

"In other words, we can look forward to a heavy cull today. Better make sure we don't waste a shot, as there's hundreds of them coming our way." Hosie grunted, taking charge of the periscope once more.

Hosie had observed enough to decide that he was able to relax his team for a little while.

He knew his boat was in a clear lane that the Japanese kept as a separation or a safety buffer zone, so kept there stopped, waiting for his torpedo team to load up again.

"Now we can have one all round No1. How are the men fore and aft T.O! Loaded up yet?"

Hosie asked, looking at the control room clock.

"Both fore and after tube space bilges are flooded. But almost complete aft sir!"

"Good work. You heard the man No1. Have both torpedo space bilges pumped dry and keep them that way. It might do our trim a bit of good anyway."

"Aye aye sir!'"

"Steward! Get hold of one of the chefs to provide a mug of tea and a sarnie for the attack team!" Hosie ordered, as Brown who was the attack team's messenger and enjoying a cigarette along with the rest of them.

"Aye aye sir!"

Soon Brown was handing out the officers their 'quartered sandwiches with their crusts removed and a pyrex cup of tea to drink from, whereas Gourdie the 'Baby Chef' gave out thick wedges pretending to be sarnies and enamel mugs of tea for the rest of them. Once scoffed with the cups and other debris removed from the control room and another 'one all round' fag, everybody felt renewed and raring to get at the next target.

Although the attack team had been closed up for nearly 3 hours, it took less than 20 minutes for Hosie to stop a battleship, sink a carrier and a destroyer, yet he still have 20 more torpedoes to sell to the Japs.

Hosie had managed to emulate a very famous German Uboat

Commander who at the start of WW1 had sunk 3 British cruisers from the Harwich Cruiser Squadron off the coast of England in 30 minutes. Naming HMS *Hogue*, *Hotspur* and *Aboukir* being the trio.

"All tubes reloaded and ready to fire sir!" T.O. reported.

"Group up! Slow ahead together. Steer 350. Up periscope! "

"Ship bearing ... that, range ... that!" he stated several times as he spun around with his periscope, while T.S reported the bearings and ranges.

"T.O! Set a sequence of firing both fore and aft. Set all torpedo depths to 10 feet unless otherwise ordered. Tubes 1 &7 range of 1500yards; 2&8 on 1200 yards; 3&9 on 1,000 yards; 4 & 10 on 1200yards and 5 on 1500yards. I'm keeping tube 6 for emergency but set depth for 8 feet!"

"Aye aye sir!"

Hosie looked at his watch then at the Perspex board for a moment, watching each bearing and ranges he took being plotted onto it.

"Port 10! Helmsman! I want you to report each bearing on each 5 degrees! T.O. I am about to conduct a little known tactic called 'The Cartwheel'. So stand by to fire 1&7 then so on with the sequence given, but on my mark. Have the ballast pump ready to drain the fore and after ends bilges otherwise they'll get flooded when they start draining down for the reload."

Hosie directed yet remained almost glued to the eyepieces of the for'ard periscope.

"350." the helmsman reported

"Mark!" Hosie ordered.•

• Imagine the boat being the hands on a clock, with the bows acting as the minute hand, and the stern the hour hand. Once the bows point to the 11 and the stern to 5, the torpedoes from each end are fired. Then pointed towards 10 and 4 and so on until it is 6 and 12 and they reach their reciprocal course for them to reload and start again The tactic is known as the 'Cartwheel' and needs precise angles and timing to have each torpedo reach its target.

"330"

"Mark!"

Hosie fired his fore and aft tubes in order as each troopship came onto the angle he was about to fire on. Thus within 5 minutes, he had fired 9 torpedoes into the columns of the oncoming troopships, knowing full well that he couldn't miss as if one torpedo was too deep for the intended target it would strike one on the other side of it. Before he completed his 'cartwheel' manoeuvre he saw that each torpedo had hit its target, as the ships blew up starting to sink, shedding several hundred more troops into the water.

Each time the torpedoes were fired the boat quivered as usual, which was virtually unnoticed among the bangs and other underwater disturbances created by the rest of the boats in the squadron who were doing their bit to sink as many enemy ships as possible within their time limit and before the next phase of the attack took place.

With complete satisfaction he observed the troops on those ships throwing Carley floats and other life rafts overboard before jumping overboard like lemmings, as not many of his victims were able to launch lifeboats in time. Yet again he had Lacey the newsman take pictures of the destruction and carnage, adding to the others he had taken since coming aboard, especially on the aftermath of each successful attack.

"2 assault ships and 7 troopships equates to over 9,500 men captain. Will you stop and pick some of them up in accordance with your hymn' For those in peril on the sea'? " Lacey asked when he was finally satisfied with his camera shots.

"Come on now, er, John! I'm in the middle of a war not on a cruise ship swanning around the place. Besides, where do you suppose I'd put them all? Start by offering your lap to sit on for a Jap armed with a machine gun in his hands, maybe?" Hosie replied with anger.

"Geneva convention and all that captain!" Lacey retorted, not to be outdone.

"Just report what you see and forget all that fancy crap! If it makes you feel better, there's a fleet of fishermen and patrol boats out there waiting to see to them. My job is to sink enemy ships not wipe their arses! Lower the after periscope." Hosie snorted then had the after periscope lowered so Lacey couldn't film anymore.

"Midships. What's our ships' head?"

"150 sir!" the helmsman reported.

"Group up full ahead together. Steer 145." Hosie ordered, explaining to the N.O. that he had turned 180 degrees and that he was going back down to the battleship.

"T.O. Let me know when I've got at least 1 stern tube loaded and 2 for'ard! I need them in case of emergency."

"Aye aye sir!"

Hosie took his boat down range to almost astern of the battleship to see that it was stopped, with a slight angle downwards at her stern, yet quite operable as witnessed by the smoke coming from her for'ard main armament.

He also saw an escort destroyer almost alongside, guessing that as the Japanese Admiral's flag had been lowered, he was transferring it to the destroyer to be able to direct the fleet from there.

"T.O.! Stand by to fire tube 6. Make range 800yards and depth of 8 feet. Signalman standby to read off the range in high power!"

Hosie made a quick all round sweep with his periscope to make sure there were no other ships coming his way.

"We have a destroyer almost alongside the battleship. Presumably come to transfer the Admiral and his flag. If he thinks that, then he'd got another think coming. He has to remain on his battleship and be isolated from any would be rescuers. We'll give them 'Unconditional Surrender' by damn. At least that's the plan. Range is.. that!"

"900 yards."

"Okay that'll do! Fire no 6 tube!" Hosie ordered, watching his last remaining torpedo speed on its way and hit the stern of the destroyer, making it sink rapidly from her stern.

"Up your kilt too! Now let's see how well the Jap navy can swim. Stop together. Take me down to 120 feet No1. I intend hiding under the battleship for safety and a bit of peace for us to reload again. That way no Jap depth charges can be thrown our way for fear of hitting their own ship." Hosie chortled, rubbing his hands gleefully again.

"Slow ahead Port. Steer 146." Hosie said, counting the time it took for his boat to get under the large floating chunk of Japanese steel. When he was satisfied, he ordered the boat to stop and remain at 120 feet.

"We have the time it takes for the fore and after ends to reload No1. One all round!" Hosie enthused then lit a cigarette in company with the rest of the control room crew.

The silent routine had been discarded due to all the bangs and noises coming from the sinking ships all around them, allowing Hosie to relax his men until the report came from the fore and after torpedo spaces that all were loaded and ready to fire again.

"It's getting a bit thick down here No1. Run the Co2 absorption unit for 30 minutes and burn 2 oxygen candles. Secure when done."

"Aye aye sir"

Stoker Williams was detailed off from the engine room and went through the control room into the accommodation space to the 'Sailors mess' and removed the covering that housed the 'abortion' unit.

"Do us a favour Signalman, and get me 4 cannisters from the rack just behind the fore ends water tight door way."

"Four John? That'll suck up what atmosphere we've got, good and proper. Better run the oxygen candles at the same time or Red the Wrecker'll have to bleed some of the B.I.B.S• for a while. That will mean extra pressure in the boat as well."

• Built In Breathing System, used for when escaping from a flooded compartment.

"Hmmm! No harm speaking in a Donald Duck voice for a while, but I'd better check up with the OOW." Williams muttered, starting up the electrically operated unit.

Soon the fuggy atmosphere was rejuvenated by the removal of most of the CO_2 and the crew could breathe much easier as the oxygen was wafted around the boat through her ventilation system.

"All tubes loaded fore and aft sir!" Sample reported.

"Slow ahead together! " Hosie breathed, and waited for a few minutes to judge if his boat had moved ahead of the battleship so he could come to periscope depth again.

To his surprise, his periscope popped up between the bows of the battleship and the stern of 2 escort destroyers starting to tow the battleship. A close explosion on their starboard for'ard side surprised the team and Hosie guessed that it was an incoming shell from one of the cruisers. Followed by another salvo that hit the starboard escort making it stagger from the multiple explosions, instantly wrecking a perfectly good ship into the bargain, solving the problem for Hosie as to which destroyer he'd sink first.

"Open outer door of tube 2. Make target range 500 yards, set depth to 10 feet and stand by to fire."

"Aye aye sir"

Hosie looked astern at the massive bows of the battleship that was slowly catching up on him, and managed to see a salvo of shells hit her for'ard gun turret, but that the shells merely bounced off it and ricocheted into the lower bridge, still with no damage to the battleship.

"Bloody hell T.S. was right! She's better than any modern battleships, and still a wonder as to how she floats with all that armour on her." He was heard to state before swiftly turning around to check his intended target.

"Fire tube 2! Port 20! Flood 'Q' Full ahead together. 200 feet!" he barked, then just before the periscope disappeared under the water, he managed to see his torpedo hit hard to sink the destroyer by her now missing stern.

"Let's get the hell out from under that lot No1and make our way up range again. We've still got 9 more fish to sell, lets do it." He said, and listened to the changes of depth being sounded out. When he was happy that the boat had corkscrewed her way out of danger he decided to get back up again so that he could see instead of trying to listen for any 'live' contacts that would come thundering through the noises of sinking ships.

"Steer 050. Keep 50 feet No1! We've been down for 8 hours now. What's the state of the batteries as we've been shaken and stirred quite violently these past few hours. In fact No1, get P.O.Harris to make a thorough check of both battery tanks."

"Aye aye sir!"

Harris came back shortly and made his report.

"We've picked up a 'sick cell' in battery No1.and a leaking one in battery 2. You have the option of giving a 'trickle charge through the first one and isolating the second one, or isolate both of them off. Either way sir, we need to have them replaced a.s.a.p."

"Very good Harris! Isolate both of them but make sure you've got rubber mats over the damaged cell in case they arc or damage adjacent ones."

"Aye aye sir." Harris responded, going aft through the engine room to the motor room to get his junior 'Amp Tramps' to get the job done.

Hosie kept at periscope depth and had Lacey photograph the sinking of Japanese ships all around him. Several ships had collided with the ones next to them, trying to get clear of the juggernaut that was still in one piece and seemingly determined to reach its landing areas.

"Captain – W/T! Flash from F.O.N.A.C. You have 1 hour to get out from under and well clear. Phase 3 has now commenced." This was the turn of the F.A.A. to come out to bomb and torpedo the main bulk of the invasion fleet, with the chance for the boats to finally snorkel or surface to get out of the area to recharge their batteries or to reload again.

Hosie saw a destroyer trying to pick up some of the hundreds of soldiers floating in the water, and decided that he'd have just one more attack before hitting the roof.

"T.O. Stand by tubes 1 & 2. I have an escort destroyer stopped virtually right in front of me. Range about 3,000 yards. Set range of 1500, depth of torpedo 8 feet."

"Aye aye sir!"

"Captain – Sonar! Picking up a fast moving multi-screwed contact bearing green 170. Suggest escort destroyer."

Hosie swung his periscope virtually 180 degrees to see what it was to discover that it was an MGB drawing the fire from the destroyer whilst an MTB following closely behind it, sneaking under the destroyers guns to make his attacking run to sink it.

"Stand down T.O. It looks as if we're about to be beaten to the punch, as one of our MTBs has just come into view from around one of the sinking ships to attack our target." Hosie grunted, and watched as the MTB. make a perfect two torpedo attack which struck the destroyer midships, sending it to join the other sinking vessels all around it. Both FPBs peeled off from the attack then sped away at a good 40 knots, leaving a large wake behind them that just seemed to reshuffle the hundreds of dead bodies floating in the water.

He looked for a large hole in the outer column and finding one, steered his boat through so as to 'get out from under'. He guessed that it would take a good 20 minutes to get out into the safety zone marked on their sea chart.

"Starboard 10 steer 010. No.1! I'm heading for our designated safety zone. I intend to come around to the back of the matrix of the Jap forces and head out towards the entrance of the gulf to catch any stricken vessels that are trying to escape. How far are we on dead reckoning to reach the zone?"

Bell took a few moments to arrive at his calculations before reporting.

"Roughly 20 minutes sir."

"Very good! No1, I intend surfacing when we reach our

safety point. So fall out attack team but go to 'Action stations Standby. We need some time for grub and get ourselves prepared to meet our public."

"Stand by to surface. OOW! We have a bit of a pressure in the boat. When you get up keep present course. Make a running charge and maintain a speed of 20 knots. Have the radar closed up and give a 5 minute sweep every 30."Hosie ordered.

"Aye aye Sir." Sample replied and climbed up the ladder with T.S. right behind him.

"Better hold on tight to my legs Signalman, or we'll be shot out of the boat and hit our heads on the conning tower deck-head."

T.S. already had items hanging around his neck to take up to the bridge, with one foot tucked under one of the ladder rungs and one hand gripping an upright, but managed to put an arm around Sample's legs as if in a rugby tackle, when Sample released the 2ⁿᵈ clip on the upper lid to open it fully.

The pressure built up in the boat was such that they had to hold on for a few seconds as a great puff of air passed over them They waited until it was over for T.S. to let go of Sample.

Both men scrambled up onto the bridge for Sample to start his O.O.W. duties, and T.S started scanning the horizon for any contacts that may be around..

"Bloody hell sir, that really was a big blow job! I got a belt around the ear from one of the binoculars." T.S. reported, wiping blood from his damaged ear.

"Yes, I hit my head on one of the clips." Sample commiserated, rubbing his sore head.

The boat was now on the surface, running full speed at an angle towards the 'back door' of the Gulf, recharging her batteries as she went along, and away from the ever-increasing carpet of dead and drowning enemy bodies that littered the sea.

The fresh air filling the boat was almost like nectar to the lungs of the crew as the hot and stuffy conditions were reversed as the a.c.u's took over giving them some relief from the heat.

Soon it was time for the crew to have their first real meal of the day.

James issued the rum ration, whilst the Chefs dished up large helpings of 'Baby's Heads' (stewed steak pudding) with peas, spuds, and gravy, followed by figgy duff and custard and all washed down with a large mug of 'rosy lea'. Afterwards, the 2nd Cox'n was busy in the fore-ends ditching 'gash' from the gash ejector, with the boat getting a tidy up, ready for the next onslaught. Only then did the crew feel a little bit more 'civilised' and in a much happier mood.

All of which taken obliviously as to what was happening all around them, for they had 'done their duty' and were retiring from the fight for somebody else to take over.

T.S. was on the bridge looking through his powerful binoculars seeing nothing but bodies floating around patches of flotsam where their ship had been only moments ago.

The boat was a safe distance away, yet having a ringside seat to witness the slaughter and the piece meal sinking of the Japanese invasion fleet by the attacking bombers.

The sudden appearance out of the smoke by the 'Baddies' destroyers was cheered by those on the bridge as they watched them dashing around chasing the fleeing Japanese escort ships. Several of the Japanese ships were easily caught and seemingly with a vengeance were literally torn to pieces before they sunk beneath the waves and for them to leave the gunners on the scavenging fishing boats to 'mop up' the survivors.

"There's literally thousands of them sir. Look, there's one of our M.G.Bs firing into a raft of lifeboats." T.S. reported.

Hoare looked around at the mayhem the boats had created before he caught sight of the first wave of Fairey and Swordfish bombers come swooping down onto the hapless Japanese fleet.

"Judging y all the dead Jap bodies, the fish will have a good feed for yonks. But does that mean they'll be able to speak Japanese sir?" T.S. asked

Hoare chuckled at the idea but didn't have time to answer as Hosie came up onto the bridge with Lacey, who had his ever-present movie camera with him to witness the start of yet another onslaught on the ruthless enemy.

T.S. tapped the shoulder of the 'After Gunner' Dodds the starboard lookout, who was one of the spare gunners, and pointed to what the boat was about to steam through.

"Look at that carpet of floating corpses, Roy. There must be hundreds of them. Unless the tide takes them out of the gulf, the beaches are going to be littered with them."•

"Serves them right not learning how to swim!" Dodds breathed.

Looking ahead they saw hundreds of bobbing heads that were the troops and sailors who were still alive from the sunken ships, waving their arms at them to stop. A little way ahead the boat was heading straight towards a raft of Carley floats with several lifeboats lashed together.

"Bloody hell! Those life rafts had better shift themselves else we'll...." was all Dodds managed to say, before the boat ploughed right through the lot of them leaving nothing but a clear path behind them with only the boat's wake now to be seen. They heard many screams and pleas to be saved but did nothing, because not only did the bridge crew not understand Japanese, they felt a great satisfaction in the knowledge that many more Japs would not 'reach the shores alive'.

Hosie tricked Lacey into concentrating on the aerial assault by the F.A.A. whilst he got clear of the patch of human debris. By then it was too late for Lacey for notice it, to record what they had just done very deliberately too.

"Serves the bastards right!" Dodds snarled, spitting over the side towards them.

* * *

• See *The Body Hunters.*

Hosie managed to hear and see the gesture of his starboard lookout, and must have realised that Lacey would perhaps highlight that incident instead of what was taking place before their very eyes.

"I think you'd better get below now John! We're about to go back onto action stations again. We'll remain on the surface for gun actions against the enemy. So I'll see that you get a few shots then." Hosie said stiffly, and ushered Lacey back down into the control room.

"We'll take about 2hours to dodge the panic stricken ships steaming everywhere yet nowhere and to get up range, so keep a sharp lookout." He ordered.

"Aye aye sir!"

The boat took a curved course towards land to give a wide berth from the ongoing absolute carnage and destruction of the Japanese invasion fleet until T.S. spotted a fishing boat signalling to them

He read the signal before reporting it to Hoare who told him to reply.

"Fishing boat, green 45 sir! Says to call on 2megs channel Bravo. That means that he wants us to contact him on their frequency of, er, er, 2121 kc/s, if I remember correctly. That's the net frequency of the FPB's as well, sir."

"Captain OOW! Fishing boat approaching, wants to speak to us on radio. T.S. says try 2121 kc/s." Hoare reported.

"Very good! Am coming up!" came the response, for Hosie to re appear back onto the bridge.

"Tell him to close me for a shout!"

"Aye aye sir." T.S said whilst returning the incoming message.

"Captain – W/T. Fishing vessel *Maid of Carpentaria* is telling us to stop immediately as we're about to enter a fresh mine field."

"Stop together! Casing party on the casing with crash mats!" Hosie directed, as T.S. gave him a loud hailer to speak to the rapidly approaching fishing vessel, which eventually came right up to the boat and stop alongside her.

"Ahoy there! This is Captain David Davidge! Who is your Captain I need to speak to him?"

"Afternoon Captain. I'm Lt Cdr Hosie the Commanding Officer speaking. What is the panic?"

"G'day Capt! You have just entered a freshly sown minefield so unless your draught is less than 10 feet like mine, then I suggest you get the hell out of here." Davidge reported.

"How far up range does it stretch? Only I can't dive for fear of ships falling on top of me. Have you some sort of a grid or something for me to steer a safe course from?"

"Negative! This minefield has been laid for any Jap ship that might wish to come this way. So far 2 of them entered further up and both are now 200 feet below us. The only thing I can do is to pilot you out of the area, but you must be prepared to reverse just as quick as moving ahead. I have 4 Army gunners on board, two of them snipers. So we might just have to shoot and blow any mines that have floated back up to the surface again."

"We have a couple of machine guns on board, with loads of ammo. But after you! Lead the way Gungadin! We'll follow your wake."

There was a pause from Davidge before he asked if Hosie could lend him a spare machine gun and maybe a box of ammo to go with it.

"Well he ain't having my Lewis nor my Vickers guns, 'cause they're mine" T.S. muttered.

Hosie heard the muttered objections and smiled at T.S. for his protectionism.

"Not to worry Signalman. I'll give him the Bren gun and the rifle. I think we can spare a box of 303 rounds to go with them. Besides it's a small price to pay if it stops us from getting blown up by our own ruddy mines." Hosie breathed, before agreeing to send them over to Davidge.

Lacey appeared onto the bridge and asked if he could be transferred over to the fishing vessel so that he can have more time recording the battle that was raging in full view of them.

"Capt'n Davidge! I have a Mr John Lacey who is a war correspondent on board who wishes to join you for the next few days. How are you fixed?"

"That's fine by me, but he'll have to bring his own rations as we're pretty low ourselves until the supply vessel turns up, whenever that is."

Hosie saw the concern written on Lacey's face, but told him that a few days provisions for him will be sent over with the rest of his equipment, along with the weapon and ammo.

"Have P.O. Hall report to the control room with the Bren gun, rifle and a box of 303. Then get the Cox'n to provide Mr Lacey with enough suitable provisions for about 3 days." Hosie ordered.

Within minutes, Lacey was waiting on the casing with his baggage and equipment, plus a large bag of groceries, who was helped on board the fishing vessel by one of their crewmen.

Guard and Kendrick emerged from the fin door with the weapons then handed them over to one of the soldiers.

"Here you are matey! These are a tad too small for what we usually handle." Kendrick stated and nodded his head towards the 4inch gun.

"We're right out of ammo as the ruddy ammo supply boat hasn't arrived yet. Maybe your boys could radio for some as we're out of shouting distance from the shore station." One of the soldiers admitted.

"Sorry pal! That box is the only ammo suitable for you as the rest is 4 inch, 20mm and 9mm rounds." Guard responded

"We're supposed to be the goalie in this part of the water. That means unless we get ammo soon, some of those ruddy Jap life boats will get past us." The other soldier informed.

Both Captains heard the conversation despite the loud bangs and explosions coming from the killing grounds.

"We'll radio for a GNAT to drop you some on our way out of here. Better get moving now." Hosie suggested, then ordered the W/T/ office to radio the base for these supplies.

"What news of my Sisters? Have you spotted them too?" He asked.

"Yes! Saw one of your lot get rammed and sunk by a destroyer as it surfaced. Shortly after that, another one was being pelted by what looked like mortar shells from the troop on a ship she was trying to dodge. A destroyer got rammed midships from a rocket firing ship, which sank before the ship had cleared the wreckage. So be careful when you go near those Japs as they seem to be able to fire back at you."

"Thanks for the tip Captain. Better you lead the way now." Hosie said appreciatively.

"Thank you Captain. I can only do 8 knots, so follow my wake with a good 2 cables distance but try not to bump into me." Davidge said with a wave to conclude the brief meeting.

Both gunners had scampered back into the fin and shut the door to return back down into the boat, for the boat to move slowly along behind the fishing vessel.

During the half hour it took them to get clear of the minefield, several Japanese assault ships had disappeared from view, with the natural assumption that they'd been sunk along with the others.

T.S. declined to be relieved as lookout, as he was mesmerised at the sight of aircraft swooping down onto the troopships unleashing yet another load of bombs into them. He saw torpedoes fired from the Swordfish and the MTBs hitting their targets, just like theirs did. The point blank broadsides from two destroyers when they had a Jap escort destroyer trapped in their cross fire. The MGBs were racing around like terriers and sinking any lifeboats that dared to stay afloat. The Hurricanes wheeling about strafing the decks of the assault ships, causing yet more fires and explosions.

"Bloody hell sir! Those Japs are sure getting a good pasting. The noise is deafening even though we're about 8,000 yards away from them." T.S. commented to Welling, who was now the OOW.

"Serves them right for coming uninvited. They know they're being hammered yet they still insist of pressing onwards down range. Perhaps this day will serve as a salutary lesson to them on how not to be so arrogant and cock sure of themselves to be able to get away with it." Welling retorted.

"Seeing as we surprised them by the instant sinking of their first wave, they sure like to think they can out-number us sir. Although judging by those two ships that have just collided with one another and about to capsize, there'll not be enough to hold a banyan on the nearest beach, if they keep on going the way they are. Excluding the raft of dead bodies that is sir."

"Yes! No doubt our two Admirals will have something to say on that when we get back."

"Glad we got shot of that War Correspondent sir. If his attitude is anything to go on, then we'll be roped in for his so-called 'war crimes'. I mean, he's not a person to do a 'Nelson' and turn a blind eye, for him to see all the lifeboats being shot to pieces."

"If it gives you any comfort Signalman, just think of it this way: the Japanese sent over a hundred thousand troops without invitation mind you, with the sole aim to invade us. It doesn't matter if they arrived in lifeboats or Carley floats, they still posed a threat to us and had to be dealt with as a hostile force for us to stop them. Anyway, pay attention to your duties in case we end up sunk by some rogue mine." Welling concluded, but T.S. was still enthralled in what he saw until he was finally relieved off the bridge to go below again.

Chapter VI

Tally Ho!

It was nearly dark when S64 approached her new position in accordance with the tactics as issued by F.O.N.A.C. for Hosie to take his 'star fix' to confirm his dead reckoning spot on the chart.

T.S. was on the bridge again, scanning the horizon on his side of the boat, whilst his opposite number scanned the other side, when he spotted a number of Japanese assault ships in line astern, moving ahead and away from him. At the same moment, the other lookout had spotted a similar number on his side.

"Some ships ahead on Red 10 sir! Same this side sir!" both lookouts reported almost in unison.

Hoare who was the duty OOW, reported these contacts to Hosie, who in turn had the radar mast raised for an all round sweep.

"Looks as if we're going faster than them, so we should be able to catch them sir!" T.S. opined.

North reported from his radar office that there were 8 vessels on a converging course ahead ranging from 7,000 to 13,000 yards on the port side and 10,000 to 17,000 on the starboard side, yet some 10,000 yards apart. Speed roughly 12 knots.

Hosie came up on to the bridge for a look, taking only a few moments to give his next string of orders.

"We should be within range in about 20 minutes, have the gun crew closed up, with the after orlekin gun manned and ready for a surface action. That goes for both bridge machine guns." He said then went below again

"Aye aye sir"

The chase to catch these escapees was an exciting one for all on board, as the boat got nearer and nearer by the minute.

T.S. managed to get a good look at the nearest one who was trying her hardest to escape, and muttered a well-known phrase.

221

Hoare heard him and sighed.

"It's Yoiks and Tally Ho! Signalman. Not 'there goes the slant-eyed, er, runts' I think you called them." he said knowingly, making both lookouts laugh.

"Fair enough sir! But as you're a hunting man, why don't you blow your little hunting horn to make it more real?" T.S. quipped.

"What are we going to do about you Signalman!" Hoare sighed again but louder, telling them to be quiet on the bridge.

"Gun crews on deck closed up sir." Hall shouted up to the bridge.

"Very good! Radar! Report on the ranges! I need to be onto the rear one at about 3,000 yards. Track the ranges of the others ahead of it. Have tubes 1 & 2 standing by in case I decide to slow them down a tad."" Hosie ordered.

"Rear target range 4,000 yards. The ones ahead of it are currently 6,000, 8,000 and 10,000 yards sir!"

"Very good. Report when each one reaches 3,000 yards."

"Aye aye sir!" Hemmings who must have relieved North, responded.

"Tubes 1 & 2 ready!" came the report from the fore ends.

"Very good. Open outer doors! Gun crew! Make your range of 3,000 yards. Use a.p. to fire at their engine room. The machine gunners aft will concentrate their fire onto their bridge as we catch up with them. Signalman will fire onto the main deck to keep the soldiers heads down in case any soldier fancies his chances to fire back." Hosie shouted down to Hall then to the gunners aft.

There was a short period of silence, as S64 crept up behind the unsuspecting troop ship, which was showing dimmed lights everywhere including a small light on her stern.

"That's kind of them to show us the target T.O!" Hosie remarked but was interrupted by the report that the target was now at 3,000 yards.

"Fire tubes 1 & 2!" Hosie commanded, for the boat to shudder as two 600 lb torpedoes were sent 'up the kilt' to the escaping troop ship.

Everybody saw the immediate effect of the ship's stern being almost blown off her for Hosie to commence his gun action.

"4 inch gun open fire!" Hosie ordered swiftly. He had his response when the short-barrelled gun barked it's first report, sending a shell crashing into the back end of the ships bridge even though the ship had started to veer off her course due to the lack of steerage.

The gun fired twice more to ripping neat holes into the side of the tall ship destroying the engines, causing the ship to finally stop. The gun aft opened fire onto the bridge creating mayhem and instant death by flying lead, whilst T.S. started to hose the decks with his favourite 'lead dispenser' dishing out a dose of 'medicine' on the crowded decks. There were sufficient lights that were shining on deck to be able to see the soldiers running every way trying to get under cover.

Some soldiers quickly got a firing party organised who started to fire back with their machine guns. There was a rattle of bullets that punched holes into the side of the fin just a few feet below the bridge, with some whizzing over the heads of those on the bridge, for the after gun to join in with T.S. to return the fire.

Within moments more enemy machine guns were firing at them, but blindly as they couldn't see their target because the boat was in the dark, whereas their ship was bathed in her own lighting. Most of the bullets fired by the enemy simply zipped into the sea as the boat was pretty well out of their ranges.

It was the intervention from the 4inch gun pumping shrapnel shells onto the deck, which put down the enemy's desire to fight back, so as their machine guns fell silent the 4inch gun crew returned to their task of methodically punching more holes into the side of the ship.

The ship started to list badly with men jumping overboard towards the boat

"Right you bastards! Open your cake-holes and say 'Ahh' for the nice Signalman!" T.S. muttered, firing at the men jumping overboard including at those already in the water.

Hosie saw T.S. killing the enemy in the water at will but decided to order him to cease-fire.

"Better save your ammo Signalman. We've still got another 3 or so to go."

"But it's the enemy, sir!" T.S. groaned but ceased fire as ordered.

Hosie had the boat race towards the next ship in the line, which was about to cross her track and at a much greater speed that she was doing previously.

"Open outer doors on tubes 5&6. Stand by to fire at a range of 3,000 yards, set depth for 10 feet." Hosie ordered, as he realised that unless that ship was sunk, it might get away.

"Tubes 5&6 ready. Both outer doors open." Came the report from P.O. Hughes in the fore ends.

"Range now 3,000 yards" Hemmings said as he interrupted the orders.

"Fire!"

The boat's bows lifted slightly again as the two lower torpedo tubes were fired, due to being on the surface. Everybody on the bridge watched the phosphorescent trace of the torpedoes as they raced to their target.

"Slow ahead! Port 15 steer 340!" Hosie ordered, thus steering his boat out of the way of the obstruction ahead of them.

Both torpedoes hit with spectacular results, as within moments the ship had capsized, with yet another load of troops learning how to swim 'Aussie' style. (Down under).

T.S. and the starboard lookout were clapping and cheering at the spectacle.

"Silence on the bridge!" Hosie bellowed, turning to them reminding them quite bluntly that they were at action stations not on 'Daddy's yacht'.

The boat was turned back onto her original track, racing towards target No3, when T.S. reported sighting 4 small warships on their port side, causing Hosie to scream down to the radar shack telling them about these craft.

"Radar! Why haven't you reported these contacts! You've got eyes to see a good 30,000 yards, yet it took just one signalman to spot them approx 5,000 yards away on our port side." He said angrily.

"Was vectoring ahead between Red 20 and Green 20, sir." Hemmings replied in his own defence.

"Well get it sorted. " Hosie concluded then turned to T.S.

"It's obvious they're too big to be Japanese fishing vessels. Establish who they are." He ordered swiftly.

T.S. looked through his binoculars in the semi-darkness as the usually bright moon was almost covered in cloud. The sea was starting to get a bit choppy with the temperature getting much cooler.

"It looks like two FMLs each towing an FPB. From their pennant numbers they're from our base sir!"

"Very good signalman! Hmm! I don't want to have any signal lamp showing, better contact them by wireless. W/T-Captain! Get in voice contact with FMLS 1640 or 1645." He ordered swiftly.

"Slow ahead together. Port 20 steer 290. I intend coming round to close them No1 and see if they need assistance." He added.

"Can the gun crew stand down now sir if we're, shall we say, suspending actions against the enemy?" Welling asked.

"Yes No1, have the gun crews remain on the casing and be prepared to receive a heaving line from them as we come alongside."

"Captain – W/T! In contact with both FMLs. Asked if we could spare some diesel, as they're getting very low on it. And we've just received an immediate signal from F.O.N.A.C. saying there's a tropical storm blowing and coming our way. Says to start returning to base." Boyall reported.

"Very good W/T. Well you heard the man No1. I'm fed up with playing the 'wet nurse' around here." Hosie moaned

"We certainly have been playing nurses sir, especially with all the medicine we've been dishing out all ruddy day. Maybe we gave out a tad too much lead this time round." Welling quipped, which made Hosie chuckle at the typical response he always gets from his officers and men.

"Get them on board for some scran and a bit of T.L.C. just like we did to those MGBs up in the islands then. Tell them Mother hen is still alive and scratching, No1." Hosie responded with is own brand of remarks.

Hosie looked at the battered FPBs and asked the captain of ML1645 what happened to them, but to come alongside and start to receive as much as he could give them.

The FPBs looked as if they were flattened almost to the waterline, with holes everywhere on the FMLs.

The 2nd Cox'n and the gunners, who made up the casing party anyway, mustered around the 4inch gun, helping them to lash securely alongside the boat.

"I'm Lt Cdr Hosie S64. Am able to assist you, we'll get a fuel transfer to the both of you." He greeted them..

"Evening sir! I'm Lt. Eddie Armitage RANVR. I think you already know Lt Topsy Turner off 2012! and Lt Harry Reynolds." Armitage replied and was given a salute by the three junior officers.

"I need more fresh provisions than fuel sir!" Reynolds stated

"You can have what you need for your vessel, but I dare say a tot of rum will go down nicely, yes?" Hosie suggested.

"I'm a brandy man, but who cares sir!" Armitage said swiftly.

"Whatever your tipple is, but you'd better get everybody on board as fast as you can, we'll give you something to satisfy your bellies too. Be quick about this as there's a storm coming our way." Hosie offered.

Soon several of the FPB crewmen appeared onto the casing, each wearing some sort of bandaging and so T.S. was sent down off the bridge to help out.

He recognised Reeves and Smith who were classified as 'walking wounded' and decided to help them personally.

226

"Bloody hell Bob! How did you lot get into this mess? It looks as if you got flattened by a dirty great big sledge hammer!" T.S. asked.

"It was a case of mistaken identity! We mistook one ship for another. When the guys in the MTB completed their attack the whole bloody lot went sky high, nearly sinking us in the ruddy blast and the virtual tidal wave it sent our way. "

"Bloody hell! You must have gone and attacked one of those bloody ammo ship by mistake! We were given strict instructions to leave it to the fly boys." T.S. said with incredulity.

"That's not all! One of your lot were on the surface trying to dodge the shells from a cruiser which turned up out of the blue from behind us catching them napping. They were hiding in between two of the tankers when the ammo ship blew, making the other one blow up, setting fire to the tankers which also blew. They didn't stand a chance, so they didn't. Mind you, that cruiser didn't get far as the *Den Helder* blasted her to pieces before she could reply. Those 4 Dutch destroyers took on the other cruiser and gave it a bloody good salvo of torpedoes before they tattooed their names onto her decks with their 4.7inchers. Bloody great it was. The only snag now is that we've all got singed bollocks from the heat of the blast. Even our 'Tiff' got it even though he was in the for'ard mess acting as a loader. Just as well I managed to get the wireless going and contact base for these FMLs to come along and give us a tow." Reeves said, accepting a fag from T.S.

"What about you then Kelvin?"

"Got hit over the head with my own ruddy gun barrel as it got blown away by the second blast even though I managed to duck the first one. Thankfully the second blast was a bloody great one as not to have bullets and other whiz bangs hurtling your way, which would do even more damage. At least it was all over once the tidal wave and the explosion shock wave hit us." Smith replied stoically, nursing a bandaged head with an eye-patch over one eye making him look like a pirate.

"Our Skipper, Cox'n and three of our gunners got hit bad and are in a very poor way. The war is over for us now as we've no ruddy ship to sail in let alone the tomato sauce we're leaking." Reeves said with an almost cheerful grin, handing Smith his half smoked cigarette to finish it off.

"Don't you ruddy believe it, Bob. Our Squadron Commander will fix us up with another one even if we've got to get out and push the damn thing. Anyway what's the score from your end of the show?" Smith asked.

"We sunk the first wave then started to make a big hole in the troopships before the flyboys took over. All we're doing now is chasing the escapees to make sure they don't come back without an invite next time." T.S. informed them which made them smile before they were gently lowered down the fore hatch into the boat for some food and a bit of TLC from the rest of the boat's crew.

Yet again S64 played mother to the much smaller vessels, managing to complete the fuel transfer before the seas started to get decidedly lumpy and too risky to open the fore hatch as it was starting to take in water.

"The weather is picking up now gentlemen, so better get going or you'll all end up mustering in Davey Jones's locker, keeping those Jap ships company before you get back to base. My orders are to return as well but I've still got a fish to fry, including a cart load of 4 inch ammo to use up. When you get back tell them you met us and we're okay." Hosie suggested.

"Thanks for the, er, pit stop sir! Had to go slow to conserve fuel, but now it'll only take us about 3 hours, maybe 4 if we have to hug the coast to keep out of the storm's way." Armitage replied, as both officers shook Hosie's hand before giving him the traditional salute between a junior and a senior officer.

T.S. was back on the bridge keeping a good lookout as the little raft of vessels went their separate ways, and Hosie ordered the boat to dive.

"Watch your depth No1! The mouth of the gulf has a lip, which restricts the depth of water to only 15 fathoms, in some cases only 5fathoms. Radar! Make an all round sweep for 2 minutes. Sonar! Keep a good listen out ahead of us." Hosie ordered, as he kept his vigil at the periscope to watch the sea getting angrier by the hour.

"Captain – W/T. Message from FONAC! Him to you only sir!" Brown reported over the intercom.

Hosie told Hoare to take over the periscope then went swiftly to the W/T office.

Lewis was setting up the decoding machine when Hosie arrived, who order him to do the business whilst he took the little tape as it got fed out from the machine.

Once the signal was decoded for Hosie to be able to read it properly, he handed it over to Lewis for him to stick it all down and bring it to him in the control room then left to make a general broadcast over the tannoy to his faithful crew.

"Do you hear there, this is the Captain speaking! Our two illustrious Admirals, F.O.N.A.C. and FOGGY have declared us the winner and have decided to cease operations forthwith. Any Japanese ships that are still afloat will be allowed to leave the area, as we've been ordered back to base. Well done everybody!" Hosie informed them with a very large grin on his face, then commenced to clap his hands like a performing seal.

Everybody cheered at this news and even gave each other a 'pals hug' before settling down again to concentrate on their immediate tasks.

"Fall out action stations No1. We'll stay below to make our way back so we can dodge the heavy weather up top. Take us down to 100 feet then go to watch dived." Hosie ordered, then turned to James..

"Cox'n! We've been shaking, rattling, and rolling for most of the day. I can smell a rum jar that has obviously got smashed open in the process. It's a pity to waste it, so issue each man, officers included, an extra large rum ration all round, for you all bloody well deserve it." Hosie said with a wink and a smile as James nodded his head and smiling at the way his captain made an undercover and unofficial way of thanking his crew without worrying about Pusser's procedure for stores issuing and the like.

"Aye aye sir! James responded, who got relieved off the after planes control to do what the man said.

The boat made her transit back to base dived, coming back up to periscope depth from time to time to keep a check on anybody else who might be around.

Fortunately the tropical storm blew itself away some few hours later, with the boat coming to periscope depth to snort and charge her batteries again. The sea was still a bit lumpy causing the snort mast to get dunked under so the powerful diesel engines sucked some of the oxygen from the boat. This caused small vacuums that made the crew's ears pop when the air was sucked back down the snort mast again. This state of affairs annoyed Hosie who decided to get to the surface and face the lumpy water rather than having a boatload of popped eardrums.

"Rig the conning tower trunking then have rags to mop up any spray coming down it No1. We can transit back safely, therefore we can cotter main vents and assume 'Passage routine."

"Aye aye sir"

"Blue watch Passage routine!" came the announcement, and the men gave a little cheer, knowing they were now on their way home and away from the 'Dead' sea.

And so it was that during sunrise of the following morning, when the sea was calm again, S64 finally reached Bradley Cove to enter the haven of their base.

As S64 came alongside the depot ship, with her Jolly Roger flag proudly dancing in the morning breeze, they were given a tremendous welcome, cheered by all who were on board it. All the supply ships that were alongside in the stores basin started to sound off their foghorns as a welcome home gesture.

T.S. had noticed that there were 2 boats tied up alongside the floating docks jetty area, none of them S60 either, and that only S65 was alongside her trot port side for Hosie to neatly tie up alongside their trot No2.

T.S made the traditional custom of piping the 'Still' in saluting a senior officer, but heard the skirl of a bagpipe coming from a lonely Piper standing on top of the depot ship's bridge.

T.S realised that the boat's crest depicted crossed thistles on the white cross of the Scottish National flag, to recognise the gesture of the piper.

"That was our reply sir!" T.S. informed Hosie, who then ordered everybody on the casing and on the conning tower to remove their caps, to wave back to the large crowd who lined the depot ship side.

Their return to base was totally mind blowingly euphoric as the crew realised that they were now back in the safety of their base and not still out at sea, still dishing out death and destruction to their fellow man, even though he was the dreaded enemy.

The implications of seeing just 2 battle-scarred boats alongside their depot ship, with the very hollow noise of the communal mess deck on board the depot ship, finally sank into the crews minds, whose boats had survived the holocaust they had caused only a few days ago, yet already seemed like an eternity.

"Remind me to return my invitation ticket, as that's one party I don't fancy going to again." T.S. muttered to his fellow sparkers as they sat eating their first breakfast back on board the depot ship.

"Yeah, me too!" Brown said glumly when he looked around the almost empty dining hall that had been full during their last visit there.

"I wonder if those FPBs got back safely, as there seems to be a lot less alongside their base than victualled for." Boyall observed.

"No doubt we'll get the S.P. from the debriefing we're going to get, if FOGGY let alone his nibs Spam Hammersley, has anything to do with it. Clear lower deck and all that." T.S. opined, finishing their after breakfast fag to wander slowly back to their mess deck.

"Oh well! As we've got a make and mend all day, we might as well take it easy. I had my eye on one of the Army girls in the Comcen so I think I'll go ashore to see what's cooking." Underwood said with a yawn.

"Not me, I've got to go and get the mail this afternoon, but before then I'm getting my head down for a few hours kip before tot time." T.S. remarked.

"What all of your head Signalman?" Crank asked, butting in as he passed them in the canteen flat.

"Yeah you just stand there and watch." T.S. replied tiredly, as nobody had the will nor the strength to argue the toss or whatever. They drifted back down into the mess, with all plans going out of the portholes when their heads hit their pillows, joining in with the heavy nasal snoring coming from others who had already succumbed to their tiredness.

"Thank God we won Chris!" T.S. whispered to his Leading Sparker, then fell fast asleep.

Chapter VII

The Wash Up

Three days later, after collecting all the evidence and details of the recent slaying and almost total annihilation of the Japanese invasion force, F.O.N.A.C. decided to hold a 'Wash Up' to see what, if anything had done wrong, what tactical lessons were to be learned from the attack, who sunk what, did what, and so on. This was to be a massed meeting in one of the aircraft hangars at the air base for everybody who was 'in the front line' was to attend.

The front row was taken up by the commanding officers of each unit and vessel, with the second and third rows having their junior officers. A small space separated them from the rows upon rows of seats for the rest of the servicemen and women, who served with them.

The general hubbub and noise of the hangar fell silent when the two Admirals walked slowly up to a raised platform and for them to take their seats.

Everybody clapped these men as they arrived and for them to wave back in acknowledgement before sitting down.

It is the tradition and custom of the Australian people to attach nicknames to no matter who they were or how lofty their office may be, for Vice Admiral 'Spam' Hammersley, and Rear Admiral FOGGY to have those nicknames.

From the word go, they treated everybody in the same manner no matter if they were an Ordinary seaman, a private in the Marines or even a four ring Captain. They would go around the command unannounced, even known on several occasions to roll their sleeves up to help out some person in difficulty or whatever. All of which made these two Admirals very popular and respected within their respective commands.

"Okay everybody settle down, and you may smoke if you

233

wish." FOGGY announced over the tannoy system, and for Hammersley to take over.

"From the map as indicated, the shores of Australia with all who live there have been delivered safely from the clutches of the, up to now, invincible Japanese Imperial forces that made war against us.

From what the intelligence boys, and our War Office and Cabinet have revealed it was truly magnificent, thanks to all of you who made it so." Hammersley announced, then went to explain each campaign that was shown.

"The Japanese task force sent to Ceylon Under Admiral Kuroshima was a powerful one, that included 4 Kondo class battleships with their plan to engage and sink the British Indian fleet under the command of Admiral Cunningham.

Admiral Cunningham already had 4 battleships of the Warspite and Sovereign class, with several heavy cruisers on station, was up to the job of taking on these would be visitors.

Somehow or another, it was watered down in favour of a major assault on Port Moresby, Midway and a 3 pronged attack on us.

The forces that were sent to land at Port Hedland on the west coast of Australia was their Left Diversionary Invasion Force (LDIF) coming from the Ceylon Task force and of sufficient power to meet and thrash our West Coast Fleet. Unfortunately for them we had a squadron of submarines and several squadrons of land-based aircraft to rely upon until our fleet under the command of Rear Admiral Mackay with his fleet raced up from Perth to engage them.

The result was that they lost most of their capital ships, a carrier and 4 destroyers by the combined forces of our submarines and land-based aircraft. A severe typhoon hit a very large part of the area, which dispersed the invasion forces ships, causing the entire operation to be abandoned, for Ceylon to be saved.

The Japanese decided to send their 24th and 5th Armies from Rabaul in New Britain to invade Port Moresby and the American half of New Guinea.

The key to it all came from the Japanese desire to conclude the destruction of the American Fleet based there then to make their way down the inside of the Great Barrier Reef smashing any of our Eastern forces in their way.

That invasion force as you can see was designated as the Right Diversionary Invasion force (RDIF) were from the main invasion force on New Guinea and of similar strength to that of the LDIF.

They were to be met by Rear Admiral Crace and his Eastern fleet when they tried to come through the narrow gaps of the Great Barrier Reef at a point near Rockhampton. There were other narrows in the reef for them to sneak through, but he had several GNAT planes dropping mines in them all to plug the gaps.

As stated, the crucial event to precipitate this RDIF was for the Japanese to win over the Americans in what will become known as 'The Battle of the Coral Sea'.

The historians will call it the Battle of Blunders as many were made by both sides, not least the fact that the Japanese seriously weakened their chances on the two major invasions by removing 2 of their fleet carriers *Zuikaku* and the *Shokaku* and 1 heavy cruiser, along with the escort carrier *Shoho* plus 1 heavy cruiser from the Australian invasion force, plus 5 submarines, sending them out to join Admiral Inouye for their planned assault on Midway.

It is of note that at the 'Battle of the Coral Sea', it was the very first time two opposing fleets were trying to knock 'ten bells of shit' out of each other from over the horizon, where nobody could see who was going where or who was doing what.

It was also the first time a major battle was fought Carrier verses Carrier, and in the end it spelled the death knell of the battleship era.

Due to the pyrrhic victory over the Japanese, the invasion forces from Rabaul were sent back there in preparation for their assault on other unsuspecting islands in the Pacific.

***

And so it comes to our own event whereby the Japanese decided to send a large yet separate invasion force virtually unprotected, given that they were hoping to draw all our naval sources away from the area and at the same time try to annihilate the Americans in the Coral Sea.

As a typical Japanese tactic, they like to plan a decent 3 prong attack on their targets as the R.T.U. and L.T.U. shows you. This includes their Main Invasion Fleet (MIF), which also had a 3 pronged attack.

The left prong was to land then make contact with the forces of the LDIF thus to cut off the Northern Territories, with the right prong landing making contact with the RDIF thus cutting off the northern part of Queensland.

The main force would land in the middle then make their way down to Melbourne to wait for the rest of their invading army reported to be around 300,000 troops.

As stated earlier this Invasion force had apart from 1 battleship, 1 carrier with 120 aircraft, 5 light cruisers and 24 destroyers, was too meagre to protect a large invasion fleet of over 100 assault ships carrying the equivalent of 5 divisions, or nearly half an army if you like, which included tanks, artillery, engineers and other support ships.

You may be aware that we only had 2 Battalions of Marines plus the remnants of the 6th and 7th Australian Infantry divisions who managed to filter back from New Guinea and other places to defend the beachheads along the entire northern half of Australia. You already know the strength of our forces, but again on paper, too little to stop this invasion force the Japanese were trying to sneak down the Gulf of Carpentaria, to land virtually unopposed into the heart of Australia.

Now we come to the reckoning and who lost what.

The Japanese Admiral Mikimoto was expected to lower his flag on his ship *Asahi* at 1700 that day, but rather than surrender his ship he had his ship scuttled in the same manner as Captain Lansdorf did with his German battleship *Graf Spe*.

At 1900, the ship went down with all guns blazing taking with it the Admiral and his entire crew. Thus ending any Japanese hostilities, allowing what remained of his invasion fleet to escape northward to get out of the Gulf.

In terms of ship losses, and I've had to wait for the result from S64 as the last one back to confirm who did what, they are as follows:

Japanese ship losses were almost 100%. According to our recce planes, only 2 escort destroyers and about 5 troop ships that managed to get away before the tropical storm hit us.

When the storm had abated and on the following morning, the recce planes went out to search the entire 'range' to find that there was not a trace of the battle we fought that day before. No ships, no life rafts, but most of all no bodies to be sighted anywhere. The storm must have cleared the entire Gulf, so perhaps we can thank Mother Nature to help us 'clean up' after ourselves. Maybe that's why we Brass Hats call this meeting 'the Wash Up'.

The total losses of the Japanese troops, is estimated to be around 125,000 out of an estimated 150,000, not including around 10,000 sailors and airmen. This then could possibly be the last time the Japanese will send a major invasion force under-protected, if ever again.

The shame of it all is that if only the Japanese military mindset adopted a 'Western' military attitude' to know when they were beaten and had enough, for them to retire and save as much lives as possible. As it was, in the aftermath, the Gulf could easily have been renamed as 'The Japanese 'Dead' Sea.'

For some of you, it may be seen as a total butchery of so many thousands of lives. But I can assure you it was the only way to stop them doing to Australia as what they did to all the other countries they subjugated under their control.

In their eyes, going into battle only means 'Death or Glory' with no thoughts of surrender or mercy shown to their opponents.

For those historians among you, we killed or drowned more men in one day than the combined total lost in both battles of the Somme, Verdun and Ypres, from WW1.

I for one, am glad each and every one of you did your duties and to live to tell the tale. The downside of this however, and from our point of view is:

We lost S61 & S62, both sunk with all hands, with S67 and S69 severely crippled due to being rammed or bomb damage etc. Only S64 and S65 survived with minimal scratches and a few dents here and there. S63 as you know had been scrapped and S60 along with S66 who arrived from the Darwin Squadron were sent down to help Admiral Crace meet the Japanese at Rockhampton.

Of the FPBs and FMLs: 3 were lost, 4 severely crippled. The F.A.A. lost 3 GNATs, 2 Swordfish and 2 Fairey bombers, and 1 Catalina. The RAAF boys only lost 1 Hurricane.

FOGGY had his British and Australian cruisers crippled by the battleship, before it was scuttled. 1 Destroyer was lost and 3 crippled. The Dutch Cruiser and her 4 destroyers got away with minimal damage, and set about sinking the Japanese warships with a vengeance, to honour the loss of their adored and much revered Admiral Karel Doorman." Hamersley said full of emotion and a powerful delivery, then paused to take a breath before winding up his speech.

"What a jolly good show! All in all, a bloody good couple of day's work! In fact, never have so many lost to so few!" He enthused.

"But there is one thought I would like you to bear in mind,

and not to put too fine a point on things. It was the Ace trump card we were able to play and one that was the crucial factor in our victory.

Our secret base and especially the Squadron of 'A' boats saved the day. For without them, it would have had a different outcome to the entire story of the war, had the Japanese battleship and her cruisers ruled the waves that day.

Perhaps a parallel of similar likeness could have been drawn about the German use of their 'Wolf Packs' during the 'Battle of the Atlantic'.

The moral of the story I'm making to you is, that you must be fully and properly kitted up with the right equipment that's up to the job for you to defend yourselves and survive to win your battles. That's why we won and the Japanese lost.

Therefore, from now on it will always be remembered and entered into the history books, to be referred to as 'THE BATTLE OF OZ' and we that survived to tell the tale, can consider that battle as being Australia's finest hours. Well done to each and everyone of you. You can now have the rest of the week off as your reward, as I don't think Emperor Hirohito and his pals will want to come and visit us without an invitation any more." Hammersley concluded almost breathless.

"All that remains to do now to observe your brave stand against the might of the Japanese fleet in saving the inhabitants of this fair continent, is for us two admirals to offer each and every one of you, a humble, yet sincere salute." Foggy stated, for the 2 Admirals to do just that.

There was a hushed and stunned silence from the men to see that their respected Admirals were actually saluting them instead of the other way round.

The total silence in the large hangar lasted for over a minute at the information given and the large map had plainly shown them

239

had finally sunk in, when the Admirals stop saluting and started a slow hand clap, that was joined by the officers who turned round to face their men, until the clapping grew into a crescendo of noise that was suddenly erupted into a frenzy by the occupants of this large hangar.

For the entire hangar full of people erupted in cheering, clapping and whistling, with hats thrown into the air with jubilation.

Every person there, without exception, was euphoric in the knowledge that for him or her, the tide of defeat after defeat had now turned to victory. That for the whole of Australia and her neighbours the New Zealanders, were now safe, and for them to breathe easy once more.

This was a time to have few days off to celebrate their famous victory because each warrior had earned it, before they were being committed once more 'into the breech'.

Postscript

The inspiration to be able to write this fictional novel was drawn from two true facts among all the others that have been mentioned throughout, but just to highlight them:-

1. The A-class Submarine was built for long-range operations in the Pacific in mind especially against the Japanese.

2. The Japanese military hierarchy and think-tank led by Admiral Ugaki and Kuroshima hatched a plan to invade Australia to co-incide with their massive invasion plans of New Guinea on the back of their attacks on the Midway and Aleutian Islands, as planned by Admiral Yamamoto and General Tojo at their Hiroshima Bay conference May 1942.

    Thus in 1942 the events of the 'Battle of the Coral Sea' and the 'Battle of Midway' took place to become entered into the annals of WW2 history, but only in this novel did 'The Battle of Oz' happen.

The uniqueness of this fictional novel is due to my idea and the concept of using real names given by those who have pledged their support in purchasing this novel, by weaving them into the fabric of the storyline as a thank you.

But for them, the characters for this novel would not have existed.

As any Aussie would say. "Good on ya Sport!"

About the Author

Frederick A Read is the author of the much acclaimed collection of novellas *Moreland and Other Stories* and the popular naval fiction series *The Adventures of John Grey*:

A Fatal Encounter
The Black Rose
The Lost Legion
Fresh Water
A Beach Party
Ice Mountains
The Repulse Bay
Perfumed Dragons
Silver Oak Leaves
Future Homes

The seventh book – *The Repulse Bay* – is due out in November 2010.

Frederick A Read

and

The
Guaranteed  *Partnership*

"Between author & publisher"

---

would like to thank the following two organisations for their assistance in the development of this special book:

and

The Royal Maritime Club

(Formerly The Royal Sailors' Home Club)